THE BOOMERANG OF DESTINY

A TALE OF THE OUTBACK

GORDON BENNETT

Edited by
HENRI RENNIE

MEREDIAN

THE BOOMERANG OF DESTINY

This edition Copyright © 2021 Henri Rennie

All rights reserved.

E-book ISBN: 978-0-6488660-4-6

Print ISBN: 978-0-6488660-5-3

Published by **Meredian Pictures & Words** *2021*

Ballina, Australia

MEREDIAN
PICTURES & WORDS

INSPIRING IMAGINATION

❀ Created with Vellum

CONTENTS

THE BOOMERANG OF DESTINY

A Tale of the Outback

By Gordon Bennett

*Published in serial form in the Daily Mail (Brisbane)
from 4 December 1922 to 30 January 1923.*

*Edited in 2021 by
Henri Rennie.*

EDITOR'S NOTE

I received this manuscript from my mother-in-law, Maggie Wild-blood. Maggie is the grand-daughter of Gordon Bennett (or 'Da' as he was known to her). It came in the form of carefully-preserved newspaper clippings, for that is the only format in which it is known to have appeared – as a serial in a number of Australian papers of 1922 and '23.

She recalls him fondly from her early childhood, her enduring memory of him in his swivel chair at his desk, the very image of one of the characters he vividly created. By that time 'Da' was living in Sydney, one of the first guiding hands of *The Bulletin*. But despite living in the 'big smoke', his mind and soul were still inextricably tied to the country.

As the newspapers' own introduction indicates, Gordon Bennett was himself very much a bushman at heart. An experienced and accomplished writer, he also had a wealth of practical knowledge and experience of his subject matter. He knew and appreciated both the good and bad of life in the bush. The drought of 1895 to 1903 would still have been uncomfortably fresh in the memory, as would the joy of the breaking of that drought, the excitement of a gold 'strike', and the loneliness of the long, dry stock routes. Those memories and those emotions are preserved here, in a story that brings the Outback of a century ago vividly to life. A time before mobile phones, commercial air travel, rapid-transit railways or road trains of massive semi-trailers thundering along a Highway One that connects the whole continent.

I've endeavoured to edit with as light a hand as possible. As the story is of its time, so too is much of Gordon's language, both style and vocabulary very much different from the LOLs and OMGs of today. But his love of words is evident, and I have attempted to preserve that as much as possible while being comprehensible to a readership one hundred years on. The pace of change in our language has been rapid, and even words that were in common usage when I was young now draw blank looks.

I'm also aware of the prospect of this book selling outside Australia – the subject is of international appeal, I believe – and terms familiar here may mean nothing to a modern European or American reader. I hope that context will help, but I have also added a Glossary to explain certain words whose meaning may have been lost, or not travelled much beyond the borders of this country.

In a very few instances I've modified Gordon's text, where he's used a term which may now be considered offensive. Gordon Bennett himself was in no way a racist man, but the everyday language of the 1920's included casual expressions which may now be interpreted as inappropriate. I've tried to be sensitive to such concerns, without losing the story's essential character. If something I've missed still causes a wince or cringe to a modern reader, I can only apologise and repeat that neither Gordon, nor I, had any intent to offend.

The Boomerang of Destiny has been a treat for me to edit, and I've greatly appreciated the opportunity that Maggie has given me. Gordon Bennett's passion for his country, and his optimism for its future, shines throughout the pages. I hope that you will gain as much pleasure from it as I have. The Australian bush is diminished now, but the Outback remains a destination that should be experienced – that "weird alluring mystery of the west, that wondrous land of toil and travail" still holds a majesty and quiet grandeur for those who seek it out. If this story encourages you to seek it out for yourself, then I will be as delighted as I'm certain that Da Bennett would have been.

Henri Rennie
Ballina 2021

1

FATE DEALS THE CARDS

Mr. James Penderby polished his glasses carefully, poised them precariously on the point of his hawk-like nose, and then, in a very formal voice, read from a very dusty document a jumble of very formal phrases.

The young man seated at the opposite side of the table endeavoured to concentrate his mind with sufficient intentness on the words of the lawyer, so that out of the seeming chaos of sound would emerge some order of intelligibility, but after many frownings and much uneasy shuffling of feet, he abandoned the task as hopeless, and waited with as much patience as he could command until Mr. Penderby had finished. In time the monotone ceased; then the young man spoke.

"Now, Mr. Penderby, will you please explain in simple language just what all that means?" he said.

"My dear young man," protested the lawyer, "I purposely avoided what is sneeringly referred to as 'legal jargon' in preparing this statement of our late client's (your father's) estate, and it astonishes me that you should find it so difficult of comprehension."

"I am sorry, Mr. Penderby," exclaimed the young man; "but I got mixed up with those 'whereases' and 'hereinafters' in the early part, so I simply did not try to follow it. Just tell me in a few words how I stand."

"Well," replied the old lawyer, in slow, precise tones, "you have practically no financial standing whatever. Beyond two or three hundred pounds, you will have nothing from your father's estate."

"Good heavens!" exclaimed his client. "Why, what becomes of all the property? Our home at Rose Bay, the cottage on the Blue Mountains, the farm at Windsor? They haven't just disappeared, you know. Property doesn't vanish like that!"

"For the last half-hour," said the lawyer, somewhat irritably, "I have been explaining to you that during the past year your father's mining speculations proved so disastrous that, in order to obtain financial accommodation, he was forced to mortgage all his properties to the uttermost limit permitted by the money-lenders and the banks; even the furniture, motor-cars and yacht were covered by bills-of-sale. When the final accounts of the estate come to be filed you will have, as I have said, perhaps three hundred pounds."

Jack Burnside, man-about-town and club idler, was palpably hit. He stared at the lawyer's sphinx-like face, twirled his hat nervously in his hands, and stamped uncertainly on the floor. After a long, shocked silence he spoke.

"Well, I'm damned!" he exploded.

The old lawyer's mask-like countenance remained unmoved. Peering keenly at the young man, he commenced to speak, holding up a bony hand for silence.

"I cannot say I feel sorry for you," he said, with what seemed to be a sinister intentness. "In fact, I feel rather pleased that you are left without means to enable you to continue your usual reckless method of life. You have been an idler and a spendthrift since you left the University under a cloud; you have no profession, no career, and no aptitude for work. You have always been content to take the money your father earned and lavish it on people unworthy to shake his hand. It was your careless and ungrateful conduct that ultimately involved him in ruin. You are a waster, and you will always remain a waster. You will sponge and loaf outrageously until at last you sink into the gutter, for you will never work. It is not in you."

Jack Burnside paled before this terrible indictment, uttered so lifelessly, yet so grimly. He sat stock-still for several moments. Then he stood defiantly before the lawyer, his eyes hard and determined, his square lower jaw thrust forward.

"I'm a waster, am I? I won't work, won't I? All my so-called friends have been saying that to me since the pater died, probably knowing all the time what I have just learned; so I intend to show you that I can. Don't forget it!"

Clapping his hat on his head, he glared for a moment at the lawyer, then turned on his heel and strode from the room without a word of farewell.

A placid smile flitted across old Mr. Penderby's face as he gathered up the yellow musty sheets of foolscap that he had been handling, and he proceeded to tie them neatly with a length of red tape. "That stung him," he muttered to himself as he put the papers away in a black tin box that bore the white-painted inscription, "Estate of Amos Burnside d'csd".

Gazing at the unromantic, scratched and dusty box, the old lawyer's face softened, and a tender light filled his eyes. "It stung him," he repeated gently, "just as I intended it should. He is no waster, and poor old Amos only realised too late that the lad was not to blame for the idle habits that he had developed, and his wasteful ways. I had often told him to give the boy a chance, but it was not until things began to go amiss with his speculations that he perceived the truth. And then he quixotically decided to realise on the remainder of his estate and hand the money to me to dole out to the lad as I thought fit. Aye, but it is a serious responsibility. I have twenty thousand pounds for Jack Burnside, invested in sound commercial concerns, the interest on which would keep the lad in idleness all his life. But no one knows of it but myself; and Amos trusted me to do the best for his boy. His boy! And he might have been my son had not Mary loved that rough, big bushman. And, then, I have my own son, Raymond. But... Yes, I will keep that money until Jack knows the true value of it; and, if I am any judge of character, he made no idle boast today, for he will show us all that he has in him the makings of a man. When that day comes, he can have his inheritance. Aye, it stung him!"

On leaving the lawyer's office, Jack Burnside found himself in Elizabeth Street, with the autumn sun shining brilliantly overhead and Sydney's traffic hurrying to and fro around him. He halted hesitantly in front of the Carlton, undecided as to whether or not he would enter. A whisky and soda would brace him up, he thought, and there would be a friend or two there. But...! Coming to a swift determination he walked past and proceeded stolidly, and with unseeing eyes, towards the Botanic Gardens. Here, in in this scented fairyland, the fairest garden in the southern seas, he sought a secluded spot and sat down to think things out.

And before his mind flashed picture after picture – the interminable mental cinema-show of remorse and regret – of days and happenings that had gone. There was his early boyhood, scarcely ever before remembered, on a farm in the back-country. He saw his father, a big, stalwart bushman, whirling a whip that writhed like a serpent and snapped like the crackle of rifle shots as weary bullocks lunged at the yokes, and a table-top wagon creaked and swayed through the sodden rain-filled waterholes. He saw his father clutching at the handles of a plough as the horses strained in the furrow, and left behind them a long, stark wound in the breast of the virgin soil. He saw his father on the "board" when the shearing machines whipped off fold on fold of snowy fleece as the wind whips the spindrift off the crest of a curling breaker, and he heard the wondrous, half-forgotten music of the frantic turmoil of a shearing shed. He saw his father at the shaft-mouth when a hide bucket was swung from a rackety windlass, and its contents of golden dirt spilled on a sheet of sap-wet stringy bark.

In all those pictures his father was the dominating figure. And he was always at work. Work, accomplished in days of burning heat, when the very birds dropped from the trees. Work, accomplished in bitter days, when biting showers swept out of the folds of the hills and the bush shivered like a tortured sentient thing. But, in no picture did he see a mother. There were women, true. Rough, kind-hearted bush women; viragoes of the shanties in the mining camps; quiet-voiced women that had taught him his letters; and one garrulous, lovable soul with gentle Irish brogue, who had packed his first school-box lunches.

And there were pictures wherein he, too, figured dominantly. But they were pictures of careless escapades at school; of being sent down from the University; of clubs, theatres, supper-rooms, racecourses, motor trips... But he could not endure these. Work! There was no picture that showed a single effort of his that was worthy.

But the pictures that seared his heart, and stirred his soul to its depths, were those of a grey-haired old man, with tired eyes and wistful, drooping figure, who had given almost his whole wealth and substance ungrudgingly to a son who had so bitterly disappointed his most cherished ambitions. And there was that vivid picture of the death-bed, when the tired old man had taken his hand and whispered feebly: "Forgive me, Jack, but whatever I have done has been for your sake."

The realisation of the pathetic heart-loneliness of his father, through all those years when he had lavished on an unworthy son that had once been bestowed on the mother who had yielded her life to bring him into the world, completely numbed Jack Burnside's understanding. He sat inert, overcome. Then the poignant pain of remorse stabbed him ruthlessly. With a cry that came from the depths of his being, he flung himself on the grass and sobbed out, "Great God, can I ever atone?!"

His grief was so absolutely sincere that he was quite oblivious of his surroundings, and entirely unaware that he was being regarded with intense anxiety by a neatly-dressed and extremely pretty young girl, who was sitting in the shade of a spreading Port Jackson fig tree only a few paces distant.

"Oh, Mr. Burnside! Whatever is wrong?" she cried, in a voice that trembled with concern.

The young man looked up, and for a few moments gazed at her with unseeing eyes. Then, recognising her, he stood upright.

"Miss Forbes. What are you doing here?" he stammered.

"I always leave the office early to come here for lunch," she said, "and when I saw you walking along the path looking so terribly miserable I just had to follow you. I've been so interested in you since you helped poor Mother when they were selling us off for rent after Dad died; and then you got me the position in Mr. Penderby's office, and I – I – I thought I might be able to help you now."

"You are very kind, Miss Forbes," the young man said, "but I am afraid that I have come to the end of my tether, and that no one will want to know or help me when the news gets around that I am practically penniless. I ..."

"Please don't say that, Mr. Burnside," the girl interrupted. "I know all about how things went wrong with your father's affairs, and I know just how you are situated. I can realise, too, what you must feel, and I know that it is not the loss of the expected money that is hurting so much now, but the thoughts in your heart of what you might have done to make things different for your dear father. I will always be your friend if you need one."

"Thank you, Molly – Miss Forbes," said the young man in a broken voice, his eyes misty. "I have just been realising to the full what an ungrateful and selfish son I have been, because an old lawyer told me the unpalatable truth. But I am determined to go to work and make my name as honoured as was my father's. I have but little money now, and no profession; so I must start from the lowest rung of the ladder. If I only had a few more hundred pounds I could go out west and start on the land."

"Mr. Burnside," said the girl, eagerly, looking into his eyes. "If two hundred pounds would help, I can lend it to you. I have a little saved in the bank, and you can have it without interest."

"Molly – why, what do you mean?" Jack Burnside's voice trembled with emotion as he spoke. "Do you think I could take your savings? No, I could never do that. But, little girl, I can never thank you sufficiently for your wonderful offer, and it has let me know that I have one friend at least. Some of my old-time friends, those that profited by my extravagance, who must have known my position when I never even suspected it, commenced to cut me in the street a week ago. Only this morning Rod Pymble, once my best chum, passed me by without a sign of recognition. They know that I am penniless, or nearly so, and they think that I am a waster. But I will show them, Molly."

"I know you will, Mr. Burnside, and I wish that I could help. I have heard what they have been saying about you; but I know that you are good and kind-hearted, and are worth them all put together. You can win out if you try, and I – I – I want you to." Her eyes were alight with eagerness, and in their depths glowed a tender radiance that stirred the young man strangely.

"You want me to win out, do you Molly?" he said, gazing into her eyes. "Why, I don't know what it is, little girl; but you have done something to change me like nothing else ever could. And it's queer, too, how I remember that for months past when anything has gone wrong, I could always think of you, and it would seem to straighten out. But Molly, perhaps it was because I, er... er..." He ceased abruptly, awed at the rapturous glory of awakened love that blazed in the girl's eyes. Then he stammered, in palpable confusion, "I must not say what I have in my mind. It would not be fair. No. It cannot be, yet."

The girl looked deep into his eyes, and seeing there all that she hoped for, the newly-kindled fires of love, she blushed warmly, and sighed a sigh of ecstatic content.

"I must go back now," she whispered. "Will you walk with me to the gates – Jack?"

"Yes Molly," he answered. And with her he walked towards the city.

2

THE NEW-CHUM JACKEROO

The train, thirty empty cattle vans, half a dozen open trucks filled with merchandise, and two dusty carriages, had grunted and rocked out of Parkes, and was panting up a slope. On each side of the line were strewn the remains of the golden era – myriads of holes and mullock-heaps of the old alluvial field.

Jack Burnside, gazing wearily out of the carriage window, speculated idly on the panorama. That introspective habit of his of conjuring up pictures out of the past had developed to a remarkable degree during the month that had elapsed since old Mr. Penderby had so rudely shattered his hopes, until he was now often amazed at the vividness of some of these visions of forgotten days and doings. And inexplicably intermingled in the themes there was Molly; so often and so realistically that there had grown upon him a sure and certain knowledge that all these things were concentrating in some mysterious fashion to help him win out. Why? He could never satisfactorily explain to himself, and he invariably ended by dismissing the whole business with some mental reference to "freaks of psychology", or an uneasy suspicion concerning "useless daydreams".

But this deserted mining field moved him strangely. The gravelly mounds, some red, some glaringly white, all raw and new, although half a century old, and with contours rounded by hundreds of summer storms, brought the flickering film of fancy's pictures into swift activity. Dimly he remembered that it was at Parkes – on the old Bushman's Lead – that his father had won a fortune in the golden gully, and thereupon, half-consciously, he began to re-people the field with the picturesque diggers, and the careless fossickers of the bygone days.

"Yes," he muttered, half audibly, "that is where old Ben Roberts' shanty was," at the same time gazing back at a prominent spot on the hill-slope.

"Wot's that?" interrupted a raucous voice. "Old Ben's shanty? Why, it vanished thirty year ago! You couldn't remember it."

Jack turned to look at the speaker, and saw a tall, gaunt bushman, whose bearded face had been burned a dull bronze with the fierce suns of the western summers. "No," he said confusedly, "I do not remember it, but something told me that it had been there. Perhaps it was merely fancy."

"Well, you're a queer bird," the old man stated emphatically, gazing at him with frank curiosity. Then speaking with the casual directness of the bush, he asked, "Where are yer goin'?"

"I am going to Bullangarra Station, somewhere out beyond Condoblin. Do you know the place? It is a large station I believe." Jack was somewhat taken aback by the question, but he answered in an endeavour to appear friendly.

"Know it? My colonial oath! It's the hungriest, forsakenest, rottenest bit of country on the Lachlan! It wouldn't fatten a bandicoot ter the square mile; an' the manager's a fair blighter." The speaker appeared quite in earnest in his denunciation of the station.

"That is rather discouraging," remarked Jack, anxiously, "for I am going there to work. I am to be a jackeroo there, whatever that is."

"Goin' ter work there! A flamin' jackeroo! Well, I'm jiggered. I work there, mostly. I've been there on an' off fifteen years come August, an' I suppose I'll peg out there," said the old bushman.

During the next two hours of their bumpy, dusty trip Jack listened to so many astounding facts about the bush, its people and its customs that he half-regretted having decided to go on the land. He learned that his fellow traveller was known from the Murray to the Territory as 'Wild Bullocks'. He learned also of "whalers", men who carry bluey and billy up one side of the river and down the other, year in and year out; of big-gun shearers, the "ringers" of the sheds; of marvellous droving feats; of bush-fires, drought and disaster. His companion, realising Jack's complete ignorance of the bush and its customs, exerted himself to the utmost in the favourite Australian pastime of "leg-pulling". And when 'Wild Bullocks' tired, some other occupant of the carriage would, with drawling voice and careless speech, take up the burden of the tales. And it was all done with a solemn imperturbability that almost dispelled the doubts that continually arose in the young man's mind. When the train drew into a wayside township, Jack was depressed, discouraged, but nevertheless determined.

At Bogan Gate, the stopping place, 'Wild Bullocks' informed Jack that the passengers would have to go up the town for dinner.

"But will the train wait?" asked Jack.

"Wait? Blimey, she waits here for three weeks sometimes!" said the old man, explosively.

They plodded through the dust, out of the station yard, and across the street, to a wooden building that was the hotel. On the verandah were seated six silent, bearded bushmen, all strangely like Jack's new-found acquaintance. Three were sprawled on a wooden stool, two were seated on empty beer casks that they occasionally wheeled into the shade as the sun moved round, and one sat on the edge of the verandah, spitting dejectedly into the dust. 'Wild Bullocks' walked straight to the bar, Jack and three other passengers bringing up the rear. As the last of the train travellers entered, the six derelicts rose simultaneously, and followed. Drinks were called for, and the six, uninvited, participated, each naming his liquor with a brief deliberateness, and the barman serving them as a matter of course. Somewhat astonished, Jack asked 'Wild Bullocks' who was paying, if the strangers were friends of his.

"Naw," said the old man. "They're just dry weather pelicans; but

I've got a few bob left, an' I'll be doin' a perish some day when one of 'em might be holdin' it."

And in the subsequent 'shouts' the penniless ones participated fully, save for the paying, and but for their mumbled, "e'luck" before they drained their glasses they spoke no word nor gave any thanks. They looked on the drinks as something justly owing to them. Then, as the bar emptied, they drifted forth to their accustomed seats to gossip for a while, and then to leave and return in time for the train next day.

After the travellers had eaten, 'Wild Bullocks' invited Jack to walk along the Bogan Road to "see an old mate o' mine. He's only about a mile up." Jack protested that they might miss the train.

"That's all right," the old bushman assured him. "Ol' Jack Costello always whistles half an hour before he starts th' train, so as th' passengers can get aboard in time. Them commercials in th' first class always has a couple o' hundred up in the billiard room after a feed."

They paid their visit, and sure enough the train whistle warned them in such good time that they had half an hour, even then, to spare before the rackety engine snorted out towards the sunset. Before they departed, Jack bought drinks again for "the dry weather pelicans" after being informed by his companion that the name had some vague connection with the bird that could consume its own weight of fish in a day, and a man that could do something of the same sort of thing in regard to beer.

3

ALONG THE LACHLAN-SIDE

W hen they had settled themselves in the carriage after their meal at Bogan Gate, to face, with stoic fortitude, the remaining dreary hours of the seemingly interminable journey, Jack Burnside noticed that the company had been increased by the addition of a Catholic priest, a little, wizened old man with a weather-beaten face and a pair of twinkling eyes. His clerical garments were of alpaca, green with age, patched and threadbare; his hat bore not the slightest resemblance to the type known as "shovel" and favoured by the clergy of all denominations, and his boots were battered and broken. Somewhat astonished at the great deference being paid to this shabby old man by the bushmen in the compartment, but more by the sudden cessation of profanity in the conversation, Jack, in an undertone, enquired of 'Wild Bullocks' as to his identity. The result proved astonishing in the extreme.

"Blimey, boys," roared 'Wild Bullocks' in tones that Stentor might have used before the walls of Troy. "Here's a bloke wot don't know Father O'Connell."

Their attention thus attracted in so startling a manner, the passengers in the carriage gaped at Jack, pretending to regard him as some hitherto undreamed-of monstrosity, and they continued to do so for such a length of time that the young man felt the prickly sensations about his neck and ears that come from extreme mental discomfort.

"I am to be excused," pleaded Jack at last, quite confusedly. "You see, I am quite a stranger to these parts."

The priest smiled genially, and when 'Wild Bullocks' had explained that "this is our new jackeroo down at Bullangarra," shook hands warmly.

"Arrah, me boy," he said, "tis after hearing a lot of Father O'Connell you will be from these wild lads, for it is forty years that I have been on the Lachlan, and I know them all, man and boy, drunk and sober, in work and out. But they do be telling stories of me at times, both good and bad, so tis sorry I'd be to have you believe them all."

After that, 'Wild Bullocks' told Jack some of these stories of the old priest's work on the western tracks, speaking in quiet tones so as not to be overheard by the subject of the conversation.

"He's a grand ol' man," said the bushman, "an' there's not a bloke in th' back country that wouldn't go to hell an' back for him. I've known him take his boots off an' give 'em to a footsore swaggie; an' once he drove into Condoblin in th' middle o' winter without a coat on, an' th' westerlies cuttin' like a shear-blade. He said he give it to a rabbiter's wife to cover up 'er sick kid in their camp down by Lake Cudgellico. Th' dead-beats an' th' busted shearers can always get a bob or two from him to help 'em on th' road, an' he don't lecture 'em neither. He just says, "Arrah, me boy, tis little I've got meself, but take this, an' when ye earn yer next cheque, remember Father O'Connell." An' they always do remember, too! I've known blokes send him a quid at Christmas from th' Gulf, or out from Cooper's Creek.

"If anybody's sick, squatter, cocky or whaler, ol' Father O'Connell's on hand. He lobs out o' th' bush just when he's wanted, seemin' ter drop from nowhere, an' him bein' a bit o' a doctor, he does a power o' good. An' he's a hard ol' case, too. I mind th' time when me an' 'Up-She-Rises' was humpin' bluey over th' Eribendry Plain, an' we lights a fire by th' six mile gate ter warm some water fer th' rum we has, it bein' the middle o' winter an' blanky cold. We sees a buggy comin' across th' plain, an' when it gets close enough we spots it's Father O'Connell. When he comes up we has th' grog pipin' hot, an' I pours out a pannikin full an' goes up ter him. Th' poor ol' bloke's blue with th' cold, him havin' no overcoat. 'Could yer do a drop o' rum, hot?' I asks him. He looks at th' steam comin' out o' th' pannikin, an' then he looks up at th' sky. 'Did I hear an angel whisper?' he says, 'an' reaches fer th' tot.

"He's a Catholic priest, but he's one o' them that don't worry everybody about not goin' ter church, an' I ain't never yet heard him mention hell. He just tries ter get us blokes ter act square, an' give everybody a fair go. Yes, he's a right man, all right. It'd do yer good ter have a yarn with him. I'll make room fer yer here."

Jack soon found Father O'Connell to be a truly interesting character, and, incidentally, he began to realise that most of the bewildering stories that he had previously listened to concerning the bush, as told by 'Wild Bullocks' and his companions, had been concocted on the spot for his especial edification. As a matter of fact the priest had hinted gently, but unmistakably, that this custom of imposing on the trusting stranger was so hallowed by time that it had become the national pastime of the back-blocks. And Jack, not slow to perceive the truth, resolved to keep up the deception so far as he was concerned, and for the sake of the fun that was in it to accept, as gospel, for the future, everything told him that was amazing and bizarre.

The train had halted at a siding, and looking across the paddocks to the south, Jack noticed a collection of buildings that appeared to be a small township nestling at the base of a steep, sparsely-timbered hill that reared itself unexpectedly out of the surrounding plain. He asked the priest what village it was.

"Arrah, me boy," said Father O'Connell. "That does not be after being a township. Tis the homesteads of Burrawang Station. You've heard of the Burrawang stud sheep, maybe? Old Thomas Edols – God rest his soul – took as great a pride in his rams as in his home. But the place is not what it used to be. More than half of it has been resumed and cut up for selectors, until now tis but a small run, as stations go.

Twas a township, true for you, in the old days at the shearing time, and tis I that have seen more than a thousand men there at the roll-call. The shed is the biggest in the world; it do be having a hundred and twenty pens, but twas never once used to its capacity, nor will it ever be now. Droughts and closer settlement brought the end of the big runs of the old days, when it was a hundred mile ride from a homestead to any of the boundary gates. Burrawang was like the rest, and now tis but the ghost of its former greatness."

"I suppose," queried Jack, "that Burrawang was one of the biggest stations here in the early days?"

"Not at all, my boy," replied the priest. "There were dozens bigger, and out in the back country from here now, there are stations half as big as Ould Erin. Burrawang ran from the Lachlan over the Bogan watershed, and there are half a dozen townships now at spots where the boundary riders and shepherds used to camp only thirty years ago. And the country that carried perhaps a hundred thousand sheep and twenty families now yields hundreds of thousands of bushels of wheat and keeps many thousand people. Tis a great thing for the country to break up the big stations – but I loved those good old days."

Looking about the paddocks, Jack noticed that the land was, save for a few patches here and there, absolutely bare of grass. As the train proceeded on its leisurely but bone-shaking way, he saw that this condition of affairs became worse, and he realised for the first time that this new country into which he was faring was in the grip of a drought. When daylight had first made the passing landscape visible he had, that morning, wondered idly at the parched appearance of the paddocks on either side of the line, and thought that a fall of rain would freshen things up. Out here, on the fringe of the great western plains, it came to him suddenly that the drought was a devastating enemy that had to be fought and conquered, a relentless foe that left desolation and despair in his train.

Although born in the country, Jack had left it as a child, and had become essentially a city-dweller. He had often visited the Blue Mountains as a man, and knew their magnificent scenery; he had sought and seen the alluring beauties of hidden bay, shining beach, shaded creek, and moaning harbour bar by the winding ways of the Hawkesbury; he had motored amid the amazing panoramas of the South Coast. When he had fared farther afield it had been to Kosciusko, to Wombeyan, to the Snowy trout streams, and he had been whirled thither in swift night trains for a few frenzied hours of pleasure, only to hurry back to his beloved city. He had rushed to Melbourne by the same night trains, by the yachting pathway, or in big steamers, to see the Cup.

He had made the same frantic rush to Brisbane to the Exhibition. Of the bush he knew nothing, and the bush folk he knew not at all. Never had he noted, save for a careless passing glance, the farms, the orchards, the stations, nor the toil-toughened bushmen, who laboured from dawn until darkness to produce the wealth of the country and to feed the teeming populace of the cities. It was now borne in upon him irresistibly how hopelessly wasted had been the best years of his life, and how sadly ignorant he was of the wonderful country that was his homeland. No wonder, he thought, the bushmen had tried to befool him with their exaggerated stories of its ways and manners; they had cynically realised his culpability, and sought to punish him in their own careless, but cutting, fashion.

In a bitter mood, Jack sucked stolidly at his unlighted pipe, and stared out across the land. He saw, away to the north, the blue outlines of a low range of barren hills, with a dead-level expanse of red, stark country, scantily timbered, flowing to their base. To the south the plains spread apparently to infinity. At odd places, he noticed, was some solitary peak rearing its scarred and stony shoulders to the horizon, and in the mid-distance, a winding length of gaunt, spreading gums that seemed to writhe along like some great, unwieldy serpent. This, he soon guessed, was the river's course; the grey, muddy Lachlan, that lost itself amid the gaping cracks in the burnt-up reed-beds down by Oxley, hundreds of miles to the west. It seemed a desolate, hopeless country, and his heart sank as he remembered his confident assertions that he would wrest a fortune from it. With the gloomiest forebodings in his mind he turned to the priest.

"It seems to me," Jack said, "that a man requires to have a heart as big as his station to try to wring a livelihood from a desert like this."

"Aye, my lad," answered the old priest, with unusual solemnity. "Tis big hearts these men out here do be having, and you'll live to find that out. But tis not always drought here; there are seasons of plenty when the land is like the Garden of Eden, and tis then you'll know it properly. But, drought or times of long, lush grasses, you'll come to love the west and its ways if you stay out here for a few years."

Within an hour, after one or two weary delays at lonely sidings, the train reached the precincts of the town of Condobolin. Jack saw ahead of him an irregular array of houses sprawled over the side of a gravelly ridge, and spreading to the river at its base. To the left was a wide sheet of water that looked like a noble stream, but which was, he learned, merely a creek that had been dammed for the town supply. Along its banks were the inevitable Chinese gardens, oases of bewildering greenery in a desert of desolation.

At the railway station, with its little wooden office, its huge galvanised-iron goods shed, its wool-loading dump and endless water-tanks, Jack, half-expecting that the advent of a stranger to such an out-of-the-way place would excite comment, was strangely disappointed that the few loungers on the platform scarcely noticed him. These men, too, appeared to be of the type and cast in the same mould as 'Wild Bullocks', his travelling companion. They were mostly tall, some lanky, burnt brown by the sun, and with keen, clear eyes that were assuredly accustomed to scanning the far-distant horizons. All were coatless, with cotton shirts open at the neck. That most of them were horsemen, Jack perceived from the long-necked spurs on their elastic-side boots, and their tight, sweat-stained trousers; but he looked in vain for the leggings of the conventional stockman and those other appurtenances of dress that city folk usually associate with the men of the bush. It was 'Wild Bullocks' who informed him later that leggings were the exception rather than the rule in country districts, explaining that a rider "could tease 'em, or grip 'em, better with the bleeders when they're pig-rootin'," by which he meant that a horseman could more satisfactorily use his spurs on a bucking animal.

Jack accompanied Father O'Connell to one of the hotels, his other travelling companions preferring to seek the rough and ready shelter of the "Bushman's Home", a dilapidated pine building, wherein travellers were permitted to camp in their own blankets for a modest threepence, and to have the use of a fire in the back-yard during the day at which to boil their 'billies'. At the hotel, the most pretentious in town, the young man found unexpected comfort and a ready welcome. It was not long before he met his future boss, Duncan Callister, manager of Bullangarra Station. That gentleman was engaged at a game of billiards in the hotel saloon when the priest introduced Jack.

"Sorry I couldn't go up to the train," Callister said. "I've been playing 'five hundred up' with old 'King Sock-em' of Euglo, and I just couldn't stop that, you know. Just go and have a drink with Father O'Connell and I'll join you later."

Jack did not know why the game could not have stopped, but he proceeded to invite his clerical friend to partake of the hospitality of the house.

4

WHEN THE STAKES ARE HIGH

It was settling day at Tattersall's Club, Sydney, and Pitt Street, for a hundred yards or more on either side of its portals, was thronged with representatives of the sporting fraternity. They were a miscellaneous lot, these men that made their living from the racing game. Hard-bitten, hard-faced, hard-voiced, they comprised bookmakers, trainers, jockeys, punters, and a big proportion of that section known as "hard heads", the whisperers, touts, spielers, urgers – crooks generally. They stood about in small groups on the roadway and on the footpath discussing in forceful and profane language the results of the big meeting just over, and at the same time interfering not inconsiderably with the traffic of the street.

Occasionally a languid police officer would stroll along and make a half-hearted request to the loiterers to "move on". The response was invariably a casual shuffle for a few yards by the "sports", and the reforming of the same old groups. Once in a while a few choice spirits would adjourn to the gaudily-decorated Marble Bar, but this was seldom, for those that live by the turf are notably abstemious where strong waters are concerned. "They can git yer when yer sober," they philosophise, "but when yer shick – Gor blimey."

Near the doorway of the club, just where the crows was thickest, a group of trainers were talking over the winnings of the bookmakers.

"It was a bad meeting for the punters, right enough," said Jim Harden, formerly a noted jockey, "and I reckon that one or two'll take the knock."

"Well," commented old Teddy Dees, "if anyone does, it'll be young Ray Penderby. He's been having a rough spin lately, and this meetin' ought to settle him."

"Yes," assented a third speaker, "he had to ask for time to settle over the Hawkesbury and Rosehill meets, and he must have done five thousand pounds over the two big events, let alone the other two days. He's a plunger, he is, and Heaven knows where he gets the brass from."

"His old man," asserted Harden emphatically. "He's a darned old fool, because he thinks the sun shines out of Ray. He's about the only bloke in Sydney that don't know what a crook the young cove is."

The conversation then turned to the probable fate of another noted plunger, and, whilst the second unlucky gambler was under discussion, Raymond Penderby himself, immaculately garbed, sauntered into the club with the air of a proprietor.

Raymond was the only son of James Penderby, one of Sydney's foremost solicitors, and was idolised by his father. He had just now attained his 22nd year, and had left behind him a brilliant university career. As a lad he had shown a marked disinclination to the law, for which his father had intended him, and, having been given his own way, as happened always where his father was concerned with him, he had chosen medicine. Study was not arduous to him, as, gifted with an unusually alert mind and a marvellously retentive memory, he was able to cram for his examinations with little effort in brief time, and emerge always with creditable passes. But, despite his abilities in this respect, his character possessed several disagreeable traits that had made him extremely unpopular with his fellow undergraduates. His intensely selfish nature often impelled him to the performance of deeds that were looked upon by his associates as being "not cricket", and which, when investigated by one with a moral sense, fully developed, were actually unscrupulous. In fact it was laid to his door that he had been directly responsible for the expulsion of Jack Burnside from the University, and it was whispered that he had never been manly enough to admit his fault. This incident was often talked about, and it was believed that Jack had been blamed for some particularly reprehensible act of Ray's because of the singular and much-commented-on likeness between the two. Those that knew both young men intimately were convinced that the conduct attributed to Jack was entirely foreign to his manly good-nature and clean, moral habits, whereas it was merely part of Raymond's everyday life.

This so-called resemblance between the young men had frequently been the cause of many innocent mistakes. Actually they were of a type that was somewhat uncommon, and many people had dubbed them, "The Twins". But, when they were placed together, the observer, who previously might have been impressed by their likeness to one another when seen apart, would often wonder, as is usual in such cases, how he had so palpably blundered in ever confusing their identity, or in seeing any resemblance between them. And, afterwards, that same observer might, as is also the usual in these cases, repeat his frequent mistake, and address the one when he believed it to be the other. Both had been friendly enough at college, and later at the University, for they were of the same age, and their fathers were the closest friends. But, after Jack's ignominious departure from the Alma Mater their paths had but seldom crossed. Raymond had confined himself to a study of his medical books, and a still more careful study of the form of racehorses and the betting markets. Jack had travelled along the easy path of pleasure; careless, extravagant, but never vicious.

As Raymond Penderby walked to the bar in the club rooms he was accosted by one of the attendants.

"Foxie wants to see you, sir," whispered the man in livery. "An' so does Jim Blackett. They're both together over at one of the settlin' tables."

The young man sought the persons named. They were two of the leviathan bookmakers, and to them he was indebted to an extent that he did not care to think upon. He found the metallicians in conference with two others of their kind, one a member of "The Big Three", and the other a noted penciller in the St. Leger. That they were discussing him he felt sure, for it was with this quartet that most of his turf business had been done.

They greeted him curtly as he halted near their table. The Leger bookie was the first to speak.

"They tell us you can't settle, and you're going to take the knock!" that individual stated aggressively.

'Taking the knock' in racing parlance, means that a punter, or taker of odds, is unable or declines to meet his liabilities. Although betting is legalised only within limits in New South Wales, a bet is regarded as a gambling transaction or a debt of honour, and if a man bets on credit with a bookmaker, and subsequently refuses or is unable to pay he cannot be sued in the courts for the money, nor is there any other legal process by which it can be obtained from him. The name of the defaulter is posted on a 'mourning board', shaped like a tombstone, in some of the clubs, but this is poor consolation to the too-trusting ringmen that have suffered, though it may be a warning to their fellows of the bag. 'Taking the knock' is more common than is imagined, and bookmakers show no mercy to a defaulter when they meet him, in so far as their language is concerned, at least.

When the question was put so bluntly to Raymond Penderby the young man flushed angrily.

"They told you a damned lie," he said sharply, "whoever they are. It is true that I am unable to settle today, and that I want time; but I will pay you, every penny of it."

"When can you find the money?" asked Foxie, drily.

"If you give me three months I will be able to settle everything. My liabilities run into six thousand pounds, and, as the four of you are my only creditors, it rests with yourselves as to whether you give me time or not. If I go to my father now he will refuse to help me, but within three months I shall be in a position to satisfy you all. It is not unreasonable for me to ask for time – you have all done the same thing yourselves on occasions, if rumour is correct – and, anyhow, I have always settled in the past. Make a fuss now, and you get nothing."

The bookmakers exchanged meaningful glances. Ultimately Blackett spoke.

"We'll give you the three months," he said, "but take a tip from me, and give the gee-gees a miss until your luck changes."

"I intend to do that," assented Raymond, "and, as this last flutter has got on my nerves, I have made up my mind to go out into the country for some little while to get right again, and to allow a scheme that I have under way to develop. You will hear from me before the time expires." And with an airy wave of his hand he turned and sauntered out of the building, nodding and smiling on the way to a multitude of acquaintances. The four bookmakers watched his exit with mingled feelings.

"There goes the makings of a damned scoundrel," muttered the Leger penciller, sagely, and the others nodded silent acquiescence.

After leaving the club Raymond Penderby walked briskly to his father's chambers in Elizabeth Street. In the outer office he found the head stenographer, Molly Forbes, busily engaged at her typewriter. The girl smiled at him brightly as she answered his greeting, and Raymond noticed, as he had often done before, that she was decidedly pretty. Indeed, Molly Forbes was of that type of Australian beauty that many artists have declared to be perfect. She was of medium height, with a beautifully-moulded figure of firm, graceful contour, alluringly attractive. Her features were those of a Madonna, and her eyes of that soft, dreamy grey so frequently discovered in the Irish-Australian maidens. Her wealth of jet-black hair was typically Irish, accentuating the beauty of her face and lending an added glory to the witchery of her sparkling eyes. The young man gazed at her with open admiration as he asked whether his father was within.

"No," replied Molly, "he has gone to the Supreme Court on Reid's case, and will not return until lunch time. He left a message that you were to take the parcel of books on his table out to Mrs. Brownlow. I will get them for you if you wish."

"Do not disturb yourself, Molly," said Raymond. "I will pick them up; and I want to write a letter."

Raymond Penderby thereupon walked into his father's sanctum to seek the parcel and to write his letter. The first object that caught his attention was a black-enamelled tin box, bearing the inscription, "Estate of Amos Burnside d'csd". He eyed it curiously for a few moments, and then, noticing that the small brass padlock on the staple was unlocked, a sudden impulse urged him to pry into its contents. He lifted the lid.

"I wonder," he muttered to himself, "if it is true that the old chap was 'broke' when he died?"

He glanced casually at two or three documents, bills of costs, probate notices, and copies of letters from his father to Jack Burnside, and from what he saw he felt convinced that the dead speculator had, in truth, died a poor man. He was preparing to restore the papers to their resting place when he noticed a large, official envelope, addressed in his father's handwriting, "John Burnside, Private and Confidential". It needed but little additional stimulus to Raymond's curiosity to induce him to discover what it contained, and the sight of a further superscription: "To be opened only by James Penderby", decided him. He carefully removed the sealing wax from the flap, and with a pen-knife managed to open the cover so that no frayed edge of paper would betray that the envelope had been tampered with. He withdrew a folded document, spread it on the desk, and read.

"Well, I'm hanged!" he ejaculated, as he realised the purport of the writing. It detailed certain transactions between his father and the elder Burnside, now deceased, wherefrom it appeared that the sum of twenty thousand pounds had been entrusted to the lawyer, to be handed to Jack Burnside at a date to be decided by the attorney at his own discretion, such moneys having been invested in the solicitor's name in reliable and prosperous commercial enterprises in Sydney. There was a further proviso, bristling with legal technicalities, wherein power was vested in James Penderby to bestow the money on charity should the said John Burnside not be, in his opinion, at the expiration of six years, "a fit and proper person to be entrusted with such sum or sums as hereinbefore specified".

Raymond Penderby stared long at the document. Thoughts of chagrin and envy filled his mind, and there welled up within him a bitter hatred of the young man whose prosperity, apparently, depended on the caprice of his father, that shrewd, calculating but kindly old lawyer. That Jack Burnside was undoubtedly unaware of his good fortune was evident from the tenor of the instrument he had read, and that that young scapegrace was bound to degenerate into a loafer in the parks of Sydney, and so lose his inheritance, seemed certain. Raymond felt a whole-hearted contempt for the man he had already injured, and as he reflected on the strange whim of the dead Amos Burnside, a sudden realisation of his own embarrassed circumstances rudely disturbed the current of his thoughts.

"By gad," he exclaimed to himself, "That money would mean twenty fortunes to me if I could get hold of it now. I could square up with those infernal bookies, and then make a fortune on Joe Burley's mare in the Epsom. She's bound to win, and unless I settle up before then I won't be able to back her. If I could only get hold of that money somehow. By Heaven, I'll try."

He hastily returned the paper to the envelope, gumming down the flap with some mucilage from a pot on the table. Then he lit a match, melted some red wax to cover the original seal, and pressed into the mass his father's seal which he had found in an unlocked drawer. Finally, having restored all the documents to the black tin box, he walked out to the stenographer's room.

"I will call for the books later, Molly," he said. "I have to go around to the Australia before lunch, but I will be back at one o'clock to see the dad."

The girl nodded, apparently not interested.

"Oh, by the way," Raymond exclaimed, "Do you know what has become of that young chap whose father died lately, and left him stranded? Burnside, I think his name is."

The girl blushed rosily. Then, with shy confusion, she informed the inquirer that Jack had left Sydney on the previous evening for

Bullangarra Station, on the Lachlan, where he had obtained a position as a jackaroo.

"You appear to know a good deal about this fellow," said Raymond, rather sharply, for he had noticed the tell-tale blush. "Anyone would imagine that you were somewhat interested in his fate."

"I am, indeed," replied the girl, in spirited tones, "and I know that he will make a success of anything he attempts."

"Then he must have changed considerably since I knew him," replied the young man, "for he was lazy, idle, and good-for-nothing. From what I have heard lately, he is becoming worse, instead of better."

The girl entered into a vigorous defence of the absent man. "No matter what happened in the past," she ended, "Jack is now a changed man, and he is going to make good – if only for my sake."

"Which means," said Raymond with a sneering smile, "that you will marry and live happily ever after?"

Molly Forbes blushed and a tender light glowed in her expressive eyes. With a wistful smile she said to the man, "That is never likely to be. He is only a friend of mine, a very dear friend. I have always known that he had a heart of gold, and that it was only evil companions that had made him reckless and careless. He was very kind to my mother when we were very poor, and I am proud to be his friend, now that he has no money, and his former so-called friends have deserted him."

"Yes; perhaps you are right," assented Raymond. "Anyhow, I hope that he can stick to his billet. Bullangarra Station, you said? Well, that is rather a coincidence. I intend going up there myself in a few weeks for a brief holiday. I will look up your paragon, and let you know how he is shaping. Ta-ta, Molly."

And with an elaborate bow, Raymond Penderby passed out into the street.

5

TAKING A CHANCE

Raymond Penderby's bachelor chambers in Phillip Street were accounted to be the most artistically decorated and expensively furnished suite of rooms in the city. Their owner took an inordinate pleasure in hunting around the auction rooms and antique shops for articles that were unusual and bizarre, and as it had always been possible for him to gratify his lightest or most extravagant whim with the unlimited moneys supplied by an indulgent father, he had filled his rooms with a collection of curios that was unique in its variety. From the quaintly-carved mahogany bedstead to the brilliant-hued Eastern tapestries, every article of furniture was a prize in itself. The rooms were greatly frequented, for he was an excellent host, but it was rather remarkable that the circle of his friends was ever changing. It was alike with men and women. The girls, many of them merely harpies in the scant guise of semi-respectability, and some eminently clean and good, seldom endured his friendship for more than a few months; the men, scarcely that time. Among themselves, many of them had sought to find the reason of this strange antipathy to Penderby, a feeling that seemed to spring up mushroom-like and unexpectedly, but none could account for it.

One young lady, a vaudeville dancer, explained her feelings to a friend.

"Do you know," she said, "I thought Ray Penderby was just the loveliest man in the world until yesterday, when something seemed to put me off him. We were at afternoon tea, and I had agreed to go motoring with him on Sunday when suddenly I sort of froze, and after that I couldn't be civil to him. I had to get outside as quickly as I could, or I should have been sick, positively I should. Whatever it was – well, it was just there, that's all."

Whatever sinister trait in his character there was, it remained a fact that of the many people that he knew there was none that he could claim as a really dependable friend. He was shrewd enough, and selfish enough, to realise that folk were disposed in friendly spirit towards him merely for what they could get out of him, and he did not hesitate to let them know this. Probably that was the great reason of his general unpopularity.

Seated in a comfortable armchair in his rooms, Raymond Penderby was surveying, mentally, the position in which he found himself.

"I've got to get that money of Burnside's," he said to himself, "but how the devil to do it beats me. I cannot get anything out of the old man; he will not stand me any more for a couple of months, although he generally pays up if I persuade him. I want about seven thousand pounds to clear off all my debts, and if I had Burnside's cash I would be right. With the extra ten or twelve thousand I could break the betting ring at Christmas time. I'll have to think up some scheme, and I reckon that I can fix it through that girl that's so interested in the waster, Molly Forbes. By Jove! She's pretty, though. I'm glad I told her I was going up to Bullangarra, although I only thought of Callister's invitation at that very moment. Well, I'll go up there, and maybe something will turn up. In the meantime I had better run along to see the old man."

Within a few minutes he was at the outer door of his father's office. Before entering, he halted to speak with Molly Forbes, and with a flashing smile said: "How is the beautiful little lady today?"

"Do you mean me, Mr. Raymond?" asked Molly, looking up in astonishment.

"That is obvious!" retorted Raymond gallantly. "Because you are the most beautiful girl in Sydney!"

"I am quite well, thank you," the girl parried. "Your father is in his office now, and is disengaged."

Accepting the dismissal philosophically, Raymond entered his father's room.

"Well, dad," he said cheerily, "how is the law business going?"

"Plenty of work, my boy," said the old man, in whose eyes shone the light of pride and affection. "Too much work, in fact! I am feeling the weight of years."

"Work gets us all at times," the young man responded, with a weary inflection in his voice. "I fagged so hard for that last exam, that I am knocked-up myself. My nerves have gone to pieces, and old Doc Burness has advised me to take a three months' trip into the bush. I would go up to Callister's, out at Bullangarra, only, to tell you the truth, I am out of funds."

"What!" exclaimed his father, in astonishment. "Out of funds? Why, it was only a few weeks ago that I gave you a cheque for seven hundred pounds. What has become of that?"

"Surely you do not think that I have wasted it, father?" answered the young man in a reproachful voice. "I would have had ample left after I paid up my few little debts but for Jack Burnside. He came to me with a story that his father had died leaving him penniless, and he pleaded for the loan of five hundred pounds to enable him to make a start on his own account. The poor fellow was so broken up that, for old friendship's sake, I gave him the money. It was only yesterday I found out that he had lost the whole lot at the races, and he has now cleared out of Sydney."

Raymond told this lie so glibly, and with such apparent sincerity that his father was convinced.

"It is a bad business, my boy," the old man said, "and that five hundred pounds is gone forever. But I will repay you myself, and take over the loan." He then proceeded to write a cheque for the amount stated, and, having blotted it, finally handed it to his son. "There! You can cash that at the bank," he continued. "And I would advise you to take that holiday at once. I do not want my son to fail in his final examination."

"I will leave tomorrow night, dad," said Raymond, in a voice that appeared to be choked with emotion. "You are too good to me."

"Do not say that, my boy," said the old man, brokenly. "I wish that I could do more for you; and I only wish that you would give up those bachelor rooms of yours, and come out to live with me. I am an old man, and very, very lonely."

"Don't, father!" Raymond commanded. "You know that subject is taboo, and we agreed not to revive it until I am a fully-fledged doctor. I am just as sorry as you that I must live in town; but it will not be for long."

"Well, my boy," the old man said, patting him on the shoulder, "have a quiet, restful holiday, and do not, ever in your life, follow the courses of Jack Burnside. By the way, do you know what has become of him?"

Raymond half-suspected that his father knew, but he lied promptly. "Yes!" he said. "He has gone to Melbourne with some of the racing crowd for the Cup. They were crooks and confidence men that he went with, so you can guess what will follow."

"Poor lad," the old man muttered, half aloud. "I am sorry for him, deeply sorry."

Raymond, assured by this that his father knew nothing of Jack Burnside's movements or intentions, made his adieu and hurried to the bank to cash the cheque, pausing on the way out to pay a flattering compliment to pretty Molly Forbes.

At the bank he received cash for the cheque, and retaining a hundred pounds in notes, he proceeded to an adjacent institution of the same kind where he had, some time previously, opened an account in another name to meet some of the doubtful contingencies that arose in the course of his varied and shady career. Here he lodged to the credit of Randolph Philpotts, his assumed name, four hundred pounds in notes. It was his habit to draw against this account on those occasions when he desired to conceal his identity, and it was in his mind at this moment that in connection with his attempt to secure Burnside's inheritance a continuance of the old practice might prove useful.

During the afternoon he busied himself preparing for the journey, packing a formidable collection of suitcases with an array of clothes and sundries that would suffice an ordinary person for a twelve-month. Later, he despatched a telegram to Callister, at Bullangarra, notifying that gentleman of his projected visit and asking that the station motor car should meet him at Condoblin on the following afternoon. Then, after completing arrangements for the care of his fastidious rooms during his absence of three months – for he intended to spend that period in the west – he sought a certain house in the dubious locality known as Surry Hills.

In this congested area, within sound of the chimes of the Town Hall clock, the worst slums of the city exist. Narrow streets, blind alleys, dirty, evil-smelling lanes, straggle over the hillsides, and dilapidated, squalid terraces frown down like wicked beings on the filthy by-ways. Little children, dirt-grimed and in rags, quarrelled or romped amid the traffic; bedraggled, slatternly, drunken women lurched and lumbered in and out of the unhealthy, miserable tenements. Slant-eyed Mongolians, swarthy, fierce-looking foreigners from the underworld of Continental cities, weedy, furtive youths and burly, toil-stained labourers lounged in the doorways or squatted on the kerbstones at each corner, talking in raucous voices or smoking stolidly. At odd corners lurked shabby hotels, unpretentious buildings that crowded back in the shadows of the terraces as though ashamed of their presence; and ever slinking in and out of the bar doorways were men, women, and even children.

As Raymond Penderby threaded his way through these unsavoury pathways he attracted little attention, although he was immaculately dressed and appeared prosperous and wealthy. Every here and there some lounger would nod to him casually, and occasionally one of the furtive youths would greet him by name audibly. That he was known to many was apparent. That his presence excited no comment was because Surry Hills had become the rendezvous and refuge of crooks, big and small, the sneak-thief and the confidence man, the burglar and the garrotter; and these fugitives from justice were not infrequently indistinguishable from the prosperous men of business of the city in so far as dress and deportment were concerned. Reaching a wretched hovel in a narrow right-of-way, Raymond knocked at a door that was flush with the footpath – and waited. An upper window in an adjoining building was cautiously opened and a head appeared, the curious one eyeing the visitor intently. Then a low whistle sounded from above and the door was opened by a slatternly female.

"Blimey, I thort it was the perlice," said the woman, apparently in explanation of the delay. "Farley's after Bill again. Come in, quick."

She closed the door hurriedly after the visitor had entered and led the way to the kitchen, which was also the dining room and reception room. In a few moments a beetle-browed, brutal-faced man, with an undershot jaw and huge, gnarled fists, came in from some mysterious hiding-place at the rear. This was Bill M'Bean, ex-bushman and now city sneak-thief.

"What d'yer want now?" he demanded of his visitor, truculently. "Got any more blokes yer want me to stoush?"

"No," said Raymond Penderby shortly. "I have a job for you, though, and one that ought to suit you. Do you want to get away from Sydney for a while?"

"My bloody oath!" replied the other, emphatically. "They're makin' it too flamin' hot fer me now, an I'm due to be lumbered any time over a bloke I did down in Kent Street. What's the lurk?"

"I want you to come out to Condoblin on tonight's train and I'll find something for you to do out there."

"Not work, is it? I mean – hard graft?"

"You need not alarm yourself; it is not hard work. I don't know myself just now what it will be, but I want you to be on hand for a job I may have. You know that part of the country, I believe?"

"I was born on the Lachlan, an' I was one of the Wongonga push fer years. I know every inch o' the country from the Abercrombie Ranges ter the Darlin' River."

"Well," proceeded Raymond, "here are ten pound notes. Get out to Strathfield as best you can and pick up the Forbes mail train tonight. See me at Parkes in the morning, but after that do not recognise me or speak to me. If I need you, I will contrive to send you a note."

"Gor blimey! Ten frog-skins! You bet I'll be there, fer I can give the demons the slip easy. I tell yer, I don't mind a free trip back ter the old parts again, an' the missus'll look after herself while I'm away."

"It will be worth fifty to you before it is finished," said Raymond, preparing to leave. "Keep clear of the police if you can, and be ready for anything."

"My bloody oath! Anythin' from pitch-an'-toss ter manslaughter!" declared Bill M'Bean.

Returning to the city Raymond debated with himself the wisdom of establishing this doubtful ally in a township that he would frequently visit, and he asked himself a dozen times what use he could make of this criminal, seeing that he had no definite plans formulated for the financial discomfiture of Jack Burnside.

"Well," he said to himself, "if M'Bean cannot be of use to me in the Burnside business I can use him in some other scheme to raise money, for I must have it, and in big lumps, pretty soon."

On the train that evening, Raymond Penderby found congenial company in a first-class smoking compartment, where several card-playing commercial travellers and a wealthy squatter were eager for a game of poker. The travellers played until Mount Victoria was reached, when the game terminated, leaving Raymond richer by more than a hundred pounds. His remarkable good fortune had been aided by a certain sinister skilfulness in dealing the cards, that had passed unobserved but which, in the past, had cost him much practice and considerable cash to acquire.

At Parkes he spoke casually to Bill M'Bean on the platform, and when the train arrived at Condoblin that afternoon he and his luggage were being whirled away by Jack Burnside in the Bullangarra motor car, while Bill was seeking a corner in the Bushman's Home and discovering many old and thirsty friends.

6

WHERE THE SEASONS COME AND GO

"You, Burnside, are to go out to the Circle Y paddock. Have a look at those wethers, and ride down the fence as far as the road to see if the netting is right. Then you can go across to Dirralong and tell McLeod, the bullocky, that he can have the grey mare for thirty pounds. After that, ride to the shed and give them a hand with the engine."

Callister was issuing the orders for the day's routine of labour to his stockmen and boundary-riders, and Jack, after a week's experience, had come to the conclusion that to carry out faithfully these daily directions the men had to work hard and for long hours. His own share of the day's toil would involve a lonely ride of fifty miles or more, and then after that, an hour would have to be spent tinkering with the cranky oil engine at the shearing shed before he got back to his bunk. Nevertheless he was enjoying every moment of his new life, and if the efforts of the day found him saddle-weary and listless as he turned his horse out at night, he ate heartily and slept as he never had before.

On the morning after his arrival at Bullangarra for the first time, Jack had decided in his own mind that he would be permitted to have at least a week of semi-idleness during which he could gradually accustom himself to his new surroundings. On that occasion he had risen with the other men when the big bell in the yard was rung at daylight by the cook, and had breakfasted with them in the rambling pine building known as "the hut". He had not been present at the stockyard when the hands had set forth to perform their various tasks, so he was somewhat disturbed half an hour later when the cook, discovering him contemplating the muddy, torpid river, advised him, with much profanity, to get up immediately and see the boss at the office.

He had found Callister busily engaged with the book-keeper, checking lists of figures, and had waited patiently on the verandah until bidden to enter. He was startled considerably, however, when he heard Callister addressing him.

"Here, you loafer," the manager roared. "Where the devil were you this morning when the jobs were going? There's no room for slackers here, and if you expect to remain on Bullangarra you'll have to make up your mind to work."

Jack was amazed and angry at the injustice of this unexpected outburst, believing that his inexperience merited some recognition, if not a little pampering, and he burst into a torrent of self-justifying explanations. Callister, however, rudely interrupted him.

"I know you are a new chum," he said, "but just remember this: you came here to work. If you won't work, it means the sack; if you will, you can stick here as long as you like, and you might be owner some day. But whatever you do, make no explanations to me." Then, continuing in a more kindly tone, he said, "Of course, I realise that you know nothing about station life, so I will take you round the run with me today, and give you an idea of what is to be done, and where the landmarks are, so that you will not get lost. Just hang around for half-an-hour until I am ready."

Jack had taken advantage of the opportunity to inspect the homestead and the river. It was a single-storey building, with wide verandahs running around three sides, and a beautiful flower garden, with tennis court and squares of carefully-clipped lawn extending to the bank of the stream. Water for gardening and other purposes was raised from the river by windmills that pumped the muddy fluid into elevated iron tanks, whence it was reticulated by means of pipes to the required spots. At the rear, some fifteen or twenty rough buildings were sprawled irregularly over an acre of ground, these comprising the kitchen, bachelors' quarters, men's barracks, store, "hut", stables, meat-house, dairy, and numerous other structures utilised for the miscellaneous purposes of a station, the whole resembling some prosperous village. Beyond this area lay the stockyards, the horse paddock, one or two small cultivation paddocks, and then the run itself. The extensive scale on which everything appeared to be laid out impressed Jack greatly, and he thought, for the first time, that the direction of the business of a big station was a work of magnitude, and truly a man's job. And it was with a feeling of newly-awakened admiration in his heart that he answered Callister's hail and made towards the stables. The two men entered the harness-room together.

"You can take that saddle, cloth, and bridle," said Callister, indicating the gear, "and it will be yours to look after so long as you are here. You told me that you can ride, but I'll give you a fairly quiet horse for a start, so come down to the yards."

The groom saddled Callister's horse, and Jack, after some racing around the yard, captured a leggy chestnut with a wicked eye, that had been pointed out to him as 'the quiet one'. He saddled the animal, which appeared to have developed a violent antipathy to him, judging by its vicious efforts to bite his shoulder as he buckled the girth, and led it to the paddock.

"He might root a bit," warned Callister as Jack prepared to mount, "so look out!"

Jack mounted quickly, but barely was he seated when the chestnut plunged forward, then sideways, and made a terrific bound into the air, landing with his head in the opposite direction to that in which he started, and with his four feet bunched together. Jack turned a graceful somersault, and landed in a sitting posture in the dust. He felt himself gingerly, and gazed with a rueful expression at the now placid horse.

"How are you feeling?" asked Callister, anxiously, as he rushed towards him.

"Oh, just a bit off," said Jack, with an effort at a grin.

Callister burst into a hearty laugh, and the groom guffawed. "Well," said the manager, "you take it all right. You can get on now with safety – he won't do it again. And don't worry about the spill, for he threw me yesterday!"

Jack remounted the chestnut, and it ambled off as unconcernedly as a horse could possibly go.

That day proved to be a revelation to Jack. Duncan Callister was the true type of a western sheepmen, one who had been born and reared on the sheep runs of the Lachlan, and whose father had, at one time, been its richest squatter. Drought, improvidence, and rash speculations had bankrupted his progenitor, and the son, in his declining years, found himself managing for a Sydney mortgage company a station that had once been owned by his family. With all the pride of his kind in his calling, he discoursed to Jack throughout the long day's ride on every phase of the pastoral industry, and, finding the young man to be an intelligent listener, he explained, with wealth of detail, his methods of working the run. Every word he uttered impressed itself upon Jack Burnside's mind; the subject interested him intensely. When the young jackeroo did not grasp the import of some point made by Callister he did not hesitate to press for enlightenment, and the manager responded with the proud eagerness of a kind-hearted teacher.

As they rode across the horse-paddock homeward, when the long shadows of the river gums were stealing across the plains and the sun, a fiery red ball, was dropping out of sight in a dusty haze to the west, Callister spoke after a long interval of silence.

"I've told you most of what I know about the business," he said, "but the real thing will only come to you by experience. This is a grand country, but every man has to work hard to wrest its wealth from it, though in the past we have worked it along the wrong lines. I can see now that drought and the lack of water, both of which can be provided against, have ruined hundreds of squatters as they did my father, but I am too old and confirmed in my ideas to make new plans now. Take my advice, Burnside, and if you intend to go on the land, learn all about irrigation, for it is the only thing that is going to save the back country."

And next day Jack commenced his duties.

The day that he rode the Circle Y paddock saw him settled down capably and contentedly in the routine of the station's work. Keen-witted, and not by any means unintelligent, he had used his powers of observation shrewdly when with the other men, and in that brief space of a week he had gained much valuable knowledge; and, what was also of infinite value to him, the goodwill and respect of his fellow-workers. It was true that they had made him the victim of dozens of practical jokes of the rough-and-ready bush order, and had told him stories that were outrageous impositions to his credulity. To the stories he listened with an air of awed interest, never expressing a doubt, and the practical jokes he took in good part, or adroitly turned them on the perpetrators. He found that there was rough good humour in the cosmopolitan collection of station hands, a loyalty to the station and the boss, and a willingness always to do to the full the work that was their share.

Riding along in the clear, fresh morning air, Jack felt the blood tingling in his veins, and an elation in his heart that he had never before experienced. Truly, he thought, the bush was the home of men. After gaining the paddock boundary he opened the netting gate and led his horse through, then spending a few moments straining with a stick a loose wire in the fence. This done, he remounted and plodded along the netted line, looking out vigilantly for gaps or breaks through which rabbits could find a passage.

Presently he found himself humming one of the old bush songs that he had heard Billy McDonald, the horse-breaker, singing in the "hut" each evening:

"Wrap me up in my stockwhip and blanket,
And bury me deep down below,
Where the dingoes and crows won't molest me,

In the shade where the coolabahs grow."

The refrain had a doleful melody, and Jack idly wondered why it was, as he had not failed to notice that most of the bushmen who indulged in song voiced so tunelessly nothing but mournful, melancholic lays. "Perhaps," he said to his horse, "the country gets on the poor beggars' nerves."

And the landscape he then saw was a dreary and desolate one. Stretching out to infinity to the west and south and north were the plains, dead-level expanses of sun-baked country almost bare of grass. Timber of stunted growth struggled for existence in clumps and patches, and between were open, flat stretches on which the mirage danced in mockery. Small mobs of listless, emaciated sheep appeared here and there; occasionally a squad of emus would run, with bobbing bodies and swaying heads, to a clump of pine scrub as his horse startled them, and a flock of brolgas in the distance would dance, on a treeless tract, a graceful minuet. Sinister, evil-voiced crows flitted down on prostrate sheep, and a scared rabbit would scurry into the raw, red patch of earth that denoted a burrow. Willy-willies, narrow spouts of whirlwind, would start skywards from the plain when not a breath of breeze disturbed the atmosphere, and carry their column of vapoury dust straight to the heavens, hanging poised, unmoving, for hours at a time. The coolabah trees and myalls hung their beautiful foliage droopingly, and the scrub pine and mallee looked like dwarfed caricatures of tender garden bushes in the heat haze. It was a drought-stricken land – and it looked it.

Jack had expressed a wonder to Callister on the occasion of his first ride as to how the sheep existed, when there appeared to be not a mouthful of feed for them, and had been astonished to learn that the grasses on the Lachlan country, the barley-grass, trefoil, crowfoot, corkscrew, and half a dozen others that he could not remember, bore a head rich in grain. This seed, being shed when ripened, collected on the ground, and when the fierce heat of summer withered the flag and stalk, and it was blown away by the whirling westerly winds, the heavy seed heaped itself in clumps against inequalities on the surface of the land, and thus provided rich and nourishing sustenance for the starving animals. And this fodder was now keeping the Bullangarra sheep alive. In another month, unless rain came, the men would have to commence lopping the edible scrubs and trees, warrior-bush, myall, coolabah, bolar, and kurrajong.

Thinking over these things, Jack recalled Callister's advice about irrigation. Remembering the rich patch of Lucerne near the homestead, irrigated carelessly and spasmodically from the river, it caused him to wonder why the thousands of acres along the frontage had not been planted with this succulent fodder and the hay stored against a lean time such as they were then experiencing on the run. He had learned that the rich red loam of the plains was wonderfully responsive to moisture, and the lack of foresight and provision against dry, rainless spells amazed him.

"If ever I get a block of land near a river," he said to himself, "I will show them what irrigation means."

It was mid-afternoon when he reached Dirralong, an adjoining station, whose homestead was near the Bullangarra boundary. He found McLeod, the bullock-driver, washing down a hunk of 'brownie' with copious draughts of tea from a jack-shay that the cook had filled. He delivered his message about the mare that was for sale, and then squatted on his heels near the old carrier to listen to the yarns that he knew would soon be forthcoming. Mac was noted for his stories all along the river.

The battered veteran of the roads soon became talkative, explaining that, while he preferred bullocks for his teams, he just now was experimenting with horses. This prompted Jack to enquire whether or not it was a fact that his reputation of being a finished artist with the whip was a well-established one.

"That reminds me," commenced McLeod, "of a new chum bloke by th' name of Attenborough – 'Orace Attenborough – what had Burrenbudgery at one time when he come out here first. He advertises for a flamin' bullocky to cart his wool into Condoblin, and I applies. When I gets to the homestead he says, 'Can you drive bovines, haw-haw?' I sez, 'What the hell is them?' 'I mean, haw, are you a capable bullock driver, haw-haw?' he comes back at me. Then when I tells him that I'll drive a team with any mongrel this side of the Cooper he gets flummoxed. 'I don't doubt your ability, me man, haw-haw,' he says. 'and as I'm in sore need of a teamster, I'll engage you, haw-haw, at fifteen shillings a week, haw-haw, and tucker, haw-haw.' I sez to him, 'You can stick yer fifteen shillings a week in yer shirt, har-har, and yer tucker, har-har, and yer flamin' bullocks, har-har, and all yer damned sheep, har-har!' He gets a bit red in the dial at this, an' then he sez, 'I might be a new-chum out here, haw-haw; but my shirt is not a travelling stock reserve, haw-haw.' I took his job after that, but on contract."

Jack laughed heartily at the droll mimicry and the quaint humour that characterised the old man's story, and to encourage him to further efforts he questioned him as to the completeness of his present team.

"Well," said McLeod, "I'll have a good team when I gets that mare, but it won't equal the first bullock team I ever had, back in the nineties. Pull! They'd pull the stars out o' heaven! I'll tell yer about one thing they did. I was drawin' fer Rand, from Bogandillon, an' has the old table-top loaded proper with wool. It was a terrible wet year, an' I got bogged in the creek near the wool-shed, an' they reckoned I would have to dig her out. Well, I straightened 'em up in the jewellery – them's the chains, yer know – an' I set 'em to it. By cripes, they tore into it an' stuck their toes a yard inter the mud. Then, with a heave, they got 'er on the run an' went fer about a hundred yards before I steadied 'em. I hears the shearers yellin', an' when I looks back, hang me if they hadn't pulled the flamin' creek bed along as well as the wagon!"

This was too much for Jack, and he burst into a roar of laughter. "So long, Mac," he said, as he went to secure his horse. "I'll come along and see the new team do a pull like that when you are ready."

"They'll do it," said the old man seriously. "S'long."

That night when Jack sat down to dinner, for he had been admitted to the manager's table after the custom with jackaroos that are approved, Callister spoke.

"I got a wire today saying that a visitor for the place will arrive at Condoblin by tomorrow's train, and I want you to go in to meet him. You can drive the car, and you had better bring him straight out, so that you can be here in time for dinner."

"I will leave here at nine o'clock, then," said Jack, "so that I can get the radiator fixed up in town. By the way, what is his name?"

"Raymond Penderby," said Callister.

Jack had many curious thoughts that night as he sat smoking on the verandah, and a disturbing premonition of impending ill-luck caused him to lie awake for hours after he had turned in.

7

A FELLOWSHIP OF EVIL

"Jack Burnside! By all that's wonderful!"

This vociferous greeting was yelled at the young jackeroo as the train came to a protesting standstill at the Condoblin station, and he saw Raymond Penderby gesticulating from the window of a first-class smoking carriage. Jack hurried to the door of the compartment. In a ten-minute interval, during which the passengers waited resignedly, as was the custom, for a leisurely porter to unlock the door and check the tickets, Jack and the visitor conversed.

"What on earth are you doing out in these God-forsaken wilds?" was the first question that Penderby asked.

"I am a full-blown jackeroo on the station that you are about to visit," replied Jack. "You see, I have had to take to hard work," he added lamely.

"I cannot tell you how pleased I am to see you," asserted the other, warmly. "And, by gad! You are looking fine. We couldn't make out what had become of you, and I, for one, was rather ashamed that I had not hunted you up so soon as I heard that your poor old dad's estate had proved so disappointing. I realised that I owed you something over that old business at the University which you so often told me had been forgiven and forgotten, and I wanted to help you. When I went to look you up, you had vanished. Why didn't you come to me? I could have given you some sort of a start, though ever so small."

All this was said with such apparent earnestness and feeling that Jack was momentarily nonplussed. He had expected some sort of veiled antagonism, or contempt at least, from this man whose attitude towards him in the past had been anything but friendly, and this protestation of a friendship so great that it included a financial gift came near to overwhelming him.

"It's rather fine of you, Penderby," said Jack after a pause. "It looked as though I had no friends after my money had gone."

"Well," said Raymond solemnly, "I want you always to count on me as one." And he again shook hands with Jack.

On their drive to the station, Raymond Penderby exerted himself to the utmost to gain Jack's complete confidence. A glib talker, suave, shrewd, and blessed with a remarkable appreciation of the humour and pathos of commonplace things, it was not long before he found that he had made a decided impression on his companion, who, it may be admitted, still cherished some longings for the life that he had been compelled by circumstances to abandon. Jack heard with absorbed interest the minor details of the city's personal gossip of folk he knew, told by a skilled raconteur, and became stirred to a degree that was swiftly appraised by the visitor.

"By the way," said Penderby, as the car passed through the boundary gates, "little Molly Forbes, the dad's head typiste, appears to have some idea that you are in Melbourne, for she told me as much when I made inquiries concerning your whereabouts. But then, perhaps you wished to cover up your tracks and put her off the scent. Women will talk, you know."

"That seems strange," said Jack in a puzzled voice. "Molly knows that I am at Bullangarra, and could have had no reason for misleading anyone." Then, in a tone of tenderness that surprised his cynical companion, he asked: "How is she? Molly, I mean. Is she quite well?"

"Blooming like a rose," the other replied, laughingly, "and half the junior barristers in Sydney hang around the old man's office all day seeking an opportunity to flirt with her."

"They are not likely to succeed," said Jack shortly, but with great confidence.

"Ah!" exclaimed Penderby with a chuckle. "So you have hopes, eh?"

Jack was somewhat nettled at the tone in which this was said, and he replied sharply, "Miss Forbes is as good as she is beautiful, and I hope, some day, to have the honour of asking her to be my wife."

Raymond Penderby laughed in apparent high humour. "Good boy!" he exclaimed. "There is nothing like working for the girl you have left behind." Then, speaking seriously he added, "You are a lucky dog to be engaged to such a remarkably pretty and clever girl, and I congratulate you heartily."

Jack then took some pains to explain that there was no engagement between them, not even a definite understanding. In the mood that was on him, an inexplicable unrest, excited by the tidings of old friends and beloved scenes, he expanded beyond his wont, and, baring his heart to this man, who was apparently his friend, told him of his most cherished ambitions, his fondest hopes. Penderby proved a sympathetic listener, and heard the story in silence. As they drew up to the homestead he spoke.

"Look here, Jack," he said earnestly, "I am going to stick to you; and you will have that girl sooner than you think."

Jack was quite emotional as he pressed his thanks, and he wrung the other's hand with fervour. "I cannot thank you enough," he said at last, "but I will repay you someday."

Penderby was welcomed by Mr. and Mrs. Callister, and conducted to his room, while Jack took the car around to the shed. Billy Prendergast, the supervisor, was there, and after assisting him to cover the machine, asked a question:

"Was that a brother of yours, Jack?" he inquired. "I mean the bloke that went inside."

"No," replied Jack, "that was Mr. Raymond Penderby, an old friend of mine, from Sydney. He's up here on a visit."

"By the Hogan's ghost, but he's the dead ring of you! I'd have sworn he was your brother," said Billy.

"I was often mistaken for him in the old days," said Jack, rather sadly, "and he for me; but there is no relationship."

During the next fortnight, Raymond Penderby employed his time, as do most visitors to an outback station, riding over the run and dropping in on the neighbours at the homesteads on adjoining holdings. It was no new experience for him to ride all day through the bush, for he had spent many former holidays on sheep and cattle stations, and considered himself somewhat of a bushman. On some of his rides he would make it a practice to accompany Jack Burnside, assisting him with his work for perhaps half a day, and edifying him with cheerful conversation the while.

Jack looked forward to these occasions, because it afforded him a melancholy pleasure to talk of former times and friends; also, it gave him a tender joy to speak of his love for Molly Forbes. Penderby always encouraged him in this direction, for he had convinced himself that his ultimate acquisition of Jack's unknown inheritance must be accomplished in some fashion through her. T was his hope that some workable plan would unfold itself as the outcome of these conversations. Although usually reserved, Jack kept nothing back from his friend. Penderby became the repository of all his hopes and fears, simply by encouraging these confidences, in the expectation that they would be of some use to him in the future.

It was during the third week that Penderby, after informing his host that he intended to ride to Jemalong to stay with the Gatenbys overnight, was cantering along the Forbes road when he overtook a sulky containing two men. As he drew abreast of the vehicle, one of its occupants recognised him.

"Hallo boss!" shouted Bill M'Bean, for it was that worthy who was driving. "Wot yer doin' up here?"

"Oh, it is you, Bill, is it?" said Penderby. "I might well inquire what you are doing here, for I have an idea that I instructed you to remain at Condoblin until I needed you."

"That's right," said M'Bean, bringing the sulky to a standstill; "but, ter tell yer the truth, I blewed all me cash, so I thought I'd hop up ter Wongonga ter see the boys, an' git a few quid. I knew it was no good puttin' the acid on you."

"I am glad you realise that much," said Penderby, with a sneer. "But where are you going now?"

"Across ter the Wongonga pub," Bill replied, "an' if yer've got time it'd pay yer ter come along with us. This bloke here is 'Brummy' Collins, a friend o' mine, an' there's a push about there's as might be of some use ter yer in some o' ther schemes o' yers."

"It will pay you to mind your own business," retorted Raymond, angrily. "I do not wish to have my affairs discussed by you or anyone else."

"It's all right, boss. Yer needn't get shirty," said Bill. "Brummy wouldn't squeak on nobody, an' the other blokes up there is keepin' clear o' the perlice too."

With that, Bill drove off, leaving Raymond Penderby to follow if he chose. The young man sat loosely in the saddle for perhaps a quarter of an hour, thinking deeply as he watched the sulky bumping across the plain. Then he dug the spurs sharply into the horse's sides. As the astonished animal bounded in pursuit of the disappearing vehicle, Penderby muttered to himself, "I am a damned fool; these chaps can give me no help!"

He trotted his horse a hundred yards or so behind the sulky for several miles, but when the shanty came into view he steadied his mount to a walk. M'Bean and his companion had alighted, and were talking to a villainous-looking individual, who proved to be the land-lord, when the horseman rode up.

"It's all right, Mister Penderby," called out M'Bean in reassuring tones, as Raymond dismounted. "There's only a couple o' the boys here. Come in an' have a drink."

The visitor tied his horse to a pepper-tree and followed the others into the bar. There he was presented, with due ceremony, to the land-lord, Mr. 'Peg-leg' Costigan, and two lanky bushmen, Joe Brady and Tommy Gillett, who immediately commenced a bitter argument as to who would shout. The impending fight between them was only avoided by the stranger claiming the honour himself, and the drinks were immediately set up amid mutual good feeling.

Like most wayside shanties, the "Drovers Rest" was a mean, single-storey building of slab walls, stringy-bark roof, and a wide, uneven verandah, on which were the inevitable stools and a half a dozen empty beer kegs. It contained some eight rooms, most of which were lean-tos, added at various periods by ambitious former licensees to the original square, four-roomed structure. The bar was its largest room, and a narrow pine counter ran across the full length of it. The shelves on the wall were well stocked with bottles of every brand of liquor – all empty though – and the walls themselves were adorned with posters of district race meetings, sporting pictures, and stallion advertisements. After each of the party had paid for a round of drinks, excepting the publican, Raymond instructed the landlord to fill the glasses once more.

"You can't have no whiskey this time," 'Peg-leg' announced sorrowfully. "The bottle's cut out, and there'll be no more until the coach comes through. Try the rum; I can recommend it."

They tried the rum, and found it of the variety usually dispensed at such establishments, fiery and nauseating. However, it vanished in the customary direction for such liquids, and within a few moments all felt its potency. Penderby was the first to notice it.

"By Jove!" he exclaimed. "That rum has a kick in it."

"Yes," responded the landlord. "I wouldn't be able to sell a drop of it if it hadn't."

The boniface then proceeded to explain to the stranger the difficulties that beset the path of an outback publican who really desired to keep wholesome liquor on tap, proving conclusively, to his own satisfaction at least, that the unappreciative thirst of the ordinary bushman could only be assuaged by stuff a little weaker than snake poison. In the meantime, M'Bean and the three horsey bushmen were talking quietly at the other end of the bar, discussing some important matter with great earnestness. Finally, Brummy Collins approached Penderby.

"D'yer want any money?" he demanded, point-blank, of the

young man.

"Why?" replied Penderby in surprise. "I have a few pounds on me, and can get what I require when I return to Bullangarra."

"I don't mean that," said the other, quietly. "Wot I mean is, big money. Two or three thousand pounds!"

"It would be very acceptable," replied Raymond, lightly, though thinking rapidly. "But how are thousands to be picked up in the bush? I would like to know more about it."

"I'm not goin' ter tell yer anything unless yer promise ter come inter the business. Bill M'Bean here tells me that yer up in these parts on some scheme that he's goin' ter help yer with. Now, as yer wouldn't be havin' Bill if yer wasn't on the cross, I thought yer might like ter get onter some big money."

Raymond Penderby swallowed the insult, and another glass of rum, but he pondered long in silence over the proposition. He needed the money badly, but he also desired to know how these men could obtain it without robbing a bank or committing some daring breach of the law. After a few moments, during which there was a dead silence in the bar, he asked Collins to walk outside with him, and moved towards the door.

"It's no good," said Collins, shaking his head as Penderby beckoned him out. "We're all in this, an' the other chaps want ter hear wot yer have ter say."

The young medical student frowned and flushed angrily. He felt annoyed and disgusted that he should find himself even listening to some proposal that was to be manifestly dishonest from such palpably disreputable individuals. He hesitated to do what the better part of him urged, to say plainly that he would have nothing to do with them or their nefarious business, and so, hesitating, he was lost.

"How long would it take to get this money?" he asked of Collins.

"About three or four months," the other replied.

"I am afraid it would have to be sooner than that to suit me," said Penderby.

"Well, stop 'ere ternight, an' we'll talk it over," Brummy suggested. "Come on, we'll 'ave another fer luck."

8

WHEN THE STOCK DUFFERS RIDE

On the day following Raymond Penderby's arrival at Bullangarra, that spirited young man had laughingly claimed, at dinner in the evening, that he deserved an especially warm welcome from his host and hostess because he had brought the rain along with him.

Truly enough, on the night of his first appearance there, the first shower for nearly twelve months had fallen, and during the ensuing three weeks the rain had pelted down almost incessantly. The disastrous times through which Bullangarra and all the other stations along the Lachlan had passed had seemed, at the date of Jack Burnside's arrival, to have been concentrating for one great, overwhelming catastrophe. Grass had disappeared from most of the runs, and those off the river that depended for water on the open tanks, great shallow excavations in the plains, and only filled by heavy storms, were in a parlous plight. Sheep had perished in hundreds of thousands throughout the Lachlan country, and already many of the smaller holders, the 'cockies', were facing ruin.

Bullangarra had, fortunately, been lightly stocked at the beginning of the dry spell, a fortuitous circumstance that had made it possible for Callister to work the various paddocks in such judicious and careful fashion that the losses had been comparatively negligible. The fact, also, that the Lachlan River formed a frontage to the widest part of the station minimised the water trouble, and the weir across the stream near the homestead impounded an inexhaustible supply. There being a fall of only a foot to the mile in the levels of the river, that nine-foot-high dam backed up the water for nearly ten river miles. Two billabongs provided water for the back portions. One of these wandering channels of the river left the main stream some forty miles to the east, and the other about twelve miles from the homestead. Both flowed back into the parent stream within a few miles of each other, a little below the western boundary of Bullangarra. Low dams across the billabongs secured water in the back paddocks of the run.

On the fourth day after the first rainfall, Jack and Callister, wearing oilskins and their oldest clothes, rode out to the Circle Y paddock, some twenty miles from the homestead. The weather was warm, and the light drizzling rain that was falling partially obscured the landscape. As their horses splashed along the track Jack was profoundly surprised to notice that the ground on every side was showing unmistakably the green tinge of newly-grown grass. He commented on the fact to his companion.

"Yes," said the manager. "That is grass, right enough, or herbage rather. A few showers make everything grow out here, either in winter or summer. You remember how bare these paddocks were – well, in another fortnight there will be feed a foot high."

"What makes it grow so quickly?" Jack asked, with some curiosity.

"I suppose," said Callister, "it is because the soil has been so thoroughly warmed by the long, hot summer that when the moisture germinates the grass seed, this heat forces its growth. Then again, all these Lachlan plains are wondrously fertile, and the soil depth ranges from four to forty feet. If it is so marvellously recuperative after drought, what would it be capable of under irrigation? That is what we want."

This remarkable characteristic of most of the back-country, its responsiveness to water, had already given Jack much food for thought. Only a fortnight before, he had received, in response to an application to the Tourist Bureau in Sydney, a pile of literature that dealt with the Yanco Irrigation Area on the Murrumbidgee, and the great Mildura settlements. From these publications he had learned how land that for years had afforded but the scantiest pasturage for stock had been metamorphosed under irrigation into smiling gardens that produced the most prolific yields of fruit and vegetables. He had read some of the statistics showing how this class of land, formerly valued at about one pound per acre, was now selling in its improved state at a hundred pounds per acre, and to his astonishment he had subsequently discovered that the men that had paid these high prices were able to make easy and prosperous livings from their tiny holdings – few greater in area than fifty acres.

Jack was pondering over this matter when they reached the Circle Y paddock. This portion of the run was so named because its former owner had used the letter Y in a circle as his stock brand, and when Bullangarra had acquired the area from the Crown as an improvement lease this explicit identification was adopted to describe the sixteen thousand acres within its netted boundaries.

There were some si thousand-odd wethers in this paddock, all of which had come through the drought in fair condition. As the riders zig-zagged across the country inspecting the sheep, Callister expressed his satisfaction at their appearance.

"These will be fit to market in another six weeks," he told Jack. "They will top off in no time on the new grass if it gets some body into it, and as prices will be high for a long time after the dry spell I think we ought to sell them quickly."

"What are they likely to realise?" inquired the jackaroo.

"If we strike a good market, they will fetch up to forty-five shillings per head; a few of those double-fleeced ones will bring a good deal more."

"That will mean a nice cheque," said Jack, with a laugh. "But would it not be better to wait until after shearing, and get the value of wool yourself?"

"Not at all," explained Callister. "The markets will be rushed after shearing, which is three months off yet on this river, and just now the butchers will pay prices for woolly sheep that easily cover the value of the fleece. The only thing that worries me, however, is the chance of a big mob being 'lifted' from this paddock by a gang of 'duffers', as we call stock stealers."

"How on earth could thieves get away with a mob of sheep?" asked Jack in surprise. "Why, it would be impossible to travel them more than twelve miles a day, and there are plenty of police and stock inspectors about."

"It does seem impossible," admitted the manager, "but they do it, nevertheless. There is a gang of sheep stealers in this district that have 'duffed' some very big mobs, and they have never been caught. We have an association of station owners for the prevention of stock stealing in this district, and although was have a standing reward of two hundred pounds for information that will bring about the conviction of any sheep or cattle 'duffers', it has never yet been claimed. Wandering swagmen, hawkers and casual travellers often kill a sheep on us, but it is only because they are in need of meat; we don't worry much about that sort of thing, but it is the lifting of a big mob that makes us savage. Two years ago they lost five thousand wethers in one mob from Melrose Plains, and the thieves are still at large."

"If you know that these thieves are about, why not have them arrested?" said Jack.

"That appears to be very sound advice," said Callister, somewhat satirically, "but unfortunately, it is impracticable. Conclusive evidence must be secured before the police can effect an arrest, and up to the present that testimony has never appeared."

"Who are the men in this gang?" questioned Jack.

"A fellow named 'Brummy' Collins is the ringleader," Callister explained. "He is a small selector with a block of about five thousand acres some six miles south from here, toward the Bland country, but his headquarters are at the shanty at Wongonga, up the river. He has a brother over at the back of Lake Cowal, who is said to work in with him in most of his schemes; and there are two young fellows, Joe

Brady and Tommy Gillett, who are mixed up with them. They are a bad lot, especially Collins, who, although only a small cocky, is a wealthy man."

"Well, we will watch out for them," said Jack cheerfully. "If I come across them I'll make it warm for them."

"You might," responded Callister, doubtfully. "But you have to catch them first."

A few minutes later the manager left to return to the homestead by way of the woolshed paddock, giving Jack instructions to spend the afternoon riding the back boundary fence and repairing any holes that might be found in the netting.

Jack picked up the boundary shortly after he had eaten a lonely lunch of cold mutton sandwiches in the shelter of a stringybark salt-lick shed. Under its rough bark roof he squatted on a huge boulder of rock salt placed there for the sheep to lick, and had munched his food thoughtfully. He was glad to be on the move again after a brief rest, although the rain was falling steadily. He had no sooner reached the fence than he discovered a wide gap in the wire netting, which he proceeded to repair with pliers and tie-wire.

These netting fences had always been a source of wonder to Jack. On Bullangarra, the exterior boundaries, as well as most of the sub-dividing fences, were all wire-netted. It must be an expensive process, he thought, to combat the rabbit pest on a big holding year in and year out, and his short experience of the west had already taught him to appreciate the fervour with which the memory of the man who introduced 'bunny' into Australia was so frequently cursed. The station on which he was employed had tackled the rabbit question boldly. Callister, knowing the country badly infested with rabbits, which only ate the tenderest and most sustaining grasses, had its carrying capacity reduced by fully two-thirds, and having unsuccessfully tried all means of extirpation, from poisoning to trapping, had at last persuaded the owners of the run to permit him to put his own idea into execution.

The result was that he had, two years before, employed big gangs of men, mostly immigrants from Great Britain, to dig out all the burrows on the whole 220,000 acres, destroy the harbour provided by fallen timber and hollow logs, and to hunt, trap, shoot or poison every rabbit that remained. These men, "emu-bobbers" as they were humorously named by the bushmen, because the bodily motions necessitated by their tasks resembled the peculiar gyrations of a flock of emus, did their work well, and it was Callister's boast, about the time of Jack's arrival, that there were not a thousand rabbits on the whole of Bullangarra. There were perhaps ten billion rabbits across the country at that time. Fifty years earlier some two million of the creatures were trapped or killed across Australia without making an appreciable impact on their numbers, so Callister's pride was well justified.

The wire netting that formed the protective barrier against invasion from neighbouring runs was some three feet above, and six inches below the ground. It was attached to the ordinary six-wire fences, the posts of which were eighteen feet apart, and strengthened by stout wire droppers at six-foot intervals. The cost of the netting alone for such a fence was more than fifty pounds per mile, and constant attention was necessary to keep it effective, more especially where crossbred sheep were depastured, for these big-framed animals delighted in butting through such an obstacle.

The Circle Y paddock had more rabbits in it than all the rest of Bullangarra run, and scores of new burrows had been opened, even during the drought. This was due to the entry of the rodents from the adjoining vacant Crown lands, on which no destruction ever took place. Callister had often complained to Jack that it was manifestly unjust that the Government, through the local administrative bodies, the Pastures Protection Boards, should compel, under penalty of heavy fines, all private landholders to exterminate rabbits, while it bred up the pest for the potential invasion of adjoining land or unoccupied country, stock routes, and reserves.

During his riding of the back boundary of Circle Y paddock, Jack had often found gaps in the netting at unexpected spots. Bullangarra running no crossbreds there, and having only the placid, easily-confined merinos, it seemed to him as if the breaks had been caused by something other than sheep. On two or three occasions latterly, Jack had suspected human agency in the matter, the meshes of the netting having apparently been cut with wire clippers, and the stout fencing wire cut through with the same implement; but, in the absence of any reason for such an act on anyone's part, he had dismissed from his mind any serious thoughts of such a possibility. On this occasion the evidence was unmistakable, however, for there were footprints in the mud and tracks of a horse near to where the break was.

A mile farther along he discovered another place where the netting had been cut and the wires pulled back from two panels of fence. The tracks of a horse led from the adjoining land onto Bullangarra, but there were no signs of its having returned. This circumstance puzzled him exceedingly as he repaired the damage in the driving rain.

An hour later he was riding leisurely down the sheep-pad that ran along the fence, his thoughts still on the matter of the broken netting, when from the depths of a patch of scrub, a horseman rode almost into him.

"G'day!" greeted the stranger.

"Good day!" exclaimed Jack, reining up in astonishment. "What on earth are you doing here?"

"Aw, nothin'," replied the other.

Jack was sufficiently accustomed to the peculiar ways of the bush, to know that it was useless pressing for enlightenment, so he waited for the man to volunteer an explanation. After a full five minutes, during which the stranger cut a fill from a plug of tobacco, rammed it into his pipe, and then lighted it, he spoke.

"I ain't seen you about here before," he said slowly. "Are you th' new jackaroo?"

"Yes," replied Jack, rather nettled.

"Sydney bloke?" inquired the other, insolently.

"Yes," answered the new-chum, maintaining his temper with an effort.

"Thought so," was the lazy comment.

Again there was a long pause, during which the stranger was busy with a stirrup-leather.

"Been ridin' the fence today?" came the query.

"Yes," Jack stated.

"Seen anythin' o' Bogan Dan along here?" the other asked, regarding the jackaroo furtively. "I was ter meet him about here this afternoon. I've rode from Condoblin terday – come by the woolshed paddock an' along the creek."

"No," answered Jack curtly. "I have met no-one."

"Queer," the stranger said. "I suppose I've missed 'im."

There was a further long pause, employed by the bushman in keenly inspecting Jack Burnside.

"Aw well, I s'pose I'd better be goin'," the man said at last.

"How are you going to get out?" Jack suddenly enquired, with unconcealed curiosity.

"Watch!" was the response.

The stranger thereupon took off his oilskin coat and spread it along the top wire of the fence. Turning his horse, he rode back some ten or fifteen yards., then whirling round sharply, he suddenly clapped spurs to the animal's sides and raced it at the wires where the coat made a visible hurdle. As Jack cried out a terrified warning the horse took off, jumped cleanly, and landed safely on the other side. The horseman wheeled around, stopped, and quietly put on his coat.

"By Jove! You took a risk with that wire!" cried out Jack admiringly. "That was a fine piece of horsemanship, and you have got a splendid animal there."

"Yairs," drawled the other, as he faced his horse about. "Yer don't catch Brummy Collins with a crook moke. S'long!"

9

FAKED BRANDS

I t may have been the effects of the fiery liquor and its subsequent inevitable demoralisation that impelled Raymond Penderby to remain at the "Drover's Rest" to learn from Collins and his gang how thousands of pounds could be made in a short time; or it may have been that some latent sinister trait in his nature suddenly tempted him, in that congenial environment, to throw off all restraint. Whatever it was, the carefully nurtured, well-educated, fashionable young medical student sat in the bar-parlour of the disreputable shanty, quite at home and on the best of terms with his still more disreputable associates.

There had been some desultory card-playing, as well as a good deal of drinking, after the evening meal, the opportunity for confidential conversation having been interfered with by the arrival of several hilarious, but inoffensive, boundary-riders just at dusk. These casual visitors departed at about nine o'clock on the twenty-mile ride to their homes, whereupon Collins and his colleagues, including the aforesaid villainous-looking landlord, sought the parlour, and settled themselves around the yarran fire that blazed in an open hearth the breadth of the whole room.

"The thing can be pulled off easy," said Collins, after there had been some casual preliminary talk between him and young Penderby, "an' all that's in it is the liftin' of a mob o' wethers off Bullangarra."

"What?" exclaimed Raymond. "Stealing sheep from Callister's place?" His instincts revolted at this suggestion that he should be a party to the unpardonable crime of robbing his host. "No," he concluded firmly. "I could not do it."

"Yer won't take it on?" demanded Collins angrily. "Wot did yer think the game was?"

"I hardly expected that you would be foolish enough to imagine that I would become a sheep-stealer, seeing that I know nothing of sheep and very little of the bush. No," he concluded, emphatically, "I will have nothing to do with the business."

This firm rejection of his proposal aroused the ire of Brummy Collins in a remarkable manner, and he leaped from his chair with such a threatening mien that Raymond apprehended a violent assault on his person. Seeing that a scuffle was imminent, M'Bean, who knew Collins' temper, hastily intervened, and forced the angry bushman back into his seat. The old publican, who was as crafty as a snake, commenced to speak in a suave and quiet voice.

"Now look here," he said. "It's no use squabbling. Mr. Penderby doesn't like the idea of sheep-stealing, but you must remember that he knows nothing of the plans you have made. Bill M'Bean has told us all that some of the sporting chaps, now in Condoblin for the races, say that our friend here has asked for time from the book-makers in Sydney. Bill also told us that they say his father won't pay, and he's got to get the money from somewhere or else take the knock, which wouldn't do for any promising young medical student. We know he wants the money badly, and we know that he can help us in this affair without the slightest risk to himself. Now let him think for a bit."

Raymond was considerably disconcerted at this brief but accurate exposition of his affairs by a stranger, but he knew that in the sporting world such matters as the losses of an unlucky punter were never secrets. Although his finer susceptibilities revolted at the crime suggested, the fear of the wrath of the bookmakers and the disgrace that would inevitably ensue in the event of his defaulting, weighed heavily on his mind. He pressed a hand nervously to his aching brow and stared gloomily into the fire. The others sat immobile. For ten long minutes there was a pregnant silence, broken only by the fitful crackling of the logs on the fire.

"Tell me the details of the scheme, Collins," Raymond said at length, in a low, level tone, "and if it is satisfactory I will consider it favourably. I will admit that I must have the money, and I suppose that it matters little how I get it."

"That's talk with hair on it," said Collins cheerfully. "Now I'll tell yer."

The sheep-stealer then proceeded to explain his scheme.

"Bullangarra," he said, "runs about six thousand wethers on the old improvement lease block; they call it the Circle Y paddock after ol' Edgar's brand. That's the mob we're goin' ter lift. Me brother, over on the Bland, is in the joke, and we've got everythin' pretty nearly fixed. I know yer don't know much about the travellin' stock laws, so I'll explain how we've fixed the get-away. About six months ago me brother took an annual lease o' them Crown lands adjoinin' Bullangarra, an' he's got six hundred o' his own sheep on there now. His home selection is in another Pastures Protection Board district ter this, so he's managed ter get the same sheep brand an' mark as Bullangarra. The stock inspector has the allottin' o' sheep brands an' marks in their different districts, an' as the range o' suitable signs ain't a wide one, a cocky in one district can get the same identical brand an' mark as a big station in another – if he wants ter. Me brother's place is eighty mile from the Lachlan, so he didn't have much trouble in getting' the Bullangarra marks, the inspector probably thinkin' his sheep'd never get across this way."

"Where do I come in, though?" asked Raymond, who had been listening attentively.

"Jus' wait a bit," continued Collins, "an' I'll explain the lot in me own way. Now, Bullangarra don't know about those sheep o' me brother's, for we've kept 'em well over on the far side; an' the lease was put through in Forbes so's nobody'd get ter know of it down about Condoblin. When me brother wants ter shift them sheep back home he's got ter get a permit an' a travellin' statement from the stock inspector. Now, he had one from the inspector in his own district when he brought 'em across, showin' the correct number, brands an' marks of his sheep, so he'll have no trouble getting' one fer the return trip from the bloke at Condoblin. Then we can pick up the Bullangarra wethers an' shift 'em across country ter the railway at Wyalong, an' truck 'em ter Sydney."

"But how can you travel six thousand wethers across the intervening stations and stock routes without exciting suspicion, especially when there are police and inspectors always on the move? The permit would only account for six hundred, anyway, and that would be unexplainable if questions were asked." Raymond could not see how the scheme was feasible.

"Aw, old Peg-leg here's a bit o' a penman," laughed Brummy, evilly. "He's fixed up plenty o' them things afore this. It's dead easy, because drovers carry 'em in their pockets mostly, where the paper gets smudged an' dirty. Anyone would have ter look close ter spot a forgery."

"Still, I fail to see how I can be of use," argued Penderby, "seeing that you do not anticipate trouble on the way, and that there will be enough drovers without me."

"That's jus' wot I'm comin' ter," Collins proceeded. "I was pokin' about Bullangarra the other day, when I comes across a new-chum jackaroo they've got there, a bloke with hair like a yeller chestnut horse an' a tough-lookin' dial. Now, I don' mean no offence, but that bloke's the dead ring fer yer. When yer caught up ter Bill an' me this afternoon I thought at first yer was him, until Bill gives me the word who yer was, dinkum. That puts me fair onter it, an' I fixed the plan comin' along, knowin' from Bill as yer needin' brass pretty bad. I reckoned it this way, that if yer'd pay Bill ter do any sort o' job fer yer, yer wouldn't baulk if a big thing came yer way."

"I am still in the dark," ventured the young man.

"I'm comin' ter it in me own way," Collins went on. "All we wants yer ter do is to give us delivery of them sheep off Bullangarra when we're ready, just as if yer was the owner, so ter speak. Then, we wants yer ter meet us on the track at different places, where we'll tell yer, so as yer can be seen; be at the truckin' yards when we're getting' the sheep away, then be in Sydney an' collect the cheque from the agents when they're sold. We trust yer, yer see; an' yer mustn't mind if we always calls yer Burnside when anybody's about."

The amazing simplicity and the undreamed-of boldness of the proposition left Raymond Penderby aghast. For more than a minute he could scarcely believe his senses. Then his calculating brain became unnaturally active, not in spite of, but probably on account of, the fiery spirits that he had swallowed. Fate, he thought, was assuredly playing into his hands. Here, ready-made for his execution, was an enterprise that would not only result in securing nearly sufficient money to pay off the clamorous and threatening betting men, but which would unquestionably involve Jack Burnside in irrevocable ruin. Already in his mind he had determined to retain sufficient of the ill-gotten proceeds from the sale of the sheep to pay off all his pressing creditors, and he was evolving some scheme whereby he could ultimately implicate the man he hated most, the young jackeroo, when Collins interrupted his cogitations.

"Wot d'yer say?" he demanded, fiercely.

"By gad, I'm with you! And here's my hand on it." And the young man impetuously wrung the gnarled fist that the sheep-stealer extended.

The others joined in the mutual felicitations with enthusiastic cheerfulness, Peg-leg so far forgetting himself as to request the company to drink success to the venture at the expense of the house. The unusually prompt acceptance of this unusual offer brought the old publican to his senses sharply, for never before had he been known to 'shout', and he instantly perceived his error. However, there being no escape, he brought in the drinks with a very bad grace, and only recovered his equanimity when Joe Brady, gulping some down the wrong way, nearly expired in the subsequent fit of coughing that shook him for fully five minutes.

When the party had settled down again comfortably, Raymond Penderby put to Collins a question that was uppermost in his mind.

"How about the division of the spoils?" was his query.

The others became instantly alert at this, although Collins, however, appeared to be reluctant to discuss the matter.

"I didn't propose ter get inter that fer now," he said, "but p'raps it's better fer us all ter know how we're goin' ter stand. It's the biggest job I've ever took on, an' I don't want ter excite any suspicions when we're on the track with the sheep, or when they're bein' sold, so that's why we've got ter trust yer, Mr. Penderby, with the cash."

Brummy then took out a greasy pocket-book and the stub of a pencil, and commenced to figure awkwardly. After a brief interval he spoke.

"I figger it this way," he said, tearing a leaf out of the book and handing it to Penderby. "I reckon that if we get all them sheep ter market, they'll fetch us fourteen thousand pounds at the lowest, an' if the market's good we'll get a couple o' thousand more. Anyhow, I'm countin' on fourteen thousand. Outer that, me an' me brother want seven-and-a-half thousand, 'cause it's our scheme, an' we're takin' the big risks. Mr. Penderby'll get three thousand, Joe, Tommy an' Bill 'ere will take a thousand each, an' we'll chuck Peg-leg five hundred out o' it."

The suggested division of the spoils provoked an angry argument in which, however, Penderby took no part. Brady and Gillett were particularly bitter and profane in their remarks, and the publican was violently furious. The two first-named and M'Bean pointed out that as besides doing the droving, they would eventually have to accompany the sheep in the trucks to Sydney on the two trips that would be necessary, the attendant risk was worth a good deal more. Peg-leg, who would take no risk whatever, and as a matter of fact, would never see either the sheep or the drovers after they had left his shanty, demanded that the division should be share and share alike.

To none of their angry protestations did Collins, apparently, pay the slightest heed. At length, when the irate disputants had exhausted their breaths or their arguments, or both, he deigned to speak.

"Youse blokes talk about risks! Be damned ter yer!" he snarled at them. "Yer a pack o' yeller-livered dingoes an' the blasted lot o' yer'd be in quod or starvin' only fer me. You, Joe Brady: didn't I git yer out o' Dubbo under the very noses o' the perlice when they was huntin' fer yer jus' after that bloke was nearly killed down the Macquarie? An' you, Tommy Gillett! Ain't I got yer off twice with an alibi when yer was up fer a cert? An' you, yer flamin', hoppin' ol' swine – wot about that bloke as was found dead out there in the scrub?"

The two stockmen looked crestfallen under this rebuke; the publican was livid with fear.

"For God's sake," he cried hoarsely, "don't bring that up!" Then, trembling convulsively, he limped into the bar, poured out a full glass of rum with palsied fingers, and swallowed it neat.

"Blimey!" burst out Brady. "I didn't mean nothin', strike me dead if I did! I'm satisfied with me cut."

"Me too," Gillett hurriedly exclaimed.

"I'm set," briefly assented Bill M'Bean.

Collins' anger was not appeased, however. "Youse blokes talk about risks," he repeated in a violent tone. "Wot about me an' me brother when they starts ter run down the tracks? Ain't we got ter find a way of accountin' fer six thousand blasted sheep we never owned? Don't yer think we ain't takin' some risk over that? A lot o' help we'll get from youse crawlin' mongrels when the perlice come nosin' round! NO! Youse'll be well over the Vic border, boozin' yer brass at some rotten shanty like this in the guts o' the scrub, an' getting' robbed o' the biggest part o' it. Then when it's gone, yer'll come sneakin' back 'ere fer me ter lay yer onter somethin' else with good money in it. Why, yer miserable cows! Yer couldn't earn a thousand blasted pounds in a lifetime!"

The now thoroughly chastened trio hastened to assure their leader that they would be content with what he chose to give them, so after a few pacificatory remarks from Penderby – who, truth to tell, had been uncomfortably concerned by the disclosures bearing upon the intimate histories of his newly-found friends – Collins became calm again.

"It strikes me," Raymond said to Brummy after a pause, "that you and your brother are certainly running a great risk if it becomes necessary to account for your possession of so many sheep, and I do not see how you can do it."

"We'll have ter account fer 'em all right," was the answer. "Don't make no mistake about that. But look 'ere!" he cried out, turning to the others. "Joe, an' youse others! Get ter hell outer this, 'cause I want ter talk private with Mister Penderby."

After the three men had joined the publican in the bar, Collins turned to the young visitor from the city.

"I didn't want them blokes 'ere while I told yer," he said. "Me brother has a pretty big place on the Bland, about eighty thousand acres, although he's only supposed ter be a cocky. But it's terrible poor country, an' it'll only carry one sheep ter twenty acres. Fer years past now he's bin sendin' in his returns ter the Stock Board showin' as how he's got twelve thousand sheep, an' he pays the rates on that number. Yer see, they charges so much a hundred head o' sheep as rates, ter keep these boards goin' and ter pay the inspectors, an' he always had some big lift like this in mind when he made them returns. No-one'd ever suspect a bloke would go on payin' taxes on a big lot o' sheep he didn't own. Now we'll consign the sheep in his name, an' if the perlice make him muster his paddocks, well, he'll have a few thousand head there an' be able ter prove by his returns that he did own the lot that he sold. The books o' the board will show that he had 'em. O' course there's always likely ter be a slip some-where, an' if I come on the scene fer the cash in Sydney it'll be too suspicious, fer me an' me brother has had a few narrer squeaks o' late, an' we don't want ter make it a welter over this. Your part'll be ter get the cash well hid in case o' trouble, which I don't think is likely ter come – and that's why I'm trustin' yer."

The worthy couple then discussed the project from all its sides until midnight, when they retired. Raymond returned to Bullangarra next morning, explaining on his arrival that he had lost his way the night before, and instead of finding Jemalong, he had been compelled to camp on the roadside with a loquacious teamster named McLeod, who, luckily, he had discovered just after night had fallen.

He had seen and spoken with McLeod, it was true, not far from the "Drover's Rest", and the veteran of the roads had hailed him as "me bloomin' jackeroo". Raymond had not troubled to mention McLeod at the time, nor to Jack Burnside later, that there had been another case of mistaken identity.

10

FIRST PAST THE POST

J ack Burnside was manifestly astonished at Callister's evident satisfaction displayed after the relation of the circumstances of the damaged netting and the later encounter with Brummy Collins.

"Good!" exclaimed the manager, after the story had been told. "It is a fortunate thing for Bullangarra that you met the damned sheep-stealer when you did."

"It looks to me," said Jack, "that he had opened that fence to enable him to drive a mob of sheep out."

"I quite agree with you," assented Callister. "But don't you see that he will guess at once that we have suspected his intention, and anticipating that we will keep a sharp watch on the paddock for the next three months, he will naturally give the place a wide berth. I am very thankful that things have turned out this way, for I cannot spare a man to ride that fence every day. Shearing is coming along, you know, and all hands will be busy enough from now on."

"I would not be inclined to risk it," argued Jack.

"There is no risk," asserted the manager, confidently. "I know Brummy and he knows me, so I will take advantage of his astuteness. You generally ride that Circle Y paddock, but we will have to take a chance there for the next two months, and let the sheep look after themselves."

"What is on?" inquired the jackeroo.

"I want five of you to start mustering the Red Tank paddock next Monday, to bring the sheep there close in to the shed for shearing. That will mean nearly a fortnight's work to clear it up; and then you have to begin on the Dead Finish blocks. I intend to leave the Circle Y until the last, for they are fairly close, and can be mustered and driven to the shed in two or three days."

Although Jack was somewhat dubious about the affair, and inclined to disagree with his boss, for he had summed up Collins as being a cool and clever customer, he concluded that Callister probably knew more than he of the possibilities, and so put the mater from his mind.

It was a week after this incident that Raymond Penderby had returned from his supposed ride to Jemalong, and work on the station was progressing in the customary routine manner. Callister had prepared his plans to shift the sheep from paddock to paddock, moving huge mobs like a chess player moves his kings and castles, and concentrating them gradually upon one point, the huge shearing shed. The days were long and hard for the station hands, the mustering and driving involving lonely camps in the bush, where the men often spent weary hours crouched over damp, feeble fires through the period of darkness, using their oilskins as inadequate shelters from the rain.

In spite of the dreary hours of riding, the body-racking jogging behind the crawling sheep, and the discomforts of wet and sodden camps, Jack Burnside revelled in every moment of it. His four or five months in the bush had wrought a marvellous alteration in him. The open-air life, the hard, strenuous days of riding through the solemn, silent bush, the easy-going but nevertheless rigorous discipline of the station, had made him a new man. His brown eyes were keen and clear with the intent alertness of the bushmen of the plains, and his muscles were hardened and as firm as those of an athlete in training. His frank, good-looking face was burned a dull bronze that that threw into relief the few freckles that spotted it, for even the winter suns had warmth. He was six feet of perfect manhood, and, because in the matter of dress he had conformed, in a measure, to the customs of the bush, he was a veritable outbacker in appearance. Save for his speech, it would have been hard to detect the city man in him at all.

Jack particularly gloried in his work among the sheep. He already owned a dog, a black kelpie that he had purchased for ten pounds from a passing drover, and he delighted in watching it work. With almost human sagacity, this black shadow would slither and glide at the side of a little flock of hurrying sheep, and silently, at the given signal, turn them in the required direction. Sometimes, a fractious sheep, "a snake-headed bastard" as the men described it, would stubbornly refuse to follow its companions, and then the dog would make its most splendid effort. Heading the rushing animal, it would spring lightly at its shoulder, turning it in another direction, repeat the performance until the harassed sheep was facing its fellows, and then, with a plunge and a threatening slither, it would rush its heels and hurry it, in terrified haste, back to the mob.

The sheepdogs on the run were kelpies and barbs, an almost identical breed, running in blacks and tans so far as colour went. They were small, lightly-built animals that seemingly never tired, and were invaluable there, as they are wherever wool is grown. In fact, were it not for these semi-human, untiring animals, the efficient and economical working of a sheep station would be impossible in a country of wide spaces and fierce, scorching summers. Jack had been surprised to learn, in the course of a fascinating chat with a man named Bob Kaleski, the greatest authority on dogs in Australia, that the breed had been evolved by the crossing of a dog fox onto a black, smooth Scotch collie, just as the blue cattle dog, another canine miracle, had been the progeny of the mating of a blue smooth Highland collie and a dingo, or native dog.

This same Bob Kaleski had also told him that the kelpie was established as a breed in Australia by a Jerilderie squatter names Elliott, who found the prick-eared pup in a litter thrown by an imported bitch, bred by an English poacher. This pup was brought across to the Lachlan, where, on Woollongough station, some forty miles from Bullangarra, it was mated with a bitch of unknown pedigree from Victoria. The result was the pure kelpie, the name being the pet appellation of the old Scotch shepherds in the backblocks for their bitches. This same bitch threw another prick-eared pup, a black one, that was different from his brothers and he proved to be of an even finer type than they. He belonged to a blackfellow who went to work on Burrawong station, and proving so useful he was entered in a contest at the Forbes show in the year that the horse "Barb" won the Melbourne Cup. As the dog also won, the name of the horse was bestowed on him, and was afterwards transmitted to his progeny to denote the breed as a whole. Jack heard that the breeding of these dogs was a business in itself, and was carried on even at that day by the descendants of the men who had first established the strain, and who sold their dogs throughout Australia.

Kaleski, a little, pleasant-faced bushman, had called at Bullangarra homestead one memorable evening, and Jack had learned more about the bush and its ways from him than he could have picked up by experience in a decade, for they yarned the whole night through.

On these very long and arduous rides Jack's thoughts very often turned yearningly towards the girl of his heart, pretty Molly Forbes. Her face was ever before him, and happy were the day-dreams and tender the fancies that he wove about her glorious being. This new life of his had deepened his feelings in regard to many things, and widened his outlook on life marvellously. It was not surprising, therefore, that he found himself, as day succeeded day, more potently stimulated in his love for this beautiful girl, and more earnestly determined to win success in order that he could claim her for his own. He had had but one letter from her since his departure from the city, a simple note that expressed a tender concern for him and his well-being; but, reading between its lines with a lover's eyes and understanding, he had found therein the outpouring of a heart that loved as fondly as his own. And, believing this, he was mightily content.

Jack and his companions had completed the muster and check-muster of the Red Tank paddock two days earlier than anticipated, and they rode into the homestead late one Friday afternoon. After he had changed and eaten, the young jackeroo reported progress to Callister, who was seated with his guest in the smokeroom, before a cosy fire.

"We were just talking about the races at Condoblin, Jack," the manager said. "They are to be held tomorrow. I suggested to Penderby that we should go in, and he has agreed to accompany me. I had intended to drive the buggy in, but, now that you are back, you had better come along and drive the car. What do you say?"

"Thanks awfully," said Jack. "I would enjoy it very much, but I had decided to take a quiet ride around the Circle Y paddock tomorrow, just to see that the fences had not been cut again."

"Don't worry about that!" exclaimed Callister, heartily. "Come along with us. Brummy Collins is not going to lift those wethers tomorrow!"

Raymond Penderby's pipe clattered to the floor, and with an angry oath he stooped to recover it. That action his livid, guilty face from the two men, who were staring at him in amazement.

"Pardon my rudeness," Raymond said, as he sat upright again, only partially recovered from the shock he had received. "I don't often go off like that, but I got a mouthful of nicotine."

"Um!" commented Callister, drily.

There was an awkward pause for a few moments, Raymond eventually breaking the silence.

"Is this 'Brummy' Collins you mentioned," he said boldly, now quite himself, "the notorious sheep-stealer one hears so much of around these parts?"

"Yes," assented Callister, "and we have good reason to know it. He has often levied toll of us, and unfortunately we have never succeeded in laying him by the heels. Jack has a suspicion that he is after our wethers in the Circle Y, because he met him there a few weeks ago on our side of the boundary, but I tell him that that very meeting will scare the noble 'duffer' away for many months to come."

"And I quite agree with that idea," said Raymond, with warmth. "But," he went on eagerly, "I can do something that will relieve Jack's mind, and make everything certain about the safety of the sheep. Let me ride that paddock occasionally during the next few weeks. I only drift about aimlessly over the run in order not to be in the way, and to avoid interfering with your station work, so let me do something useful at last."

"That is a rattling good suggestion, and it is deuced good of you, old chap," said the manager, gratefully. "A casual look at the place about twice per week will do."

"That's agreed," Penderby stated. "And now, Jack, what about the races tomorrow?"

"I'll come," said the jackeroo, eagerly.

It was early next morning when the Bullangarra party arrived at Condoblin, and drew up at the Royal Hotel. As the car came to a standstill, vociferous greetings were shouted to Callister and his friends from the folk on the verandah, and as they gained the foot-path there were many cordial hand-clasps and cheery words.

A big crowd of people thronged the street. Squatters, cockies, boundary-riders, shearers, swagmen, trainers, jockeys and the usual sprinkling of blackfellows, had all foregathered for the sport. These men had come from far and wide across the Lachlan Plains, some from two hundred miles away, to enjoy that rarest of outing for the bushman – a country race meeting. Jack, already well-known to many of the landowners and young men of the district, was soon chatting animatedly with a group of friends, and consequently he did not notice Raymond Penderby walk into the hotel bar with a disreputable, sporty-looking individual, who appeared to be a jockey of sorts.

After Penderby and his companion had taken a drink, they left the bar and walked to the stables at the rear of the hotel. In a loose-box the jockey pointed out a beautifully-proportioned, bright bay mare, clothed and saddled to go to the course. The animal was pawing impatiently at the half-opened door, and snatching at the bit.

"She's a beaut, ain't she?" said the jockey, enthusiastically stroking the mare's soft muzzle, and instantly quieting her.

"Yes, she looks fit enough," commented Penderby. "But do you think that she can win here?"

"She's home on the bit, Mister Penderby," answered the boy, proudly. "Home an' dried. They'll have to scratch gravel to pip me t'day in the Lachlander Cup."

"Well, if you want me to back her and give you a 'cut' of the winnings you will have to make a cert of it," said Raymond.

"S'help me Gawd! She'll win, Mister Penderby," said the boy, eagerly.

"What odds are they offering around town?" asked Raymond.

"Yer can get even money," was the reply.

"Damn it, Benny! That's no good to me!" exploded the young city man. "Do you think that I can get a decent win at that price? I've only got a couple of hundred with me, and at evens that would be no good." He turned on his heel to walk away, when suddenly a thought struck him.

"What is the next best thing in the race?" he asked the jockey.

"Well, if the mare was out, nothin' would beat Birrimboo; he'd be a stone moral," replied the boy.

"And the next best after him?" was the further query.

"The Rat!" said Benny. "They're offerin' tens an' twelves about him. All the rest'll run like hairy dogs."

"Who owns Birrimboo?" Penderby asked.

"Ol' Joe Taylor; he's down at McIntosh's pub," was the reply.

"Well," said Penderby, after thinking a while, "if you can take hold of your mare, and I can fix Taylor to 'stiffen' Birrimboo, I'll go for a big win on The Rat. You will be riding, and with the help of Taylor's boy you can settle anything that looks dangerous. Are you willing to take that on?"

"My flamin' oath!" replied Benny. "So long as you give us a fair cut. But fix Taylor up first!"

As they walked away, a half-drunken bushman lurched out of the adjoining stall, and staggered unsteadily after them. He was muttering to himself as he made difficult progress, "Penderby, eh?

Goin' ter work a'ready! I'll get in this joke. But how does his name come ter be Penderby?"

Taylor, who was one of the many half-bankrupt trainer-owners that follow bush race meetings, was easily 'fixed for the joke", and Raymond Penderby was not long in putting a hundred pounds on The Rat, at twelve to one, with the bookmakers who were operating at the various hotels about the town.

After lunch, the Bullangarra party drove to the course. On the way out, Callister mentioned to his guest that he had heard that he was backing The Rat.

"Oh yes," said Penderby. "I know the boy that is to ride him, and he tells me that he has a good chance of winning. I have only invested a tenner, though."

"You can count it as lost," laughed Callister. "There is nothing here today that can beat the bay mare of Benny Bingham's. She won the double at Forbes last week without being troubled."

"Oh," was all that Penderby said.

The Condoblin racecourse was like most others in the bush. The track, marked by peeled saplings, ran around the side of a hill, the 'straight' being along a flat shoulder on the gentle rise. Patches of thick scrub hid the horses and riders at several points, but this mattered very little. The grandstand, a rough, shed-like structure, was capable of accommodating perhaps two hundred people, and the publican's booth, which was largely patronised, was a framework of unbarked pine poles covered with a tarpaulin, and having a bar-counter of unplaned, sawn planks.

Jack Burnside had invested a five-pound note on the winner of the first race, at the solicitation of Raymond Penderby, and had the pleasure of receiving twenty pounds from the bookmaker after the event. Raymond claimed to have laid a similar sum, but Benny Bingham had handed him over two hundred pounds in notes in a quiet corner, this being the result of a commission that the jockey had executed on the young medical student's behalf.

The second race was won by a six-to-one chance, on which Jack had invested the full twenty pounds that he had previously collected.

He had been reluctant to lay out this sum, for he now regarded money as something to be held on to tenaciously, but Penderby had overborne his scruples.

When the boys were saddling for the Lachlander Cup, Jack sought his friend from the city.

"Are you going to put any more on The Rat?" he asked.

"No," replied Raymond. "I had a good win on the last; so I will have a flutter on Bingham's mare, Marigold. She is favourite, and they tell me that she cannot be beaten."

Jack turned to seek a bookmaker with whom to invest another twenty pounds, when he felt himself seized roughly by the arm. Turning sharply, he discovered that his assailant was his former acquaintance of the train trip, 'Wild Bullocks', and that that gentleman was very drunk.

"Don't back Mar'gol'," said the old bushman, mysteriously. "Come over 'ere an' I'll tell yer jokesh."

Jack tolerantly permitted himself to be dragged by the ancient, rather than led, to a patch of scrub at the back of the stand, for he had ample time in which to make his wagers. When they were well away from observation, 'Wild Bullocks' in tones rendered thick and only half-coherent by drink, told his story. He informed Jack that during the morning he had been sleeping off the effects of the drink in one of the loose boxes of the Royal, and had awakened to hear a flash Sydney bloke and a little jockey planning that the Lachlander Cup should be arranged for The Rat to win. When the conspirators had walked away, 'Wild Bullocks' had followed them, because he had for the moment mistaken the Sydney man for Jack, although he had heard him called Penderby. On this account he had decided to hold his tongue about the matter, and profit by the information if he could borrow enough money to bet with; but, seeing the two men together on the course and having heard the conspirator tell Jack to back the favourite, which he knew was 'dead', he had determined to speak.

Jack was astounded at the information, and at first had thoughts of complaining to the committee. Knowing something of the racing game, however, he realised that he would be laughed at for his pains, as he could prove nothing, and if the parties were accused, they would make indignant denials. In a quandary, he addressed himself to the bushman.

"What shall I do?" he asked.

"Why, back The blanky Rat!" answered the other, gravely.

"I suppose that is good advice, after all," said Jack.

"Yairs!" responded 'Wild Bullocks'. "An' say! What's that flash bloke's proper name – the chap that rigged the joke?"

"His name is Raymond Penderby, a friend of Callister's," answered Jack.

"Is that fair dinkum?? Raymond Penderby?" cried the other, in startled tones.

"Yes, that is his name. His father is a lawyer in Sydney," answered Jack.

"It's true, then eh? Well, I'm damned!" said 'Wild Bullocks', turning away abruptly.

For want of better, Jack took the advice given by the old bushman who had acted so strangely at the end of their interview. He thought that, perhaps, the old man had been mistaken after all, for he did not credit Raymond with being a likely person to bother about faking a race at a little country meeting. He put sixty pounds on The Rat at 10 to 1. 'Wild Bullocks' similarly invested the five-pound note that Jack had given him.

There were nine starters in the race for the Lachlander Cup, and the field got away on even terms. At the seven furlongs, Loyalty took the lead, with Sting, The Rat, Birrimboo and the favourite close at hand. The track was heavy owing to the rains, and the pace was slow, a circumstance that caused excited punters to vociferously predict the failure of the top-weights. With Loyalty still two lengths in front the field swung into the straight, The Rat, hard-held by his rider Casey, preparing to make his run. At the distance Casey had brought The Rat to the front with a rush, and was plying his whip vigorously. Birrimboo and the favourite, running neck for neck, were a length behind, with the riders whipping also. Twenty yards from home Marigold drew in front of Loyalty, now a beaten horse, and apparently made a desperate effort to head The Rat. Birrimboo held her half-a-neck behind. Whips flashed, hoofs thundered, the crowd yelled itself hoarse, and the three leading horses dashed past the post in a bunch. A blanket would have covered the trio.

The crowd was mad with excitement. They swarmed around the judge's stand, some claiming that it was a dead-heat; others, that the favourite had won, still others that it was Birrimboo. The judge, old 'King Sock-em' Burcher, the 'straightest' squatter on the Lachlan, turned to Stenhouse, the secretary.

"The Rat first, by a neck; Marigold second, and Birrimboo third," he said briefly.

Stenhouse hoisted the numbers, and the weight flag was soon flying in the breeze.

The interval between the Cup and the succeeding race was filled by the crowd with animated discussions on the wonderfully close finish that they had witnessed. Winners and losers alike were apparently satisfied, although the bookmakers appeared to be annoyed over something. Jack Burnside, after collecting his winnings, walked across thoughtfully to the car. In doing so, he saw Raymond slip towards the scrub, where the racehorses were tied up. There he saw him enter into conversation with Taylor and the little jockey, Benny Bingham. After that, he became more thoughtful still.

Penderby duly paid over to his two fellow-conspirators the sum of three hundred pounds apiece. Each expressed the liveliest satisfaction as he pocketed the notes.

"My word, Benny," said Penderby. "You cut it pretty fine at the finish."

"I was safe," replied the jockey. "I belted me ridin' boot till I caught The Rat, an' when I got up, I belted him."

Jack bet no more that day. Penderby was fortunate over the last two events, and actually forced Callister to back the winners. The party drove homeward in the dusk with mingled feelings. Callister, who had won about two hundred pounds, was jubilant. Penderby, who had netted something like three thousand pounds, was quietly pleased. Jack, although in pocket to the extent of something like seven hundred pounds, was inwardly perturbed.

And in the town, the owner of The Rat was cursing himself for not having a solitary shilling on his own horse, and wondering why the bookmakers were abusing him for being a sly bird, a take-down, and other things that were uncomplimentary and untrue. Further, too, he could not understand his friends, all of whom appeared to be under the impression that he had effected quite a coup by neglecting to give them the tip and so spoil his market.

11

"ALL'S FAIR…"

It was about three weeks after the Condoblin races when Raymond Penderby, who had been feigning an indisposition to his friends at the station, informed Callister that he intended visiting Sydney to consult a specialist.

"My nerves are still bad," he told the kindly old manager, "and my heart is playing tricks that I, as a medical student, do not like. I will be away for a few days only – perhaps a week – and then return for the shearing, if you'll have me."

"You are always welcome at Bullangarra," said Callister, heartily, still remembering his win at the races. "Come back when you like; but I may say that we will not call the roll for the shearing for three weeks yet."

"Oh! Anyhow, a week in Sydney will do me," laughed Raymond, and he departed to pack up his things.

During those three weeks Raymond had ridden the Circle Y paddock every second or third day, and, to the intense satisfaction of the manager, had reported that everything there was in order. The young man, however, omitted to mention that on each of his rides he had spent the day in the company of Brummy Collins and the three companions of that enterprising 'duffer'; that the sheep were being quietly concentrated at the back of the run with such constant driving and harrying by dogs that they were likely to remain in the near vicinity of the back fence for a considerable time. Perhaps this slipped his memory.

Penderby departed on the morning following his conversation, the knockabout man driving him to the station in a sulky. Jack, being out at the Dead Finish, did not learn of his departure until two days later, on his return to the homestead. There he found a letter from Molly, couched in the usual affectionate terms, and he set forth to the Black Rock paddock next day with a light heart.

Raymond Penderby's sense of filial duty was not developed in any marked degree. Instead of seeking father immediately upon arrival in Sydney, to cheer the old man with a welcome presence that would allay an anxiety created by the two brief, hurried letters that had been sent him from Bullangarra, the young man went straight to his flat in Phillip Street. Removing the traces of travel, he telephoned to a young lady friend and informed her that he would be along for breakfast.

He kept this appointment, spending the greater part of the morning in the company of the girl. At eleven o'clock he took an affectionate farewell of her and proceeded to Tattersall's Club in Pitt Street. The first man that he encountered was the Leger bookmaker.

"Here you are, yer blanky scaler!" snarled the metallicians. "I got yer flamin' note askin' fer another month, an' I wouldn't have given it only fer Foxie. Can yer pay now?"

"I can pay you anyhow, you miserable hound!" exclaimed Raymond wrathfully. "It was a thousand, wasn't it? Well here, take this. And I will never make another bet with you as long as you live." With that he thrust ten hundred-pound notes into the bookmaker's face.

"I didn't mean no offence, Mister Penderby," said the other, in a cringing tone, as he counted and pocketed the money. "You was always a toff, you was, as I said ter Foxie when we all got your letters. I've had a rough trot meself lately, or I wouldn't have asked you fer the money, s'help me I wouldn't."

"Well, you're paid now, so get – quick!" said the young man, angrily.

The bookmaker departed with alacrity and in high good humour. Penderby spent the next hour compromising with his other creditors of the ring. As they were far more prosperous than the one who had been paid in full, he had no compunction in asking them for further time. Foxie, whose claim was the largest, cheerfully accepted the proffered proportion of cash and the promise of a full settlement within another two months, a course that compelled the others to do likewise. The matter being arranged to the satisfaction of all parties concerned, Raymond parted from them amid expressions of mutual good-will. Then he met and lunched with a fellow student, a former friend of his at the University.

At three o'clock he entered the door of his father's chambers. Molly Forbes sat in the outer office, busily tapping at a typewriter. She looked up in expectant surprise as he greeted her.

"Oh, Mr. Ray! How are you?" she exclaimed. "And how is Jack?"

Raymond was a consummate actor. He gazed sadly at the eager face of the girl, shook his head slowly, made as though to speak, hesitated, and then turned away to look mournfully out the door. The hopeful, happy look on the girl's face rapidly gave place to one of consternation. She paled, and clasped her hands across her heaving bosom.

"Oh my God!" she sobbed out. "Is he dead? Tell me!"

"No," replied Raymond, facing her again. "He is not dead. It were better that he were."

"Oh! What has happened to him?" Molly cried in puzzled, but broken tones.

"I do not wish to be uncharitable towards one to whom you have evinced such interest," answered Raymond, "but if you ever harboured any romantic thoughts of that young man I am truly sorry for you."

"But what has he done?" asked the girl in anguished tones.

"If there is a thing that he has not done out there in the west that is wicked and criminal," Raymond said impressively, "it is murder.

No! He has not been charged with that – yet. He was bad enough before he left Sydney," the young man continued in a level voice, "but up there he has cast aside all restraint and decency. He has become a drunken sot, a loafer, and the associate of thieves. He is mixed up with a gang of sheep-stealers, and I would not be surprised to read of his arrest in the papers any day. He only kept his position on the station through my intervention on his behalf, and partly because labour is scarce at shearing time, for on a sheep-run, even a dissolute, half-drunken mustered is better than none. Heaven alone knows what will become of him! In one of his moments of remorse he spoke to me of suicide, but I believe that he is too great a coward for even that final act of cowardice."

With that, Raymond passed into his father's room. In turning to close the door behind him he saw the huddled, pathetic figure of the girl drooping over the table, and heard her heart-broken sobs. Then he hailed his parent with a boisterous joviality.

"Yes, as fit as a fiddle, dad," he exclaimed, wringing the old man's hand. "I just ran down to get another overhauling – not that I need it, but for safety's sake – and then I'm off back to Bullangarra for another month. Don't I look well?"

Old Mr. Penderby stood back a few paces, proudly surveying his son. There was an unwonted mistiness about his usually piercing eyes, and an unaccustomed tremor in his voice as he spoke.

"You look the picture of health, my boy," he said, and shook hands again.

Certainly, Raymond Penderby had benefitted vastly in a physical sense during his brief stay in the bush, for he was bronzed and clear-eyed, despite his frequent carousals with the sheep-stealers in the scrub. The open air and the hard riding had given him a firmness of muscle and a and a lightness of tread that were unmistakably obvious. His doting father had good reason to be delighted at the change he saw. The pair talked for half an hour at the office, Raymond eventually accompanying the old man to the family home. There they spent a pleasant evening.

Raymond described to his father some of his experiences on

Bullangarra. He was an accomplished conversationalist, adorning his reminiscences with interesting stories and humorous quips and gibes until his proud parent was boisterously mirthful. The talk of the bush awakened in the old man's mind memories of his youth, spent far from the cities, and he too expanded in a manner of which the young man had never believed him capable of, telling of wild days, wilder nights, and the wildest escapades it would be possible to conceive. As they parted, Raymond insisting on returning to his flat, the old man asked his son to call at the office early on the following morning. To this the young man gave a ready assent.

As Raymond clambered into a taxi that he hailed on the street, he muttered to himself, "The old dad has something human in him, after all." Then he fell to wondering whether he had been wise to refrain from mentioning to his father anything concerning Jack Burnside. Although, as part of a plan that his scheming brain was already formulating, he had lied to Molly Forbes, it were perhaps, better, he thought, to keep his father in the dark regarding old Amos Burnside's son; and if necessity ever arose at a future date for an explanation of this silence he felt capable of inventing one that would prove satisfactory. The girl, he knew, would not mention Jack to the old lawyer, for his father, although as considerate employer, had never yet been known to converse with his typistes or any of the articled clerks on any matters save those that related exclusively to the work of the office. That night Raymond retired in high spirits.

On the following morning he reached his father's office a few moments after the old lawyer had left for one of the courts. Raymond's arrival had been carefully timed, inasmuch as he had spent fully half an hour in a hotel on the opposite corner waiting and watching until his parent had departed, and he had been rather impatient at the old man's unpunctuality. As he entered the room in which Molly Forbes was engaged at her accustomed tasks, Raymond, cynical and callous-hearted as he was, felt a pang of remorse for his shameless untruths of the previous afternoon.

The girl's face was haggard and tense with suffering. The wide grey eyes held sombre depths of sorrow, and the dark black lines beneath them startlingly intensified their anguish. Her figure seemed bent and burdened down beneath the dead weight of her misery; she was the personification of unutterable despair.

"Great heavens, Molly! What is the matter?" exclaimed the young man, and there was genuine concern in his voice as he spoke.

"Nothing is the matter, now," she answered in a dead, listless voice.

"It is I that have done this thing, Molly," said Raymond, still affected, "in telling you of Jack Burnside! I wish that my tongue had withered before it uttered one word that would give you pain. I only wish to God that I could recall my words!"

"It is not your fault, Mister Raymond," the girl replied, weeping quietly. "Do not blame yourself. I – I – I thought that he might have tried to do better things out there, but perhaps the temptations have been too great. And perhaps the loneliness of the bush stung into being again the terrible disappointment he must have felt at the ruin of his hopes and expectations, and drove him to despair. Oh! If he had only had someone there to help him at first!" And burying her face in her arms she sobbed aloud.

Raymond Penderby then laid himself out to comfort the heart-broken girl, and it was his uncanny ability to appraise correctly the deeper feelings of others that crowned with success his efforts on this occasion. Although, at the time, he had no definite object in doing so, he skilfully won such approval as the young girl was capable of then showing him for what he had described as his own unselfish and unsuccessful endeavours to rescue Jack Burnside from the degradation in which he wallowed. With devilish ingenuity he plumbed the depths of her soul and found that it had been only her pure, confiding love for the other, her virginal innocence, that had been revolted and had been content credulously to accept the story of Jack's supposed debasement and dishonour. He realised that her love for Jack, not as she then thought him to be, but as she had believed him to be in the first joyous days of the awakening of her heart, still burned within her breast with undiminished lustre. But now it was an ideal only that she loved with such vehement passion.

Raymond's experience with women, and it had been a long and varied one, told him that in Molly's bitter disappointment this loss of both an ideal and an actual lover would leave her peculiarly susceptible to tender influences wherein something else might eventually take the place of that which was gone. He knew that the heart of a girl, wrung with the grief of a loss of one loved so dearly, instinctively turned at the moment of its greatest sorrow to a sympathetic comforter; and thus, at the end of an hour he had calmed the raging fierceness of Molly's despair. He took his departure from the room at what he considered to be the opportune moment. Saying farewell, he pressed the girl's cold hands within his own.

"I cannot thank you enough," the girl said, emotionally. "But for you I could not have borne it any longer."

That night Molly wrote to Jack. The letter cost her many hours of poignant pain in the composition, and it expressed the agony of unshed tears. Having accepted as true the malicious and wretched story told by Raymond Penderby, she did not seek to reproach Jack for his, to her mind, unforgivable conduct, it having been forced to her conviction that if her half-expressed love before they had parted could not have kept him, thenceforward, on the path of righteousness, it could now avail nothing when he had sped so far along the way of degradation. Nor did she write of what she had been told, nor ask for explanations. To her it seemed as though Jack had ruthlessly and brutally flung back in her face the love that she had offered. In the letter, as it was ultimately written, she told him that she had been seriously considering her position, and their mutual attitude towards life, and had come to the conclusion that, perhaps, it were better that she did not write to him again, nor he to her. "And," she wrote, in concluding, "if the future should alter for you in the manner I will pray that it may, and you can some day find it in you to win success, please think, just now and then, in your happier hours, of your broken-hearted Molly."

The next three days were spent by Raymond Penderby in remarkable fashion. During the mornings he would talk with Molly at the office, laying siege to her heart by craftily bestowing on her a tender, earnest sympathy, and by subtly besmirching the reputation of Jack Burnside. The afternoons were spent by him about the offices of the stock salesmen, and the hotels frequented by men from the sheep-stations outback. On the sale-day he was at the busy, bustling yards at Homebush, making himself a conspicuous figure. When he set forth to seek the company of those who sold stock and those who bred them, he carefully dressed for the occasion, turning out in the unmistakable clothes and the distinctive wide felt hat of the bush-man. He met squatters from the four quarters of the continent, and, because he told them that he was dealing in sheep in a large way on the Lachlan, and would be selling some big lines at an early date, and because he spent his money liberally, he was accepted as one of themselves. Curiously enough, he had given his name as Burnside, a circumstance that was the outcome of a peculiar incident on one occasion.

A fellow-student, who had taken a good deal too much liquor, had greeted him in a hotel as Penderby, and had been quite taken aback when Raymond had denied his identity. With drunken insistence the student had maintained that he was correct, and went so far as to offer to wager on it, but Raymond turned on his heel and left him. Someone then told the argumentative one that the man addressed was named Burnside, not Penderby, whereupon he had called out to Raymond:

"So you're at it again, are you? Well, it must be something crooked, and I warn everyone in this bar that you are an imposter!" The indignant student shouted this loudly, and all eyes were turned toward Raymond.

"Bah! You are drunk!" Penderby said, and left the bar unhurriedly.

At the saleyards Raymond met a young selector from the Lachlan, and was hailed gladly as Jack Burnside.

"Down with sheep?" the selector asked.

"Yes, we have a few in today," said Penderby, uneasily. "Er – excuse me, I have to go round to the agent's office just now, but I'll see you later." And he rushed off towards the buildings where the salesmen and their clerks were accommodated; but he took care to keep out of the way of the inquisitive bushman during the remainder of the day.

The conduct of the sales proved absorbingly interesting to Penderby, as it does to anyone that cares to visit the great live-meat mart of Sydney. The yards, covering a vast tract of land, lay alongside the railway line; the stock were unloaded from the trucks onto ramps that opened into receiving yards. Here the cattle were swum in huge tanks, and the sheep watered and fed. Drafting-yards led them to the selling pens, whence, after sale, they were driven over a hill to the abattoirs, a mile distant. On top of the selling pens ran a platform of planks, along which the auctioneer and his clerk walked, the buyers following below along a pathway between the yards, and clambering to the cap of the rails when the selling commenced. A veterinary officer and two assistants preceded the auctioneers, marking with green paint any stock showing signs of disease or too emaciated to be fit for human consumption.

The selling was, as it always is, marvellous for its rapidity. Usually from sixty thousand to ninety thousand sheep, and from five thousand to nine thousand cattle were disposed of within a few hours. Some of the salesmen would knock down five thousand sheep, in small lots, in ten minutes, obtaining prices that were the full market value. The buyers – butchers, exporters and dealers – were keen appraisers of the worth of meat on the hoof, and amazingly correct in their estimate of the weight of the animals. Bids, therefore, would come out with the rapidity of machine-gun fire, and as the auctioneer was just as well acquainted with the values, the yards of sheep and cattle would be knocked down out of hand, with no useless waste of time.

The scene on sale-days is one of bustle and excitement. The raucous voice of the auctioneer, the sharp staccato yelps of the buyers calling their bids, the barking of dogs, the shouts of the drovers, the bellowing of the bullocks, the complaining bleats of the sheep, make a medley of sound that is indescribable. Above all hangs the red, impalpable dust of the yards, and permeating everything is the pungent, acrid but agreeable odour of the livestock.

As Raymond Penderby betook himself home, late on the afternoon of the sale, he felt satisfied that he had spent a very edifying time.

At the end of a week he returned to Bullangarra. In taking leave of Molly, he had made no open avowal of love, nor had he even protested anything more than sincere friendship; but he had contrived to create the impression that he was willing to fill Jack Burnside's place in her heart. Indeed, Molly sought in her memories of his kindness and sympathy for something definite in this respect, just as he intended that she should, but could seize upon no particular thing. And this encouraged in her mind still further tender thoughts of him, just as Raymond had intended also.

12

"WOOL AWAY!"

J ack Burnside did not receive Molly's letter until a week after its arrival. He had been moving rapidly over the run with the other station hands, shifting sheep from paddock to paddock, and there had been no one at the homestead who could be spared for what was regarded, at that juncture at least, as the quite unnecessary task of "carrying letters all over the run". To say that he was both pained and amazed at what had been written is to inadequately describe his feelings. When the precious missive had been delivered to him by Callister, after dinner one evening, he had hurriedly excused himself from the company in the dining room, and sought the seclusion of his own apartment to peruse it.

He was thankful that he had done so after he had read the letter, for his face expressed only too plainly the agonising emotion that he felt. He sensed that Molly had gone through some soul-searing ordeal, else she would not have written in such fashion, but he was completely bewildered in his attempts to account satisfactorily for it, or to formulate any convincing explanation. He had so much trust in her, and was so confident and assured in his own love for her that he did not for a moment suspect that the treachery of a trusted friend might have been responsible for such a change in her feelings.

He made no attempt to go to bed, but walking out into the night sought a favourite seat of his by the river, close to where the stream was spilling noisily over the weir-top. There he gave himself up to thought. During those dark hours of misery there came to assail him the demons of jealousy, and his fevered imagination conjured up pictures of Molly and some unknown other man who had captured her heart. These fancies persisted, try to suppress them as he would, and his sensitive tempera-ment and that trick of introspective reasoning that had grown upon him, encouraged a belief that she had, all along, regarded him with nothing more than mere maidenly pity, while she had given her love to some other man who had spurned it. Never did it occur to him to connect Raymond Penderby with the matter, but he resolved to question him on the morrow, never-theless.

During the early hours of the morning he wrote to Molly. He had at length brought himself to believe that she had been betrayed by some unprincipled villain, although that very thought made a raw, rankling wound in his heart, and that she sorely needed some loyal friend to stand at her side. Movingly, he told of his own feelings towards her, his great love, his boundless trust; and he offered, if she would but be content to take his name and share her sorrows with him, to lead her to the altar at once. He covered many pages, pouring out unreservedly the magnitude of his love, and addressed the enve-lope with fingers that trembled.

He found an opportunity to speak with Raymond early next morning. His face bore traces of his night of suffering, but he was calm and restrained.

"Did you see Molly when you were in Sydney?" he asked, anxiously.

"Only once," replied Raymond. "She looked ghastly, as though she were seriously ill. My dad told me that she had been absent from the office a good deal during the past two months, and when she was there she could not do her work because she appeared to be worrying over something. He could not account for it, because she had always been such a quiet and reserved girl, but he thought it may have been a love affair."

"Did you speak to her?" Jack queried, in even tones.

"Yes," replied Raymond, "but only on one occasion. That was the only time she was at the office during the week that I was down. I told her that you were getting along splendidly, and that you sent affectionate remembrances, whereupon she appeared to become quite incensed. This came as a great surprise after what you had confided in me, but of course, I could not be inquisitive, so I left her without pressing for any explanations."

Jack then told him how he suspected that some sorrow had overwhelmed the girl because of the tenor of a letter that he had received, and Raymond, luring him into further confidence by subtly-expressed sympathy, soon learned of the other's noble, generous-hearted offer.

"I have written to her," said Jack, "making that offer. Will you post the letter today for me? I have to ride out this morning to Black Rock, and cannot get away to meet the mailman. If you ride across to the main road through the Circle Y paddock and catch the mailman on the Forbes coach about noon, she will receive it two days earlier than if I send it to Condoblin in the station bag."

"I will take it, Jack, old man," said Raymond warmly. "I would ride a thousand miles to catch the coach with it if necessary. Just trust me and I will get it away safely. It is a chivalrous offer, and you are a true gentleman."

"Thanks, Ray," said Jack huskily, turning to go for his horse. "You are a friend in need."

Raymond watched Jack saddle his horse, pass through the gate into the horse-paddock, and gallop across the plain. Then he sauntered carelessly into the kitchen, and when the cook had passed outside, bound on some culinary errand, he buried the letter in the heart of the roaring fire on the hearth. As he scattered its ashes he smiled grimly to himself. "That settles that little business," he muttered to himself; "but it looks as though I am going to have a girl left on my hands."

Later in the morning Raymond found Callister at the stockyard, where half a dozen musterers were receiving orders for the day. He strolled up as the manager was concluding a warm argument with Billy Prendergast, the overseer.

"I suppose you ought to know best, Billy," Callister was saying. "If the grass in those paddocks won't stand that mob, you had better go out to the Circle Y today and start the wethers in from there. I did intend to have had them shorn last of all, but now we will have to put them through first. We might send them to the Dead Finish after they are shorn."

"Righto!" said Billy, nodding. "Get a move on, boys!" And with a clatter of hoofs and much barking of dogs, the cavalcade moved off.

"What? Are you going to move the sheep in from Circle Y?" Raymond demanded of Callister, in great concern.

"Have to," replied the other brusquely, not noting Penderby's manifest perturbation. "Too many too close in on the home paddocks where we want to reserve the grass, so it is a case of necessity."

Raymond was greatly dismayed at this totally unanticipated turn of affairs, but he managed to conceal his chagrin and control his voice as he fell into step with Callister, who was walking towards the gate with a bridle on his arm.

"By Jove!" he exclaimed. "I consider that I have a proprietary right in that paddock, so if you don't think I'll be in the way I will ride out after the men and lend a hand."

"I'd be mighty thankful if you would," said Callister. "An extra man makes a wonderful difference in a big paddock like that."

Raymond immediately saddled a horse and raced at a good round gallop across the plain in the tracks of Prendergast and his riders. He had notified Collins of his return from Sydney immediately he had arrived at Condoblin, and he knew that the sheep-stealer and his gang were at that moment camped somewhere near the back Bullangarra boundary. It would be decidedly unfortunate, he thought, if the musterers should encounter Brummy and his companions, more especially if they chanced to be inside the netting fence. He knew that the station men would make at once for the boundary in order to start cleaning up the paddock from that fence, driving all the sheep in front of them towards the woolshed; and he intended to prevent this if possible.

After a hard ride he overtook the men. Prendergast was issuing instructions, and had apparently allotted each man a particular range of country over which to work, for he was pointing in various directions across the paddock.

"Hullo!" greeted the overseer as Penderby rode up. "After a job?"

"Yes," was the reply, "I have come out to give you a hand with the mustering."

"Goodo," said Prendergast. "As you know the paddock, what about starting at the east corner, where the billabong comes in, and picking up what sheep you can find between there and the salt-lick? It's a pretty big stretch; but there won't be many over that side. Simmons will pick you up after lunch."

"All right, I suppose so," Raymond responded, absently, wondering whether he would be lucky enough to meet any of the sheep-stealers in that quarter.

Penderby rode off, and within an hour had picked up his appointed position. He found a large mob of sheep feeding over a fairly extensive range, and within a short time had them together in a 'ringing' bunch in the midst of a little clearing. Having no dog, he experienced some trouble in starting them in the required direction, and was consequently riding hard for some time, backwards and forwards at the rear of the stupid, crowding mass, yelling the usual startling cries of the musterer. He was deeply engrossed in the task of moving the sheep off when he heard, with a start, someone calling his name.

Brummy Collins rode out of the scrub and greeted him. Raymond, in anxious tones, hastily explained the situation, which caused the sheep-stealer to explode in a fury of profanity. However, after a few moments he realised the futility of his outburst and became thoughtful.

"It'll mean waitin' another month," Collins said, "an' providin', o' course, they bring them wethers back inter this paddock. Aw well, I suppose we'll have ter make the best of it, but yer'll have ter do yer damnedest ter get 'em back here. The worst o' it all is we'll lose a few thousand quid by the loss o' the wool."

"Rather queer to look at it as our loss, don't you think?" commented Raymond, drily.

After further hurried discussion of future plans, Collins rode off, and jumped his horse over the netting into the adjoining block. As he disappeared, Bob Simmons rode up and sent his dogs around the sheep.

"Did yer see anybody about here this morning?" he asked Penderby. "I seen some fresh horse tracks about that don't belong to the station mokes, an' it looks to me as if someone's been working these sheep lately."

"I have seen no-one," was the abrupt reply, and Raymond rode quickly to the other side of the mob.

Two days later the sheep were well in towards the homestead, disposed of in a handy paddock, and ready to be taken to the shed at a moment's notice. There, complete preparations had been made for the greatest event of the year throughout the back-country, the shearing, and already the shearers and rouseabouts were arriving at the station. Everything was bustle and excitement in the vicinity of the woolshed. The engine, a portable oil engine, had been installed in a lean-to near the main building; the belting had been connected with the pulleys on the shafting that extended overhead along 'the board' and which drove the machines. The pressers had overhauled the wool-press, the men's huts had been cleaned up, the cook's galley refurnished, wood piled close at hand; in fact, everything placed in readiness for the commencement of the great undertaking.

Bullangarra shore, on a yearly average, sixty thousand sheep, there being stands for twenty-eight men. The shed was a huge, T-shaped building of unpainted sawn-pine planks, the shearing 'board', pens, and wool tables extending along the top, the base accommodating the wool-pressers, the branded bales, and the odds and ends of the shearing. The 'board' and its pens were raised some six feet above the floor of the pressing room, and the sheep were driven from drafting yards at the rear into these pens beneath the roof. When the sheep had been shorn they were pushed unceremoniously down shuts that lodged them in counting pens below, whence they were taken through the branding races and drafting yards, back to their destined paddocks. The fleece of the sheep was taken off by machines, similar in action to the hair-clippers of a barber, but on a larger and more solid scale, necessarily, to stand the speed of the engine drive. These shearing machines, which are purely an Australian invention, have long since superseded the old blades, the 'tongs' as they were humorously termed by the old hands, save on small selections where the cocky himself, or some veteran 'battler', hand-cuts the tiny clip inside a few days.

On the day prior to the commencement of the shearing there were nigh upon two hundred men at the Bullangarra shed, all seeking, or allegedly so, something to do. In accordance with long-established custom these men enjoyed the hospitality of the station from the hour of their arrival up to the "roll-call" – that is, the actual engagement of the labour required for the shearing. Those that were unsuccessful in securing employment received sufficient rations to carry them to the next run. They were a motley crew, these toilers of the bush, young boys and grizzled veterans with sixty summers behind them, with all ages in between. Some of the lads were scarcely fourteen years old, but even thus young they had worked as "tar-boys" or rouseabouts at several shearings, and proudly earned their union tickets.

The men came to Bullangarra in various fashions. Many, with swag and 'nose-bag' slung across broad shoulders and 'billy' in hand, trudged through the scrub from their last station down the river, a method of progression that was, aforetime, most common. Others had their mounts and pack-horses, a few, the "Goulburn cockies" – small selectors who supplemented the meagre income afforded by their holdings with the proceeds of hard work at any occupation, including shearing – drove sulkies, and camped and ate apart from the other men. The rest came per coach, hawker's van, or any other chance conveyance that availed. They were bronzed, hard-muscled, hard-living men, with clear, fearless eyes filled with the spirit of a boundless independence, and for whom no work was too arduous. If they earned big cheques in a few short weeks and "blewed" their money in the reckless dissipation of the outback shanties in as few days, they showed little sign physically of their excesses. They toiled frenziedly, honestly, for the wherewithal to 'spree', and, the debauch over, they worked once more as hard as they had lately drunk.

At the roll-call when the names of the men that had bespoken pens were announced, twenty answered. The vacancies were filled from the waiting ranks. Then the "boss of the board", Prendergast, who practically ran the shearing, signed on the wool-rollers, piece-pickers, tar-boys, rouseabouts, and pressers. The expert, or 'the squirt' as the men called him, looked after the engine, ground the combs and cutters, and fixed the handpieces of the machines. The wool-classer sorted the fleeces according to length and quality of staple. These two last-named were the aristocratic employees of the shed, being non-union, and therefore merely tolerated by the rest of the true-blue 'ticket-takers'. The cook was chosen by the shearers by ballot, it being part of the business of sheep-shearing that the men that take off the fleece shall feed themselves at their own expense, whereas all the other employees are fed by the station. The shearers are a tribe distinct, with many strange rites and privileges that are jealously guarded. The cook – 'poisoner' they term him – on his appointment selected his 'off-sider' or 'slushy', who was a friend, to assist him in his work.

On the following morning, when the east was greying with the first faint hints of dawn, a whistle sounded shrilly in the engine-house. Men and boys tumbled out of their bunks, performed a hasty toilet, snatched a pannikin of steaming tea, gulped it down, and hurried to their stations in the shed. So soon as it was light enough, work commenced.

The shearers found the pens behind their stands filled with wethers from the Circle Y paddock, and when the starting whistle gave the signal each shearer seized one of the struggling animals, dragged it out to the board, squatted it on its haunches between his knees, pulled the lever that set his machine in motion, and plunged the cutters into the wool along its belly. In wide swathes the fleece folded out and lay in snowy circles about the feet of the shearers, until in one piece the whole of the wool of each sheep was taken off. Then a few hurried trimmings about face and ears completed the operation, and the naked-looking animal was pushed roughly back into the pen.

The men worked with frenzied haste. So as soon as one sheep was shorn the shearer cried, "Wool away!" whereupon a boy seized upon the fleece and with a dexterous twist threw it outspread upon a handy wool-table. Here it was, in turn, again seized upon by the piece-picker or the wool-roller, trimmed of its dirt-encrusted fringes, and rolled into a neat ball, to be passed on to the classers' bins.

Lads scurried along the boards with brooms, sweeping up stray scraps of wool, keeping the floor absolutely clean. Occasionally would ring out the cry, "Tar!" when some shearer in his haste had sliced inches of skin from a sheep's side, or the wrinkles on the neck. Then a boy, with a tin of tar and a brush, would dab gouts of the reeking antiseptic into the gaping, bleeding wound. This cutting of the sheep is not uncommon where such speed is maintained; and, towards the end of shearing, when a shed has been long delayed, and men have pens engaged elsewhere, they will, not infrequently, deliberately injure the animals, in the hope of being discharged. This is known as "shearing for the sack".

At eight o'clock the men halted for breakfast, and within half an hour were at it again. Top-speed is necessary at shearing for many reasons. During the spring months the light fails early in the afternoon, and few sheds have artificial illuminant. Then again, wet weather is frequent, and no shearer will handle sheep on which even a point of rain has fallen. The damp heat of the 'yolk', or saponaceous cholsterine, in the wool, causes, so they aver, acute rheumatism in the fingers and arms, or serious festering sores. And of course, the station owner or manager is anxious to get the sheep back into the paddocks and his wool onto the selling floors as speedily as possible.

Shearers are paid at a certain rate per hundred sheep shorn. In the old days the price was twenty shillings per hundred, but when the bush workers organised industrially, and after hard and bitter struggles formed the Australian Workers' Union, the strongest of its kind in the Commonwealth, wages increased all round. Today the union's organisers are ever on the move among the nomads of the back-blocks. Every shed at shearing time has its "rep", a spokesman elected from the workers on the job, who represents the union, and acts as between it and the employer. But conditions have altered considerably in other respects. The old-time, careless, easy-going shearers have largely given place to young, alert, saving men who work for contractors. The contracting firms undertake, for a certain figure per sheep, to conduct the whole of the shearing, the station only providing the sheep and the wool-classer. These firms have teams of picked men that they move about over the country from shed to shed in motor cars or other swift conveyances, and the shearing is put through far more rapidly than in former times. The firms do remarkably well, the stations are well-served, and some of the 'big-gun' shearers – the "ringers" – earn more than a thousand pounds per year. It is nothing for a whole team to average two hundred sheep per day for four weeks, the 'ringer' often cutting 260 or 270.

Thus the shearing at Bullangarra proceeded, and within a month the shed "cut out". The wool was carted away on huge tabletop wagons to the railway station at Condoblin, consigned to the selling brokers in Sydney.

On the third day of the shearing, the six thousand wethers were sent back to the Circle Y paddock, Raymond Penderby assisting in the droving of them. A week later, Brummy Collins and his gang had driven them out across the Crown lands to the main road. Raymond Penderby was present, dressed remarkably like Jack Burnside. In fact, two or three casual travellers who had previously seen Jack noticed his supposed presence on this momentous occasion, and therefore thought little of the circumstances of a big mob of Bullangarra sheep faring south when a station employee was apparently giving delivery of them to the drovers. Raymond turned up, too, at different points along the route of travel during the next week, when the sheep were being driven toward Wyalong, and his presence was generally observed. He attended the sales in Sydney, and in due course was paid, on behalf of the Collins brothers, cheques totalling fourteen thousand, seven hundred and twenty pounds, for which he gave the required receipt – in the name of J. Collins.

13

BLACK SHEEP AND A BAY HORSE

Bullangarra shed had been cut out for a fortnight. The huge, barn-like building was deserted; the ashes in the cook's fireplace scattered to the four winds; the boisterous shearers and rouseabouts swallowed up in the scrub. A strange silence brooded where for a brief space half-naked, sweating men had worked with a frantic, clamorous haste that shattered the quietude of the bush. The memory of the uproar, the profanity, the hurrying, the excitement, was well-nigh forgotten. And well-nigh forgotten too, was Raymond Penderby, the young city visitor, who had been so affable, so self-effacing, so easily entertained. He, pleading that he had been called urgently to Sydney by his father, had departed, bag and baggage, at the end of the second week of shearing.

The sheep had been drafted back to their accustomed paddocks; the great rush of the year had expended itself. The station hands were ready, once again, to take up the broken threads of Bullangarra's humdrum routine. Issuing orders on this particular morning, Callister directed Jack Burnside to ride up to Thomas's at Baroo, to take delivery of a yearling blood colt that had been purchased for the station stud, and to fetch him home.

Jack started out at daybreak. Although early, the sun shone with a glowing warmth, tempered by a cool, wattle-scented wind that lightly stirred the foliage of the trees. The air was clear and invigorating as it only can be in the wide, open spaces of the bush. The country presented a remarkable contrast to what it had been when he first arrived at Bullangarra, a little over six months before. Then it had been parched, withered and desolate. That day it was a picture of rich, green proliferation. On every hand the long, lush grasses waved feathery tops against his horse's sides. The billabongs, dams and tanks were filled to overflowing. The scrub and bush timber had assumed a lighter and gayer tint in their sombre foliage. Bird life teemed everywhere; as he rode along a creek-bank a cloud of wood-ducks rose with a hurried whir-r-r, and winged swiftly and silently to the river. Fat, lazy sheep scurried perfunctorily a few yards from his approach, and big-eyed sleek bullocks stared incuriously at him as he passed. Prosperity was writ large upon the land, and he marvelled that such a miraculous transformation was possible in so short a space of time. And pondering on the affairs of his world in the bush, his thoughts travelled to the city and the girl who had apparently cast him from her life.

Jack had anxiously expected a reply to the letter that he had given to Penderby to post, but none had come. In the first few weeks of his disappointment he had thought to rush to the city to learn from Molly's own lips the story of her sorrow. He had, in fact, mentioned to Raymond that he intended to follow such a course. That astute individual, however, had cunningly persuaded him that the girl would have written had she needed him, or had intended to accept his offer, and also had convinced the love-sick and jealous jackeroo that she had either satisfactorily settled her trouble, or else intended her silence as an intimation that Jack was not required to interfere any further in her affairs. Jack, permitting himself to be dissuaded from his intention, had then endeavoured, but futilely, to banish her from his thoughts. He still loved her to adoration, and on this glorious spring morning he sorrowfully acknowledged to himself that she would ever remain the object of his affections.

Jack had extracted a promise from Raymond, prior to that young man's departure from the station, that if he found Molly he would write and explain her attitude. No letter had come, so Jack concluded sadly that she had left the city. With his mind still completely engrossed with these disquieting thoughts he rode slowly along the stock-route, oblivious of his surroundings for many a mile. His day-dreams, however, were rudely shattered as he was passing a low bush shanty on the roadside, whose existence he had not even noticed. There smote his senses an angry voice, demanding peremptorily that he should halt. Glancing up in surprise, he saw a villainous-looking individual limping nimbly towards him.

"You blasted thief!" roared the lame man. "It's like your damned hide to brazenly turn up here after robbing us! What have you done with the money for them sheep, you bloody bushranger?" Then the excited individual danced about in a fighting attitude right under the horse's nose.

Jack was astonished, but amused.

"What's up?" he asked, smilingly. "Been taking too much of the snake-juice in there?"

This provoked such a storm of vituperation that Jack became annoyed. Spurring his horse, he wheeled sharply to avoid the excited stranger, and cantered off along the track. The other shook his fist at him in rage, Jack hearing him shout out:

"All right, Mister bloody Penderby; if Brummy don't fix you, I will!"

Jack was entirely at a loss to account for the inexplicable conduct of the man at the hotel, and it caused him no small amount of concern. He was still in a state of wonder when he rode up to Thomas's place half-an-hour later. A little, old man, who resembled a retired and prosperous jockey – which he was – gave him a greeting as he approached the house.

"Hallo!" said Thomas. "How are you going? Have you come for the colt? It's a couple of weeks since I saw you last, eh?"

Jack explained that he was in good health, and that he had come for the colt; but he denied emphatically that he had ever seen the old man before in his life.

"Why," said Thomas, looking at him intently, "I had a drink with you last Monday fortnight over at the Wongonga pub. Didn't old Peg-leg drive you out to the Marsden turn-off that afternoon?"

"No," answered Jack, "not me. You are evidently mistaken."

"All right," said Thomas curtly, "have it your own way; it's not my business, I suppose. Well, come along and get the colt."

Jack accompanied the old man to his stables at the rear, and then saw, from the point of a slight eminence on which the homestead was erected, one of the finest farms that he had ever beheld. The property lay in a wide bend of the river, bulging in a generous sweep at the lower end and contracting like a bottle's neck near the homestead. Four or five cultivation paddocks, vividly green amid the surrounding lush-grassed lands, lay along the stream; an orchard that seemed a garden of rare, fragrant blossoms extended over a wide area. The place was literally alive with sheep, cattle and horses, and the dozens of haystacks dotted over the domain looked like some grotesque, pre-Adamite monsters grazing contentedly among them. Jack halted, sweeping the farm with admiring gaze.

"By Jove!" he exclaimed, enthusiastically. "What a magnificent place you have! There is nothing else like this in Australia, surely?"

The old man was manifestly pleased at this laudatory outburst. His soft spot had been discovered. Forgetting his pique of a moment before, he answered elatedly.

"You are nearly right," he said. "It will take some beating, although I say it myself. I am proud of my place, and proud of the hard work that I did to make it like it is. But I am prouder still that I have shown people on the Lachlan that you can do anything with irrigation."

A few deftly-put questions opened the floodgates of the old man's eloquence. He told Jack that he had taken up the selection of 2560 acres some years before, with the object of showing what could be done under irrigation with land that was apparently unfit for anything else, save light grazing. The lay of the farm made it possible to irrigate by gravitation practically the whole area, so hat when he had constructed a five-foot weir in the river, he had water sufficient for all his requirements. Thirty acres had been first put under lucerne, and with proper tillage this land had established in two years, and he was now getting a cut from it every month. Forty acres had been planted with Japanese millet, forty acres with oats, and forty acres with barley, some twenty acres being devoted to maize. These crops provided green fodder, hay, and cereal in abundance. The orchard of citrus and stone fruits occupied thirty acres, and was just commencing to bear. The total cost of installing a pumping plant, constructing the earthwork weir and opening ditches had been under two thousand pounds.

"Does it pay you?" queried Jack.

"Pay!" echoed the old man. "Pay? Well, I should smile. Right through last season's drought I ran and kept fat three-and-a-half thousand sheep, three hundred sixty head of cattle, and eighty horses on this little block with the fodder that I have grown. Those sheep on the flat there are all sold now; sixty-three shillings per head in the paddock. Before I started irrigating, this country would not have carried more than a sheep to two acres, and in a dry time most of them would have starved."

"You have certainly shown that you can grow some things, providing you have plenty of water," Jack said.

"You can grow anything here," said the old man, warmly. "I have tried all sorts of experiments with all manner of fruits, grasses, fodder plants and grain, and proved it. They all regarded me as a sort of harmless lunatic when I first started in here, but I have a suspicion that that opinion has altered a good deal since the drought. Some of the neighbours are queer, too," the old man rattled on. "When I was sowing grasses on the pasture they all rushed me with advice about the best English varieties to put in. I just went ahead and planted native grasses, Mitchell, blue, kangaroo, about six local trefoils and clovers, and one or two new sorts from the back of Queensland. I did that because they are all built for this climate, and in the summer stand for months longer than the imported ones. This little place will do me!"

Jack took charge of the colt, a fine up-standing bay, with the staying Musket blood in his veins, after inspecting Thomas's brood mares and sires. The old man bred blood-stock on a fairly extensive scale, and the horses from his stud had carried winning colours all over Australia. As he was leaving, Jack expressed a wish to return at some later date for a more leisurely and closer inspection of the property.

"You are welcome," said Thomas. "Come any time you like. But, by the way, you haven't given me your name."

"I'm awfully sorry," was the apologetic reply. "It is Burnside, Jack Burnside."

"Um! I thought it was something else," commented the old man, drily.

Jack led the colt along quietly, and when nearing the hotel later on he saw the lame man take up a position in the roadway.

"Hallo," he muttered to himself. "Here's the old lunatic again." He halted within a few yards of the man.

"Oh, Mr. Burnside!" exclaimed the waiting pedestrian. "I want to apologise for my goings-on this morning. I had a few drinks too many, and didn't know what I was doing. My name's Costigan; I'm the publican here, so come in and have a taste."

"It is all right," replied Jack. "I wondered what was up. But why did you call me Penderby?"

"Blowed if I know," Peg-leg answered. "Must have been because you're like a chap by that name I used to know in Sydney."

"Ah yes," said Jack, thoughtfully. "Raymond Penderby, I suppose."

"That's him," was the answer.

As this conversation was going on four men lounged out from the hotel to the roadway. Jack recognised one as Brummy Collins.

"Good day, Mister Collins! He said. "Been doing any more sensational jumping lately?"

"No," replied Brummy, but someone else will before long. Nice sort of colt youse got there"

"Yes," said Jack. "Twelve hundred guineas worth, so he ought to be good! But I will have to be moving to get him home tonight. So long!"

"S'long!" said the men.

Jack proceeded slowly for the sake of the unshod colt, and darkness overtook him some six miles from the homestead. He was riding through a patch of scrub, sitting loosely in the saddle, and wondering how the publican first, as he knew, and Thomas afterwards, as he guessed, had come to mistake him for Raymond Penderby, seeing that it was impossible for them to have known the young medical student, in that locality at least. His own innate honesty not prompting him to seek for anything sinister in the coincidence, he merely speculated vaguely as to the reason. He was thinking of the doubt that Thomas had shown, when his horse suddenly propped stiffly with a snort of fear, nearly unseating him.

"Now!" yelled a voice from the murky darkness.

He glimpsed in the dim starlight a masked figure on horseback at his side, and a stirrup-iron swung downwards by a man's arm. Then something crashed into his brain like millions of flashes of consuming lightning – and darkness closed about him. He heard voices that sounded far away as though someone were talking about the colt – and then nothing more.

It was broad daylight when Jack returned to consciousness. His head ached grievously where the stirrup-iron had struck, but there was no wound, for the soft felt hat had lessened the impact. Very painfully he collected his senses, and then realising that he had been attacked for some unknown reason, he sat up and looked about him. His horse, tied carefully to a nearby sapling, first caught his wandering gaze, but there was no sign of the colt. Strangely enough, too, his boots were both unlaced. Then he realised that the blood horse must have been the reason for the attack. It had been stolen!

He was quickly on his feet to look for tracks, and he found footprints of men and the marks of shod horses inextricably mixed. After an interval he discovered that the hoof-tracks took some order, leading through the scrub towards the back of the run. Then, realising that the case was one for a black tracker, he mounted and galloped in to the homestead.

"Where the devil have you been?" queried Callister, as Jack reined up to the front of the office. "Where's the colt?"

"Someone knocked me on the head with a stirrup-iron in the Moonbi paddock about seven last night, and I lay there unconscious until this morning. My assailants took the colt, for there are tracks of shod horses and one unshod leading towards the road paddock."

"By God!" exclaimed Callister, in passionate anger. "It's Brummy Collins! And I'll have him this time if I chase him to hell!" Then he turned to Jack and in withering tones said, "Why the hell didn't you put up a fight? You're big enough."

Jack quailed at the utter injustice of this, but did not venture an explanation. Instead, he said, "Will you ring up Sergeant Cahalan at Condoblin, and ask him to bring the tracker out? The thieves can be run down easily."

Callister stared hard at him for a moment, then turned abruptly on his heel and rushed inside to communicate with the police. That afternoon the sergeant and Moolbong, the tracker, accompanied by Callister and Jack, proceeded to the scene of the assault. The tracker ran back the trail of Jack's mount for about a quarter of a mile, and then returned to pick up the others leading off the run. With amazing speed he cantered through the bush, following tracks that were invisible to the others. From the boundary gate the tracks led to the road, and here the blackfellow paused.

"That feller, Mister Jack, he turn back along here," he announced.

"What do you mean?" demanded the sergeant.

"That feller jackeroo, Mister Burnside, he come alonga fence, then ridem back again," said Moolbong, oracularly.

"But they knocked me out," explained Jack, greatly perturbed.

"Oh!" said Callister. "One of the gang rode your horse to the fence; that is what he means."

"By cripes, no, boss," said the tracker. "Bootmarks here belong Jack."

The party then went on in silence. For a mile the blackfellow held the lead, chattering excitedly all the while. Then he halted suddenly.

"Plenty big feller mob sheep lie down belonga here," he said. "Track bin losem."

For an hour he searched the very distant traces of the sheep until he reached the travelling mob that made them. But on neither side could he find the faintest traces of shod hoofs. The tracker was completely baffled. The drovers had seen nothing of horsemen or even swagmen, they said, and, being strangers and knowing nothing of Collins, they were believed.

"Mine bin thinkit they walk alonga top wire of fence," said Moolbong with a grin.

"You shut your mouth!" roared the sergeant, angrily.

On the return trip Callister and the sergeant rode well in the rear of Jack and the tracker. The sound of an angry argument between the two often floated towards the jackeroo, and he wondered what subject it was that so stirred them both. When they again reached the scene of the assault, Jack was sent ahead, the sergeant calling the tracker to examine the spot once more. As his horse jogged slowly along, the horrible thought flashed across the young man's mind that they might suspect him of complicity in some nefarious scheme to sell the colt or to dispose of it in some dishonest manner. He turned his horse with the intention of demanding an explanation, but he saw the others coming rapidly towards him.

"The police will make enquiries tomorrow, up around Wongonga," said Callister to Jack as he came up. "The sergeant thinks he can get him this time."

"But what about the tracks?" questioned Jack, anxiously.

"Oh, Brummy can do wonderful things, and can fake a track as cleverly as he can fake a brand."

That night, after dinner, Callister and Jack sat smoking on the long, wide verandah of the homestead. After a long silence, during which each had been busy with his own thoughts, the manager spoke.

"Do you know, Jack," he said, "that stupid old sergeant wanted to arrest you on suspicion today, and I had a hard job to persuade him otherwise."

"Arrest me! Good God! For stealing the colt?" cried Jack, dazedly.

"Yes, something like that," answered Callister, simply.

At that moment Billy Prendergast walked rapidly onto the veran-dah. He was plainly weary with fatigue, but also visibly labouring under the stress of some tremendous excitement.

"Boss!" he shouted, hysterically. "There's not a hoof in the Circle Y paddock! The back fence is cut, and there's old tracks where the mob was drove out. I ran 'em to the Marsden road, and they end there. It must be a month since they was lifted!"

"Well – I'm damned!" exclaimed Callister and Jack together.

14

BACK O'BEYOND

The news of the 'lifting' of six thousand wethers from Bullangarra, and the sensational theft of a twelve-hundred-guinea blood colt, caused a great stir throughout the Lachlan countryside. Callister was in a state of rage, bordering on insanity. An inspector from the head office of the company that owned the station – an old bushman he was, into the bargain – had arrived to take charge of the inquiries into the matter, and to assist and direct the police in their investigations. Jack had proffered his help to this big, silent stranger, but experienced the mortification of having it curtly rejected.

"We'll know where to get you when we want you," the inspector had added, grimly.

The police soon discovered that James Collins had trucked six thousand wethers to the Sydney market from Wyalong nearly a month before, for which he had been able to account in an apparently satisfactory manner. They also ascertained that a man answering the description of Jack Burnside had been seen frequently in the company of Brummy Collins at the Wongonga Hotel before and about the supposed time of the theft. McLeod the bullocky bore reluctant witness to that effect; Thomas, the stud-master saw someone like him, so he informed the police, but at the time Jack had claimed, when questioned at Baroo, that it must have been someone else. Two travellers had seen Burnside, and they would swear it, with the very sheep on the main road, not far from the Bullangarra boundary, during the second week of the shearing. All of which, so the police and inspector argued, pointed conclusively to Jack's being implicated in the conspiracy to a degree that they had yet to establish.

The inspector, knowing much of sheep-stealers and their ways, had pursued diligent enquiries concerning James Collins' annual lease and the sheep that had been on it. The stock inspector at Condoblin had kept no accurate record of the number of sheep mentioned on the permit that he had issued in connection with that individual's return trip to his holding. It might have been six hundred, he said vaguely, or it might have been six thousand. The figures on the carbon duplicate were faint and blurred. There were so many sheep on the move at that time that he could not remember any particular permit definitely. Collins, however, disposed of any doubt by producing the soiled and creased document clearly showing the number to be six thousand.

Then again, Bullangarra stockmen, under the supervision of the inspector and the police, had mustered Collins' holding; finding, after the inspector had twice counted the sheep, that the discrepancy between the number returned to the Pastures Protection Board for taxing purposes and those on the run corresponded within a thousand of the lot sold. This thousand, so Collins averred, had perished during the drought. And because there was no shadow of a doubt that the sheep that had been sold had borne the Bullangarra brand and mark, it was hoped that Collins would be implicated in that way, but those same signs, the astute selector proved, were also legally recorded in the name of James Collins – himself. Neither the inspector nor the police had the slightest doubt but that Collins and his brother 'Brummy', aided and abetted by Jack Burnside, had stolen and sold the sheep, but it would be impossible to convict them before any jury on the evidence that could be submitted.

Of the colt not the slightest trace had been discovered, a fact that worried the inspector as much as the disappearance of the sheep. Thomas was the only man that knew and could identify the animal, which was unbranded, and in a year it would have almost grown even out of his recognition. The blood-horse, therefore, like the sheep, appeared to have vanished forever so far as Bullangarra was concerned.

After a month of futile effort, the police abandoned the search, and the inspector departed for Sydney. On the morning that the disappointed and furious officer left the station, Callister called Jack into his office.

"Here are your wages to date, with a week extra in lieu of notice," he said, handing Jack a cheque.

"Why! What is this for?" queried Jack in consternation.

"You're sacked," said Callister, "by orders from headquarters."

Then the manager told the young jackeroo that Williams, the inspector, had expressed himself as being firmly convinced of Jack's connection with Collins and his gang, a belief that, unfortunately, had also gained acceptance throughout the district, and therefore had directed his discharge. "I pointed out to him," Callister went on, "that you could not be guilty as, apart from your upright character, which I may say I have come to appreciate, I showed him how, on some of the dates when you were supposed to have "been seen" near Wyalong or up about Wongonga, you were actually in my company here. However, he had made up his mind that you had to go, so there was no altering it."

"I thank you, Mr. Callister," said Jack, greatly moved, both by the news of the inspector's suspicion and the expression of the manager's trust. "you know that I am guiltless of even carelessness over these matters, and your trust in me compensates for the many bitter feelings that I will have when leaving Bullangarra. Although you do not know it, the track to Bullangarra led me to a cleaner, happier and better life than I had led before, and I will part from you all here with feelings of the sincerest sorrow."

"Don't talk about parting yet, my boy," said Callister, with a sympathetic smile. "I am sacking you in my capacity as manager of this station, at the direction of my superiors; but as your friend I am going to ask you to enter into a little partnership with me. I know that you have about a thousand pounds by you, so I propose to put up the same figure. Will you come in?"

Jack was quite overcome by the offer, and for the moment could find no words with which to express his thanks. "Yes," he said brokenly, "I'll come in, Mr. Callister, if you can trust me."

"Tu-tut!" said the old manager. "I know you, that's enough. But you have not heard what the proposition is. Well, I'll explain. You know something about sheep by this time, or my teaching has gone for nothing, and you are not afraid of hard work. The company has a big lease over near Fifield, about forty miles across towards the Bogan, that they have turned over to me for a year. There are no sheep on it, but you can pick up a few cheap lines in the district through the agents – up to, say, two thousand pounds worth – fatten them, and sell them. There will be plenty of grass there to the end of the summer, and we ought to clear a thousand apiece if you buy well. We're halves in the dealing business. Then, I have a mining lease on the platinum fields there, and I want you to oversee the puddling operations, which will start next month. I will give you 25% of the profits from the wash-up. Now, are you agreeable?"

Jack expressed his readiness to start at once, after he had again expressed his gratitude to his friend. As he was preparing to leave, Callister said to him quietly, "I wonder if Raymond Penderby, who is deuced like you sometimes, had anything to do with those sheep-stealers?"

"Ah, I wonder..." said Jack, thoughtfully.

A week later, Jack Burnside had bought fifteen hundred travelling sheep, in low condition, and turned them onto The Wilgas, as the Fifield lease was called. It was a rough place, somewhat heavily timbered, comprising twenty-five thousand acres, held from the Crown as a scrub lease at an annual rental of thirty pounds. It was well grassed, however, and watered by a few tanks that were full to the top of the batter. The homestead was built of bark and kerosene tins, there being a complete suite of rooms all in one, about twelve by fourteen feet. Jack, finding "Wild Bullocks" in Condoblin, out of work and out of money, although he had drawn sixty pounds at the Bullangarra 'cut-out', engaged him on the spot as assistant manager, cook, rouseabout and boundary rider. When the sheep had been disposed of on the new run, he repaired to Fifield to locate the platinum mines.

Jack found Fifield to be a typical outback village. Perched on the side of a low ridge, it fronted a stretch of dusty road that apparently led from nowhere to nowhere, and was composed of a tiny, wide-verandahed hotel, a store, a police station, a blacksmith's shop, a one-room school, and three or four shabby, unpainted houses. A huge open tank on the plain constituted the town's water supply, wherein goats and dogs bathed with the children as the fit took them. They told him at the hotel that the tank was also the winning post when they held races, and that at a meeting not long before one of the competing horses had been galloped into the water by an excited boundary-rider, who had only been rescued by great effort on the part of an equally excited crowd. The horse, unfortunately, had been drowned, but had been removed a few days later by the policeman.

The mines were located a mile to the south, at a place that was called Platina. This proved to be a collection of miners' humpies, rough, comfortless, and poor-looking. To his surprise he learned that there was only one other place in the world besides this where that precious mineral, platinum, was to be found in anything like payable quantities, and it astonished him considerably to hear that the metal was worth about fourteen pounds per ounce.

He found Callister's claim being worked by two venerable fossickers who looked as they were the original discoverers of the country. They had five hundred loads of dirt waiting to be washed at Jack Jones' puddler, and were ready to commence at once. Jones, who owned the one puddling plant on the field, could only work it when rain had filled the nearby tank, a circumstance in that droughty locality that often left the miners with hundreds of loads of dirt on hand for sometimes a whole twelve-month.

The platinum-bearing dirt lay below a few feet of easy sinking in loose alluvial that ran in a well-defined line for over a mile, and the whole area of the field was riddled with pot-holes and studded with mullock heaps. When the dirt was carted to the puddler it was washed through a series of sluice-boxes, irregularly corrugated with wooden ripples that saved the precious metal in similar fashion to alluvial gold. The dirt did not carry any heavy proportion of the dull-lead-coloured mineral, but the average yield was consistently profitable. After three weeks' working, Jack took charge of just on one hundred ounces of platinum, which, with the telegraphed approval of Callister, he sold to the local storekeeper, who represented an English firm of buyers, for thirteen-hundred and ninety pounds. His own share of the profits, after the deduction of certain expenses, totalled two hundred and eighty pounds, a sum that he regarded in the light of a direct gift from his friend.

During the next six months Jack attended strictly to business with the sheep, buying and selling big and small lines, fattening some of The Wilgas, snapping up other lots travelling on the stock-routes, and quitting them shortly afterwards at a higher figure, often without even taking delivery. Luck seemed to follow in his footsteps, and he could not make a mistake. Within nine months he had cleared more than three thousand pounds, and before the twelve months had expired, when the lease was to be again taken over by the company, his shrewd dealing had brought the total to four thousand, six hundred pounds. "Wild Bullocks" had helped him in many ways. While the old bushman was a keen judge of sheep, he was, perhaps, a keener judge of men, so his advice was always sought before a deal was concluded. These excellent precautionary conferences on Jack's part had averted what might have been several serious losses, for which he was more than thankful, and as they prepared to ride to Parkes, where Callister was to meet Jack and receive a final settlement, the young man enquired as to the future movements of his companion.

"Aw, I reckon I can strike a job back at Bullangarra, if I wants ter," said the old man, "but, ter tell yer the blasted truth, I've took a fancy to yer, an' if yer goin' in fer any more dealin' I'll come in with yer. I've always boozed me money up before, but I'd like yer ter give me wages a flutter with yer own cash so as I'll get enough ter go back ter me old home town fer a holiday."

"You can come with me for so long as I have a feed to divide," said Jack, greatly touched by the old man's words. "I want some old friend like you that I can depend upon for good advice. I will make a few hundred for you, anyway, and then I will go back with you, if you like to your old town, which, I suppose, is Sydney?"

"Naw," said the old man, sadly, and with a far-away look in his age-dimmed eyes. "It's Dungog, a little place up among the hills in the Williams Valley. There's a clear river there as runs along between big willers an' ironwoods; the flats is always thick with grass an' the hills is always green. They never have no droughts there. Me old father an' mother used ter live there, but I s'pose they're dead by now, fer I heard on 'em fer nigh up forty year. I've got a couple o' brothers an' a sister about there too, I believe, but they wouldn't know me now. I were the eldest, an' I cleared out when I were a lad, an' I never writ home. The only news I ever got about 'em was from some shearin' mate who might o' come from about there, but I ain't been game ter enquire this last ten-year."

"Well," said Jack briskly, "we'll take a trip up there together after I have settled with Callister, and I will give you a good time. I have always wanted to see that part of the country and I might buy a farm there. But, er... er, there's just one thing that I would like to know. It is a delicate question to ask, and I hope that it will not offend you. What is your real name? I have never heard it."

"Raymond Penderby," was the quiet answer.

"Good God!" exclaimed Jack. For a minute he sat staring in blank astonishment at the face of the man before him. Then he cried, "Do you remember a young fellow of that name being at Bullangarra when the sheep were stolen last year? You must have seen him. Was he a relation of yours?"

"Yes," said "Wild Bullocks" calmly. "I seen him, and don't yer remember me warnin' yer about him at the races? He was the dead ring of what me young brother Jim was as a lad, although he were taller. I tipped he were a relation when yer told me his name on the

Condoblin course, but I never let on, cos I spotted him as a crook. I'm
pretty rough meself, but I've always acted square ter me mates."

They went to Parkes. Callister was astounded, and delighted, at
the result of the year's work, and demanded indignantly that Jack
should take two-thirds of the profits. This suggestion was strenuously
combated by the young man who, for his part, warmly insisted on his
friend taking the lion's share. A friendly settlement was ultimately
effected by Jack agreeing to a liberal deduction for expenses from
Callister's original capital, a 'half-and-half' division of the balance,
and a hundred-pound contribution to "Wild Bullocks". Then, in the
highest spirits, they talked of the future. Jack, although successful as
a stock-dealer, had been attacked by the 'mining fever' during his
year in the vicinity of Fifield, and had long before determined to
spend a few months prospecting along the great mineral belt that
extends from the head of the Lachlan across to the great Cobar
copper mines. This he told to his friend, who, to his great satisfaction,
hailed the proposal with delight.

"Halves!" cried Callister, enthusiastically. "I'm in on it! I will pay
the tucker bills, and you do the work. Will that suit?"

"Yes," said Jack laughingly. "But it will have to be thirds. "Wild
Bullocks" comes with me!"

"That old whaler?" said Callister, somewhat doubtfully.

"Yes, that old whaler," answered Jack. "He's my mate, and I owe
him a good deal more than you suspect."

"You are sound right through, Jack," cried Callister, impulsively.
"Always stick to your friends. Thirds it shall be, and here is my hand
on it."

"Wild Bullocks" did not take his long-looked-for trip to Dungog
just then. News came to Parkes of a big find on Burra Creek, some five
or six miles beyond Fifield, just as he and Jack were preparing to
leave for the coast. There was gold there, so it was shouted around
the town, in bucketsful. The tidings aroused a frenzy of excitement in
the young man, as they did in every soul in the township, the consequence being that Jack and his ancient companion were amongst the

first to peg out a claim at the new rush. Jack felt success in his blood as he drove in his pick to open their shaft.

Before he left Parkes, he had been greatly attracted by a fine-looking colt he had seen in a stall at one of the hotels, and had enquired if it were for sale. The owner, an evil-looking individual with a battered face, asked eighty pounds for the animal, whereupon Jack immediately closed with the bargain. Father O'Connell, who lived in Parkes, chanced to come upon the scene at the moment of the sale, and as the late owner of the horse wrote out the receipt, the old priest congratulated Jack on his purchase.

"Tis after winning races you'll be with him," said the old cleric, "for he has some blood in him, if I am a judge."

"Yes," the late owner said, "he's well enough bred, but we don't know his pedigree. I bought him at Molong from a drover bloke, who said he come from Melbourne."

The horse accompanied Jack and "Wild Bullocks" to the mining field.

15

PLUNGING FOR A FORTUNE

After Raymond Penderby had collected the sum of fourteen thousand, seven hundred and twenty pounds from the auctioneers who had sold the sheep stolen from Bullangarra station, he had lodged the whole of the money in the private account that he maintained in the name of Randolph Philpotts. For a day and a night, the burden of his malefaction bore heavily upon his conscience; he neither slept nor ate, but instead, drank fiercely in the hope that the alcohol would benumb his senses into forgetfulness. The liquor, for a time, had an entirely opposite effect, as it seduced his imagination into creating such an array of terrors and fears that he was shaken to the core. But after twenty tortured hours his evil genius took complete possession of his being. He had done this thing which could not be undone, and he had now sufficient money to pay his gambling debts, the one obstacle that prevented him from betting again to any great extent on the racecourses. If only the whole amount were his, he thought, he could cripple the bookmakers at the spring meeting in a fortnight's time. What a revenge that would be!

This train of thought set him considering the degree of his crime. The other men, he argued to himself, were thieves, had always been thieves, and could never be anything but thieves – and they cared nothing for those that they robbed. They had prospered, too, in their misconduct – or at least, the shrewd ones had. Why, therefore, should he not retain the whole of the money, and let them taste some of their own bitter medicine? They dare not say anything, nor make any exposure. It would be no greater degree of theft than he had already been guilty of. In fact, he thought, and he wondered why it had never struck him before in that light, it was one and the same theft. Having arrived at this brilliant and eminently satisfactory conclusion, he determined to keep the whole of the money, and then went to bed and slept for sixteen hours on end.

He awoke invigorated and refreshed, bodily and mentally. He attired himself with meticulous care, let himself out of his rooms, and hurried to the bank that held the account of the fictitious Philpotts. He drew sufficient money in notes to pay off the three bookmakers, and a further thousand pounds to invest in several big doubles on the Epsom and Metropolitan Handicaps, the classic events of the Australian Jockey Club's spring carnival. Ten minutes later he was settling in Tattersall's Club.

No thought of his duplicity disturbed the serenity of his mind, nor did he fear any overt approach from Collins and his friends for some time to come. He paid his debts with heartiness, tempered by profuse apologies for the delay that had been occasioned by his temporary embarrassment. Then he further astonished and delighted the bookmakers by investing a thousand pounds between the three, to win him a fortune if Barbary and Kelp won the Epsom and Metropolitan double.

"I am going to break the ring this meeting," said Raymond, as he noted the wagers in his pocket-book, "and I have the cash to put in. No more booking for me."

"That's the style," said Foxie, with a knowing wink at the others, "and if you have the cash we'll take all the bets you want to make."

"I will have you asking for time within three weeks," asserted Raymond, half-jokingly, half in earnest.

"You'll have to win a million, then," replied Blackett, drily.

Leaving the club, Raymond sought his father's chambers.

Entering briskly, he hurried through the typiste's office, scarcely condescending to glance at Molly Forbes. As his father was absent he was compelled to face the girl, and speak to her.

"Well, Molly, how are you? The dad's out again, I see. I wanted him urgently." He spoke rapidly, and looked ill at ease.

He was shocked at the changed appearance of the girl in the few short weeks since he had seen her last. Her cheeks were pinched and pale, her eyes dull and heavy, and encircled by ghastly, discoloured shadows. Her very figure appeared to have shrunken. She brightened perceptibly when Raymond spoke, a fact that he was quick to notice.

"Your father has gone to the Newcastle Sessions, and will not return for three days," the girl stated quietly.

"You have not told me how you are, Molly," said Raymond in a tender voice, for to do him justice he was greatly moved by her pathetic appearance.

"I have not been well, Mister Raymond," she said tremulously, "but I am much better now, thank you."

"Now look here, Molly," said Raymond, putting some enthusiasm into his voice, "this sort of thing will never do. You have been moping too much, so I am just going to make you come out to dinner with me tonight, and to the theatre afterwards."

"Thank you, Mister Raymond, but I could not go," Molly answered sadly.

"It is no use your saying 'No' to me, Molly," said Raymond firmly. "You will come if I have to carry you!"

After some further refusals, which were gallantly overborne by Raymond, the girl gave a reluctant consent. She was burning with repressed eagerness to ask for some news of Jack, but because she had received no answer to her last letter some feeling of offended maidenly pride checked her impulse. Jack in his degradation must have indeed forgotten her, else he would have written. It was this painful reflection that finally decided her in accepting Raymond's invitation.

As Penderby waited for Molly Forbes at six-thirty, in the lounge at the Australia, sipping a whiskey and soda, he asked himself why he had invited her to spend the evening with him. No satisfactory reason being forthcoming he decided that he would have to make the best of it in any case, admitting that he owed her something for the sorrow that he had so callously and unnecessarily brought her. He no longer needed Jack Burnside's inheritance, he reflected cheerfully, and it amused him to think that he had laid up a store of trouble for that self-satisfied, quixotic, young fool. Molly, well-dressed, and with her troubles apparently forgotten, would prove an attractive figure amid any surroundings, and he was fond of the company of pretty women.

As the girl entered the foyer of the hotel Raymond met her with an open admiration that was unquestionably genuine. In her simple evening frock of some sequinned, white material, Molly shimmered radiantly like some queen of faerie. Her eyes blazed with a strange, eager light, her cheeks were warmly flushed, and her sad smile was sweetly alluring. All the male loungers stared at her with unconcealed interest.

"By Jove, Molly! You look stunning!" greeted Raymond, warmly. "Why, you are beautiful! One would never recognise you now as the white-faced young lady I saw this afternoon."

Whether it was the unusual excitement of the dinner or the glass of champagne that Raymond persuaded her to drink that lightened her spirits and lifted the load of sorrow momentarily from her mind, Molly could not guess, but at the theatre she found. With a sudden feeling of dismay and disappointment, that she had been actually enjoying the comedy being enacted on the stage. Could she really have been right, she wondered anxiously, in that vow registered by her in the first agony of her sorrow to consecrate the remainder of her life to the memories of her lost lover? It had been so easy at first, she realised, but now, when there was mirth and happiness all about her, and the friendship of a handsome, sympathetic young man laid at her feet, it appeared to be difficult, if not unreasonable. And then, she thought, as Jack had so callously rejected her, he had, no doubt, entirely forgotten her by this time. Well, she could do the same.

As he said good-night to her at her mother's home, Raymond was strangely stirred by Molly's radiant, alluring presence.

"Will you come out again with me, Molly?" he asked, tenderly, pressing her hand within his own.

"Yes, Ray, if you wish it," she answered, doubtfully.

"Wish it?" he exclaimed passionately. "Great heavens, Molly! I want you to be happy, and I want you to be with me always. You beautiful angel!"

The girl, unwontedly moved by the excitement of the evening, swayed slightly as though under the fierceness of his emotion. In an instant she was in his arms and his lips were caressing hers with burning kisses. For a moment she lay passive, helpless, overcome by the intensity of her feelings. Then with a fierce anger she tore herself away and fled up the path.

"Oh, oh!" she moaned, and reaching the shelter of a vine-hung verandah she threw herself, sobbing, into a chair. An hour later she crept, white-faced and dry-eyed, into her bed.

With a thoughtful mood upon him, Raymond Penderby walked to his flat. In searching his heart, he was concerned to find that this girl had made an impression on him, the like of which he had never before experienced. Accustomed by now to face matters squarely with his own conscience, and to make the best of them for his own selfish ends, he quickly realised that he desired Molly as he had wanted no other woman. What it was in her that appealed to him he did not trouble to discover; it was enough that he wanted her. That, to him, meant that he would henceforward use every means in his power to obtain her. He foresaw, with satisfaction, that no great difficulty lay in the way, for his cunningly-laid scheme to kill her love for Jack Burnside would inevitably incline the girl to seek elsewhere sympathy and consolation for her empty heart. That night he dreamed of Molly Forbes and the future.

During the ensuing fortnight Molly and Raymond Penderby spent many evenings together at the theatre, down the harbour, in a motor launch, or motoring along some of the favoured suburban roads. The young man made love sincerely, but restrainedly. On none of their excursions, nor at any of their partings, did he again attempt to embrace her. Molly, on one occasion, found herself disappointed in a way that she could not understand, because he had not essayed to kiss her, although she had perversely made up her mind to resist him had he made the attempt. She still thought very often of Jack, and while she unashamedly admitted to herself that she had loved him ardently, and even yet loved the ideal of him, she thought that she was punishing him in some unexplained fashion by flirting with Raymond. She was intensely human, after all, and needed a strong man's love.

Raymond had no fair companion at the spring races. He desired to be free and unimpeded by any woman in order to carry out his grand assault on the bookmakers. Like all gamblers, the lust of risky chances permeated his being. The monetary gain from his successful coups meant little to him, for, again like the born gambler, he won or lost with absolute unconcern. If he were successful, the money provided easy pleasure; if he lost, something invariably turned up in the end to enable him to pay. He was the true gambler, in that he was devoid of conscience, and could take hazardous risks with perfect equanimity.

Randwick racecourse, the best appointed in the world, was a picture of beauty on the Epsom day. The lawns, the dazzling blossoms of the flower beds, the gorgeous green of the hedges, the rich verdure on the hill, where the steeplechase track wound giddily, reflected the glory of the Australian spring. The huge, three-decker stands in the "paddock" were packed with a dense mass of excited racegoers, and out on "the flat", or the "shilling touch", surging crowds piled about the betting ring and the totalisator.

Raymond was a prominent figure in the betting ring of the "paddock", the principal enclosure, for the bookmakers knew, by some inexplicable means, that his cheque was good for twelve thousand pounds at least, and all of them were consequently eager to write a big share of his business. He was a noted 'plunger', and they knew that the inexorable laws that governed their calling would encompass him in financial confusion either early or late. His investments on the first two races were heavy, and he saw, with something of disgust, both his fancies finish in second places. Had he patronised the totalisator, with its mechanical odds – 11% of the investments to the Government and the club, with the balance divided between the first, second and third horses in the ratio of sixty, twenty and twenty percent – he would have won a considerable amount. Both his placed horses had paid over three pounds for every ten shillings invested on the 'tote'. The bookmakers paid nothing for the placed horses. Legislation prohibited place-betting.

For the principal event thirty horses sported silk. They represented the best sprinters the country could produce, all aristocratically bred, from an equine point of view, and all worth small fortunes individually. Barbary was an outsider, quoted at 33 to 1 in the ring, but inspection showed her to look capable of doing great things. Her owner had advised Raymond that her recent track work had been phenomenal, and that she had shown him a gallop of "forty-one" with heavy shoes and a ten-stone boy up, all of which pointed to the fact that she would be likely to break a record in the race, in which she was called upon to carry only six stone seven pounds.

Raymond accordingly 'plunged'. He invested nearly five thousand pounds, backing the mare from 33 to 1 down to 6 to 1, and still the bookmakers clamoured for more of his money. The first and second favourites were consistently and heavily backed by the shrewd 'hard-heads' of the game – a fact that in no wise disconcerted the young medical student. He strolled up to the members' stand just as the horses left the bird-cage.

The contestants made an inspiriting picture as they raced by the judge's stand in the preliminary canter. Beautiful, eager animals they were, with flashing eyes and wide, quivering nostrils, reefing and tearing at the restraining bits as they skimmed along the turf. As they flashed by in a galaxy of riotous colour, shining coat of horse and shimmering jacket of rider, Raymond felt his blood tingle. For who could remain unstirred by the excitement of a race on that historic convincing ground, or who would not be thrilled by the very exhilaration in the air?

As the starting-bell clanged the crowd strained silently to watch, with concentrated gaze, the packed field as it swung along the back of the course. At the half-mile, as two horses emerged from the ruck, loud exultant shouts proclaimed them to be the two favourites. On swept the field to the turn. Entering the straight, a big black mare shot to the front, and was soon lengths ahead of the leaders, but running wide and near the fence on the far side of the rails.

"Barbary! Barbary!" shrieked the crowd.

It was Barbary that was making this magnificent run. At the Leger stand she was three lengths ahead of the favourites, who were running neck-and-neck, well ahead of the nearest of a stringing field.

Suddenly a roar of dismay rent the air. "Barbary's down!" yelled the crowd, frenziedly.

On the hard-packed path, in the rough going, just where the crowds trudge across the racing track from the outer gates of the St. Leger to "The Flat" in the centre of the course, Barbary had blundered. The mare faltered, stumbled to her knees, and then rolled over. The boy, flung clear, sprang to his feet uninjured, and grabbed the loose reins. The field thundered past, and in another two seconds the first favourite had won by a nose.

"Damned bad luck!" was all Raymond's comment to the owner of Barbary, as they partook of a drink at the bar some five minutes later.

Motoring homeward that afternoon, Raymond Penderby calculated that he had lost over seven thousand pounds. This circumstance failed to disturb him to any great extent, however, for with the genuine optimism of the gambler he intended to recoup it all on the Monday. His doubles had gone all awry, it was true, owing to Barbary's unlucky fall, but he could easily win with straight-out bets on Metropolitan day.

Unfortunately for him, the Monday proved more disastrous still; he did not back a single winner. It ended by his being in debt to the bookmakers once more to the tune of three thousand pounds.

Seated in his room that night he reviewed his position seriously. He had hoped to have won a fortune, but by an unlucky stroke of fate he had failed. This, in itself, was of little concern, save that, had he been successful, he could have quietened Brummy Collins and his gang who, he knew only too well, would shortly seek him out. Now,

however, he would shortly have to ask his old enemies, the bookmakers, once more for time to pay. They could not refuse him very well,
he knew, so he would settle so far as was possible, reserving a thousand pounds for contingencies that he guessed were bound to arise
ere long.

The more he considered the situation, however, the more
perturbed he became at the possibility of some violent aggression on
the part of Collins, a desperate character at any time, but now
assuredly unlikely to hesitate even at murder so soon as he discovered that he had been completely tricked. Jack Burnside's inheritance
again came to his mind. If he could only obtain that, it would be easy
to settle everything. But, unfortunately, his return to the Lachlan was
effectually prevented by fear of the sheep-stealers; nor did he think it
possible to lure Jack to Sydney where he could be involved in some
way. Then there was the girl, Molly Forbes. He thought of her for a
long while.

"Yes," he muttered to himself, "it will have to be the girl, after all. I
will use her somehow to get that money, and then I will get her, too. I
want her now as badly as I want that damned cash."

Just then there reached his ears the low, muffled sound of
knocking at the door of his flat. As it was long past midnight he was
puzzled to know who the visitor could be. Some premonition of
danger warned him against answering the summons, but an irresistible impulse drew him, against his will, to the door. He unlocked it
quietly, and opening it but a few inches, looked out. Brummy Collins
and Bill M'Bean stood on the threshold.

As they recognised him, both men burst into angry vituperation.
Uttering fearful oaths, they sprang at the door, and Raymond scarcely
had time to close it before they furiously dashed their bodies against
it. He shrank back into the passage, dismayed, unnerved. Outside, the
violence of the uproar was terrific. It echoed loudly through the
deserted street, awakening sleepers, and causing windows to be
hurriedly thrown open. Presently above the cursing and shouting of
the infuriated sheep-stealers Raymond heard gruff, peremptory tones
commanding silence. The police, he guessed. Then he recognised the

voice of a sergeant that he knew. Opening the door hastily, he walked outside.

"Sergeant!" he exclaimed hurriedly. "I want you to take these drunks in charge! They are shearers, on a 'soiree'. I met them up country recently, and they have been endeavouring to force themselves on me at my home tonight. I have been subjected to a great deal of annoyance by them!"

There were three police officers present, and they laid rough hands on Collins and his companion. Both resisted violently, but they were soon overpowered and handcuffed. As they were being marched off to the lock-up Collins turned and glared malevolently at Penderby.

"I'm goin' ter get yer, yer bastard!" he gritted out menacingly. "I'll get yer fer keeps, too, s'help me Gawd!"

As the prisoners departed Raymond called the sergeant inside, and poured out a stiff glass of whiskey for him.

"Look, sergeant," he said. "You know what pests these drunken bushmen become if they think they know a man. I want you to get them both out of Sydney tomorrow night. Send them back to Forbes or Condoblin; they come from the Lachlan. You policemen have the means of doing that sort of thing, and you might see that they are kept in the backblocks for a month or two."

"I'll do it for ye," answered the sergeant. "I owe your father something for many a good turn he's done me. It'll be easy, for I know one of the men, M'Bean, as an old offender."

16

WHEN A MAIDEN LOVES

R aymond Penderby was completely unnerved by the night visit from Collins and M'Bean, and no little concerned at the danger that threatened from these desperate characters. He knew that the sergeant would be as good as his word, in that the pair would be compelled to keep out of the city for a few weeks at least. In this knowledge he found very little comfort, however, for he was certain that ere a month went by the duped and angry desperadoes would be on his track again. In his imagination he already felt a questing bullet plunging into his brain, and a gleaming knife biting into his vitals. Despondently he realised that Sydney was no longer safe for him; that for his own security he would have to fly. His studies at the University, already interrupted, would have to stand over for a year, perhaps for all time. It mattered little which. All he knew was that he must escape the impending vengeance of his former confederates.

It was probably the inexplicable complexity of his character that impelled him to formulate, even in his panic, shadowy plans for the future. He, who had helped a gang of thieves to rob his host, and had later robbed those very thieves without a qualm, planned to settle his 'debts of honour' with the bookmakers on the morrow, to the extent of his available finances. He made up his mind to convince his father that a year's sea trip through the East was vital to his health. In that twelve months many things would be forgotten, and when he returned he could seek out some way of laying hold of Jack Burnside's money.

These thoughts brought Molly before him. Yes, a trip through the golden East, with Molly as his wife. It would be a honeymoon indeed. But their marriage would have to be a secret one; he could not afford to tell his father of it, because he was aware that the old lawyer had plans already made about that matter – some alliance with a country cousin that he had not seen since she was a tiny child, and who lived on some sort of a farm up Dungog way. Molly he wanted, not his cousin; and Molly he was determined to have for his wife.

It was on the third day after his encounter with the bushmen that he again sought his father's office – and Molly. As he entered the outer room he saw a tall, bronzed bushman, who had been enquiring for his father. The lawyer had chanced to be absent.

"Good morning Molly. Good morning, Mr. Williams," he cried out cheerfully.

Both responded to the salutation, Molly smiling happily as she turned to her machine.

"Haven't seen you about lately, Williams," said Raymond. "Where have you been hiding?"

"I was out at Bullangarra, one of our stations," replied the inspector, "inquiring into one of the biggest sheep 'lifts' we've had in many years."

"What? Sheep stolen from Bullangarra?" exclaimed Raymond, simulating amazement.

"Too true," answered the other, briefly. "Six thousand wethers 'lifted' as clean as a blue-gum sapling."

"Did you catch the thieves?" asked Raymond, with some anxiety.

"No," replied Williams. "But it was the Collins gang, without doubt. You were up there just before the sheep were stolen, so I believe, and you probably have heard something about this Brummy."

"Yes," answered Raymond, deliberately, wondering whether this shrewd bushman suspected him in the matter. "I often heard Callister speak of the gang. That jackeroo, Burnside, seemed to be very interested in the stories of their exploits."

"Interested!" burst out the other, angrily. "He was one of the thieves. He was mixed up in the theft of a twelve-hundred-guinea blood horse afterwards, and the evidence was absolutely clear against him Only for Callister I would have had him arrested."

"Where is he now?" asked Raymond eagerly.

"The devil knows!" said Williams. "I had him sacked, and I told Callister to chase him off the run. I believe that he has cleared out farther west, on to the Darling River country. He's no loss, wherever he is, the damned thief!"

A sudden crash behind them caused both men to turn swiftly. Molly Forbes, pale as death, was lying in a huddled heap on the floor. She had overheard everything, and shocked beyond conception at the terrible revelation, had fallen in a dead faint. Williams, the big, tender-hearted bushman, lifted her up as gently as though she had been a little child, and placed her in a comfortable chair. Raymond stood by helplessly. The inspector's calls, however, soon brought two of the other typists from an adjoining room, and restoratives were conjured from nowhere, seemingly, and promptly applied by these tearfully sympathetic young ladies. After a few minutes Molly regained consciousness, gazing around her in a bewildered fashion. Then the recognition of Raymond and Williams bringing to her mind the damning accusation that she had just heard, she burst into hysterical sobbing.

The two men, nonplussed and quite unable to do anything of service, took a discomfited departure. Outside on the pavement, Williams gave expression to his amazement.

"I wonder what the deuce made her tumble over like that?" he said.

"Hanged if I know!" said Raymond, who had guessed the reason, and was considerably annoyed in consequence. "Girls get queer spasms at times, I suppose."

That evening Raymond motored out to his father's suburban home to dine with the old man. The strain of the untoward incidents of the past week had left vivid traces on his face, which were accentuated by a deadly fear of Collins and his gang that laid gripping fingers about his heart. As he sat at the table, with the glare of the electric light full upon his face, his father could not but note the tragic change in his appearance.

"Raymond, my boy," the old lawyer questioned, "are you ill?"

"I am far from well, father," said the son, in a melancholy voice. "I thought that my holiday at Bullangarra would have recuperated me, but I must now admit that it did not. I was so bad today that I allowed old Dr. Rothwell to give me a thorough overhauling, and his verdict has completely upset me."

Mr. Penderby Senior was apprehensively solicitous. "What did he tell you, my boy?" he asked in tones tremulous with anxiety. "Nothing serious, surely!"

"Serious enough, father," was the reply, "and unfortunately too true, for my experience tells me that he is right. It is the heart, dad, and my only chance is a year's trip around the East and the Islands, so he says. I told Rothwell that it was impossible for me to abandon my studies at this juncture, and that I would not ask you to foot the bill for a holiday jaunt. Then he gave me six months, at the limit, to live!"

His father was overwhelmed. "But you must go!" he cried, greatly moved. "What does your degree matter? And how insignificant are a few thousand pounds compared with your life? You must go!"

"No, father," said Raymond, in tones that sounded as convincingly contrite as they were hopeless. "I have taken your money too often without making you any return whatever, and this final imposition would be too much. I will stay."

The argument that followed was long and anxious. Anxious, indeed, for the doting father who, disappointed in an earlier love, had lavished all the warm affection of a generous, kindly heart, hidden beneath a rough exterior, on this reprobate son, and who now only wished to give the object of that love a long respite from threatening death. Anxious, too, for the stony-hearted, deceitful son, until he saw that his crafty renunciation of the chance for health afforded in the proffered holiday had so steeled the old man's determination that he should take it that no refusal would be tolerated.

At last Raymond accepted, with reluctant gratitude, his father's offer to provide him with a thousand pounds for the voyage, and the visible manifestations of uncertainty, sorrow and wounded pride that accompanied the acceptance moved the doting old man almost to tears. It was arranged that Raymond should leave Sydney within two days in order to join an Eastern boat in Brisbane, the young man exhibiting, when a discussion of his itinerary followed, a peculiarly accurate knowledge of steamer timetables, names of boats, and fares.

He took his departure from his father's home late that evening, with a countenance that expressed the humblest gratitude – but with a heart filled with the most impious elation. As he sped back to his rooms he chuckled to himself at the ease with which he had accomplished his object so far as his father was concerned. "He was easy," he muttered to himself. "Dead easy. Now, I'll keep a thousand from the betting wreck, and with the dad's little cheque, and Molly, I can have a good time on the other side of the world until Collins is safely in gaol." With comforting reflections such as these he sought his bed, and slept.

When he visited his father's office next morning he learned that Molly's mother had telephoned to say that her daughter was ill and could not come in to work that day. This news disturbed him greatly, for he intended to have persuaded the girl to consent to a hasty marriage that very afternoon. He must see her, however, and so, acting on an impulse, he proceeded to call a taxi to take him out to her residence.

He found the young girl lying on a couch in the darkened parlour of her home. So soon as her mother had left them together, he threw himself on his knees beside her, and essayed to take her into his arms, murmuring words of endearing sympathy as he did so. For a moment Molly remained impassive. Then, with a great effort, she threw him from her.

"Go away, please," she entreated. "Go away, and let me die!"

"My poor, darling girl! What is the matter?" asked Raymond, with soft, caressing voice.

"Go away!" she again pleaded. "Do go, please, for I do not wish to see you again."

Raymond paid no heed to her broken-hearted supplication. Seizing one of her ice-cold hands and pressing it tenderly, he told her of his great love for her; how she had become the queen of his heart, and now he must have her for his wife. He pleaded in tense, quivering accents that she would marry him on the morrow, and set out with him on a honeymoon that would be a dream of happiness unmarred by sorrow or remorse. His words throbbed with passion, and to the girl they seemed to burn with the wondrous lustre of truth. Perhaps just then they did.

For fully five minutes after his impetuous declaration she was silent, lying with eyes half-closed, lips parted – but with her hand still in his.

And through that brief interval of time, that seemed like aeons, what thoughts passed through her stricken brain? She liked this man, she admitted to herself, and he offered her honourable marriage and a great love. The man she really loved had spurned her, and had soiled that love of hers by his degradation. She would marry; she would forget – forget the man that was a criminal flying from justice. Then she saw the hunted fugitive, the man she really loved, a lonely, broken, frightened thing flying always from a pursuing vengeance. This was Jack, he whom she loved, harried by the remorseless laws of the land into the barren desert wastes and the mocking mirages of the far-back bush. She pictured him tramping with bleeding, blistered feet through the molten leagues of great spinifex deserts, his face haggard with despair, his eyes tragic with suffering. She saw him huddled in the bed of a dust-dry tank, perishing with thirst, and it seemed to her that he raised his head, and with tired, sad eyes looking into hers, cried, "Molly, dear sweetheart, I love you! I am coming back to you!" The vivid reality of her fancy overpowered her.

With a heart-broken cry, she sat upright, and swiftly withdrew her hand from Raymond's clasp. Then, sobbing bitterly she whispered, "No; I do not love you. Please go away. I can never marry you, because, God pity me, I love Jack Burnside with all the strength of my body and soul!"

And, with a gesture of grief-stricken despair, she pointed towards the door, swayed helplessly for a minute, and fell fainting back on to the couch.

Raymond left the house with his mind inflamed strangely by his emotions. He had convinced himself long before, that he had really and sincerely loved Molly Forbes for herself alone, and during the first brief period of his disappointment he had indulged in many comforting thoughts of self-pity. These, however, gave place to an unreasoning anger that this chit of a girl, a mere employee of his father's, should so reject his offer of marriage, and, what was worse, insult him by triumphantly proclaiming her love for a bush-whacking, penniless jackeroo. He was virtuously indignant at the whole business, but after he had had a few drinks at the Tattersall's Club, and had satisfactorily settled his 'debts of honour', he was inclined to view it in a more equable light. By the afternoon he had forgotten all about Molly in the excitement of packing for his protracted absence from Sydney. Such was his remarkable nature.

Old Mr. Penderby was in a thoughtful mood as Raymond bade him farewell. "There is just one thing, Raymond," he said, "that I would like to say before we part for this long, long year. I heard a very disquieting thing from an old friend today, up at the Supreme Court, and it was that you had lost over ten thousand pounds at the races. You are not escaping from Sydney to avoid any awkward consequences of your betting, are you?"

Raymond appeared to be greatly concerned. "I did lose a few hundreds, dad, but they represented my winnings up at Condoblin. Where would I get ten thousand pounds to bet with? And what bookmaker would trust me to that extent? Whoever told you that story, father, intended to do me an injury, for it is a dastardly lie."

"It was Williams, my son," said the old man, "the inspector of the

Commonwealth Mortgage Company, and he would have no object in telling such an untruth to me."

"Well, if you do not believe me, dad," answered Raymond virtuously, "ring up Foxie or Blackett, the only two bookmakers with whom I do business. Or wait! I will ring them up, and you may listen at the other receiver!"

Before his father could protest the young man had reached the telephone, and soon had Foxie speaking at the other end. In reply to Raymond's question, the old metallicians announced that their account was nearly square, and that the difference owing was so insignificant that it could wait indefinitely. Blackett, in turn, made similar expression of the position with him. The old man's face as he hung up the receiver, was a picture of happy contentment.

"I knew you could not lie to me, Ray, my boy," he said, trustfully.

Raymond secretly congratulated himself on having taken precautionary measures on the previous day that resulted in the bookmakers giving these ambiguous replies in answer to his telephoned inquiries. He certainly had not anticipated from his father an awkward question, such as had been sprung on him, but he had decided, on general principles, to work off something of the sort on others who he knew were bound to be inquisitive, as a guarantee of good faith, so to speak.

The parting between father and son was tender in the extreme. Raymond, however, was heartily relieved when he was out in the street again and on his way to the railway station to board the Brisbane mail train. But, after he had left, the old man sat for a long while in his private office, thinking sorrowful, dreary thoughts. And, after an hour, he took from its recesses an old, black, tin box bearing the device in white letters on its front – "Estate of Amos Burnside, d'csd".

Raymond Penderby caught the *Mataram* at Brisbane, and left for India, via Java and Singapore. Among his fellow-passengers he found a number of horse buyers who had been operating in the various Australian States on behalf of the Indian Government, purchasing remounts for the British cavalry and blood horses for princes, rajahs, and nabobs. Within a few days he was a boon companion of the members of this strange company, far-faring Australians, born in the bush and reared in the saddle, who, for their marvellous judgement of horses, were the chosen agents of those who wanted the best animals that could be procured. They were bushmen in speech, in dress, in figure, although they had sailed the seven seas, and had bought and sold in all the horse marts of the wide world. With all their knowledge of the ways and the men of foreign climes, they loved Australia best, and with rough, rude oaths each proclaimed his home town the best part of Australia. The Australian horse, they unanimously affirmed, had no equal in the world. The 'waler', the sturdy stock horse from the cattle stations in the ranges or the sheep runs on the wide western plains, was to them an equine miracle. Untiring, splendidly-proportioned, dauntless, the bush-bred horse was, they swore, the rarest product of the country, and their praise of the gallant animals that, perchance, afterwards fattened the vultures in some battle-scarred Afghan defile, was whole-heartedly sincere.

They told Raymond of the success of Australian racehorses in India. How the last Viceroy's Cup had been won by a blood-colt that had led the greatest fields to victory a year before at Randwick. How Australian trainers prepared these racehorses among the millions of dark-skinned people, and how Australian jockeys piloted them down the grassy straights. Their talk was of the horse always, and the young medical student, who was no mean judge of an animal himself, soon became as enthusiastic as the most vociferous of them. It was not surprising, therefore, that before the boat touched at Singapore, he had entered into a partnership with Mr. Jimmy Elliott, relating to the matter of horse-dealing that, within a year, put a further few thousand pounds into his pockets.

17

THE GLEAM OF GOLD

"Four blanky ounces for three months' work. Rotten," exclaimed "Wild Bullocks", wiping the sweat from his face as he stood leaning on the handle of the windlass.

"Yes," replied Jack Burnside. "And I have just bottomed on the pipeclay band." He swung himself out of the greenhide bag in which he had been hauled from the bottom of the shaft, and squatted on the mullock-heap. "Do you know, we ought to go through that pipeclay, for I have feeling that there is wash dirt or a big reef below it. Those leaders in the clay most likely go straight through to some reef deep down beneath."

"Aw, hell," yelled the old man in disgust. "Why, if we come at that, the blokes what's left about here'd reckon that was the dead finish of us. I've heard 'em say pretty often that we're barmy, as it is."

"Let them talk," said Jack, "but we are going to try it."

"Right-oh. You're boss, so have yer own flamin' way," said "Wild Bullocks", with an air of exaggerated resignation.

Jack and his mate had worked like galley slaves and lived like blackfellows for three months on their claim at the Burra Creek diggings, to gain a financial result of about fifteen pounds. Although they had been amongst the first arrivals on the field, they had found,

even at that time, hundreds ahead of them, and they had consequently been compelled to peg-out a show nearly half a mile from
the "reward claim", or original double-area, taken up by the first
discoverer. They were on the line of the wash-dirt, but in some
extraordinary manner they appeared to have chosen the one claim
that seemed to be the poorest of the lot. During the first week over
three thousand men had rushed to the field. Tents sprang up in the
night like mushrooms; mullock-heaps and rough-and-ready wind-
lasses appeared in mysterious multitudes in all the bush around. For
a week every man had worked in a fever of excitement, those with
claims delving frenziedly through the surface, sinking to the wash-
dirt, the newcomers cutting datum pegs to define the boundaries of
their blocks, or pitching tents in the scrub. Every now and then a
pandemonium of delirious shouting and a maddened stampede of
diggers towards some particular 'show' told that one lucky fossicker
had unearthed a rich, glistening nugget. Then, after a few minutes,
men had rushed back to their own pot-holes, feverish with the lust of
desire for what they had just beheld, and had set to work more impatiently than before.

During the first week the spirits of the miners were mercurial.
Many abandoned good, paying claims to rush to a locality where
some big nugget had been discovered, only to be rewarded with a few
meagre colours. Others, like Jack and his mate, sticking resolutely to
their first claims, would either strike the pay-dirt or the pipeclay
band. Within a fortnight the rush had petered out, and thousands
had already departed to the Carlisle diggings, in towards
Condobolin. At the end of a month there were hardly three hundred
miners on the field. But enormous quantities of gold dust had been
won, even in that brief time, and the escorts had taken away
hundreds of thousands of pounds worth of the precious metal to
the Mint.

The old miners, who had been tutored by the hard and varied
experience of a hundred such 'rushes', claimed that the pay-dirt
always ended at the pipeclay band, the strata of white, pulpy earth
above which the gold was found. They had seen the same thing on

the Turon, at Lambing Flat in the old days, at Parkes, at Forbes – at any number of places. Burra was played out, and it was best to move on. The old-timers moved, but there were those who were content to thoroughly test their claims and be satisfied with small returns. "Chinamen's claims" they called them. The many holes that Jack and "Wild Bullocks" had sunk had always bottomed on the pipeclay, but Jack had an idea that there was something rich below, on account of the tiny 'stringers', or leaders, that had been frequently noticed by him in the white, soft clay. It was, however, only when the prospect of payable dirt above it was utterly hopeless that he determined to seek beneath, follow one of these leaders, and prove whether it really indicated a reef below or led to the basic igneous rock.

As they completed the timbering and laddering of their shaft, to make deep working safe, they had high hopes. When the last pole was in place, they climbed to the top for a smoko. Jack was altered out of recognition. He had been rather fastidious about his clothes and appearance before the lure of gold had led him to Burra, and he had hated to be untidy. Now, however, he was a miner, purely and simply. He had grown a full beard that, when the dust and clay streaked his face, gave him the air of a man of forty. His hands were cracked and calloused by the arduousness of his labours; his feet were encased in huge, nail-studded bluchers, that had never known a blacking brush. For clothes he wore dirty moleskin trousers, held up with a green-hide belt that "Wild Bullocks" had plaited, and a grey, thick flannel shirt, that was ever open at the neck. A coat, in that climate, formed no part of the miner's costume. His hat was a battered felt one, the original colour of which had long since been lost under a coating of clay. Yet, despite it all, he looked a hearty, healthy gentleman.

Physically, too, he was a changed man. His muscles were as hard as steel, and his chest had expanded enormously with the exercise of his labours, until it was that of a giant. But in his eyes was a wistful, far-away look, that was never absent. For more than a year his heart had ached numbly for the love of that one fair girl whose vision was ever present before him. Day and night, Molly Forbes filled his thoughts, and everything he did was, so he whispered to himself, for her sweet sake. After those first days of bitter anguish when he had thought her lost to him, he had determined to be steadfast in his love for her, whatever might befall. He had given his heart wholly to her, and none but her, or the fragrant consoling memories of her, could ever find a place in it. He had studiously avoided the company of other women – and there had been many that had sought him in the bush townships with luring glance and challenging smile – for he now regarded his love for Molly as something inviolate, enshrined within his memory; something that must never be polluted by sacrilegious intrusion. Every action of his was directed by a sad, but nevertheless chivalrous and high-souled devotion to this beatified spirit of his lost love.

Jack attacked the pipeclay, so he believed, for Molly's sake. The sinking was easy, and within a week they had struck the country rock below. For another week after this they sank through the solid stone, following a tiny, almost imperceptible leader, and using fracteur to break it out. One evening, after they had fired the two shots that were to be their last, if indications failed to prove more favourable, Jack determined to descend to see the result, and so end the suspense. He was lowered in the hide-bucket, and lighted a candle in the wire 'spider' that was stuck on a rocky projection. With a crowbar he prised up several big pieces of stone dislodged by the explosion, and as the rock fell apart, a peculiar, but unmistakable glitter on a piece of bluey-grey quartz rivetted his alert attention. He hurriedly seized it and held it up to the light.

"Hooray!" he yelled excitedly to his mate, sixty feet above. "We've struck it at last!"

He put one foot into the bucket, calling for "Wild Bullocks" to haul him to the surface. Suddenly espying another specimen, he leaned forward to pick it up. At that moment the old man turned at the windlass like mad. Jack's foot was abruptly drawn up in the air, and before he could clutch at the rope the bucket was flying towards the top. As he picked himself up and sprang at the ladder, he heard his mate yell disgustedly, "Struck it! My oath, a reef o' blasted hot air!"

That night the two discussed future plans. "Wild Bullocks", when first shown the gold, had become greatly excited, and had given an impromptu recital for the benefit of the landscape in general, and a very few terrified rabbits, consisting of the most realistic imitation of a mob of thirst-maddened cattle. After tea, and during the discussion of ways and means and prospects for the future, he was compelled at frequent intervals to get outside the tent and go through similar performances to relieve his feelings, hugely edifying Jack by traversing the gamut of bovine bellows and roars with exquisite technique, if unmelodious elegance. Ultimately, being reduced to reasonable quiescence by sheer exhaustion, he consented to listen.

Jack knew enough of mining by this time to realise that to work even a rich reef required considerable capital – very much more than he could command – and he, therefore, suggested that without performing any further developmental work they should sell the mine, or float it into a company. The specimens on closer inspection were not so rich as to suggest that there was likely to be unlimited gold in the reef, but as they came from a well-defined quartz band they indicated the existence of a rich lode somewhere in the vicinity. It might take a year of driving, sinking, or cross-cutting to locate that reef, so, after all, it would be more advantageous in the long run to sell at once. "Wild Bullocks" at first opposed the proposition with great spirit, but soon became convinced when Jack pointed out to him that speculators were on fire to invest in new shows in that district, and that there would be little difficulty in their clearing perhaps two thousand pounds each. The old man excitedly expressed his readiness to start then and there for the city to clinch the bargain with some of the mining men that are supposed to linger in the vicinity of the Exchange, waiting for such plums as the one he could give them.

It was at last decided that they should allow Callister, who was a shareholder with them, to dispose of the mine, for he was in touch with many of the financial magnates of the city. They prepared to set out for Bullangarra on the morrow.

In due course Callister floated the proposition as the Burra Creek Gold-mining Co., No-liability, for twenty thousand pounds, the vendors taking a fourth of the sum in cash in consideration of their interests in the mine, and 4990 fully paid up shares in the company. This mine was afterwards worked for many years, and paid a dividend of five percent per month on each share, until a big amalgamation of interests on the field gave back the lucky shareholders five times the amount of their original investment.

The proportion that fell to "Wild Bullocks" made the old bushman rich beyond his most extravagant dreams. For a whole day after the first cheque for his share had been paid to him, he had locked himself in his room at the hotel in Condobolin, where he and Jack were temporarily located, thereby causing much speculation among his erstwhile many and thirsty friends as to his sanity. To them all, old swagmen and battlers of the overlanding routes, it was inexplicable that a man with a few thousand pounds at his disposal should be absent from the bar for a single moment, and they debated the matter freely and with great feeling in the shade of the big kurrajongs in front of the hotel. As he walked on to the verandah a cheer rang up from the assembled 'hard-cases'.

"Make it open house!" yelled Billy the Dodger.

"Blow the bleedin' lot in, Bullocks! We'll shepherd yer!" suggested Bogan Dan.

"Bai Jove, old chappie! But it will be a rare symposium, a carousal for the Vikings of the Lachlan tracks! Skald! Bring forth the horns of foaming mead!" This was called out by Old Bart, in a cultured voice. This venerable loafer, the dirtiest and most disreputably clad of a motley band, enjoyed a yearly remittance from 'Home'. He was alleged to be the scion of an aristocratic English family, and had had his peculiar name bestowed on him on an occasion when an inquisitive mate had seen on a discarded envelope addressed to the old fellow from a firm of English solicitors, "Sir Ponsonby Champneys, Bart." The mate, believing that the concluding contraction of the title, actually an abbreviation of 'Baronet', was some manner of a surname, promptly rejected the knight's former nickname of Darkie the Hum, and thereafter respectfully addressed him as Bart. The relation of the whole circumstances by the aforementioned mate had set the fashion, and as Bart the old wreck was known far and wide.

"Wild Bullocks" eyed his former companions with a dispassionate gaze.

"Where's Jack Burnside?" he queried, briefly.

"Down at McIntosh's pub," was the information, volunteered enthusiastically.

"After I've seen him, I'm with yer," he announced, and set out towards the abode of the publican whose 'straightness' was an honoured theme throughout the backblocks. The thirsty ones followed in his wake.

At McIntosh's, "Wild Bullocks" found his friend and partner, who, with the publican, accompanied him to a private parlour. After drinks had been served, the old man, sipping his with an air of extreme indecision, spoke.

"Look here, Jack," he said, "this is the first time in me blanky life that I've got a few quid tergether, an' I'm reckonin' on takin' a pull. I don't want ter blow this cheque in like I've done the others I've earned by a darned sight harder yakka, 'cause I'm getting' ter be an old bloke an' I'll be peggin' out before many years. What I've got'll about run me till the cut-out, if someone yards it fer me an' lets a little mob o' notes out through the crush when I call, jus' ter keep me pen full. But if I lobs it ter the bank, me old mates out there'll reckon I've turned dog on 'em, so I'm damned if I know what ter do. Fer God's sake, you an' Mac tell me!"

Both Jack and the publican warmly applauded the old man's good intention, and urged him strongly to lodge the whole amount in the bank until such time as it could be suitably invested. They impressed on him the foolishness of dissipating any of it in liquoring up his old-time mates, strenuously opposing the wasting of a single penny in this fashion. "Wild Bullocks" listened to them in grave silence, and only spoke when McIntosh and Jack had no more to say.

"No," he told them. "I couldn't come at that. I've got ter shout fer the mob, 'cause even if none o' 'em's holdin' now, they always stood me in when they was knockin' down their cheques an' I was stiff ter the world. I'll spend fifty quid on 'em; put a tenner in at five o' the pubs, an' they can drink till it's cut out. But I ain't goin' ter join 'em, Jack. I'm getting' off the booze here fer good. It don't mean I'm goin' ter turn inter a blanky tee-templar, but I won't never get drunk again so long as I live, by Gawd!"

Thus it was decided how "Wild Bullocks" should celebrate his accession to wealth. Within an hour twenty sun-baked swagmen were uproariously drunk. At midnight, as their aforetime mate sunk into slumber, he heard their distant voices raised in discordant song, carolling the refrain of an old bush ditty –

"Old Baldy broke the yoke,
Poked out the leader's eye;
And the dog hid in the tucker-box,
Nine miles from Gundagai."

And if, in every fibre of his being, he yearned to be with these old mates – men with whom he had tramped and toiled through days of drought and rain, of fullness and of stint, of cruel, parching thirst on the track, or reckless wasted hours of riot in wayside shanties – who is there to think the less of him for it? Through those lonely hours of the night, within that cheerless room, he fought his greatest fight – and won. The next day found him exultant and content, and with a new, great purpose in his life.

As Jack and "Wild Bullocks" lounged outside the post office one afternoon, idly watching Jack Buckley lash the down-river bags to the onto the back of the thorough-braced 'shanghai' that did duty for the transport of His Majesty's mail to the stations in the 'Never-Never', the 'Back o' Beyond', the 'West o' Sunset', the 'God-Forgot', as the further-west country was picturesquely named by bushmen, the old man asked his friend whether he had ever taken a trip on a mail coach.

"No," replied Jack, "and I have no ambition to – yet."

"Well it ain't too bad," said the old man reminiscently. "I've had some good ol' times on that 'shanghai' o' Jack's there. Say, Buckley!" The driver came over to them. "D'yer remember that trip we had down ter Euabalong with the Guv'ment Inspector bloke?"

"My oath," said the mailman, tersely.

"What was that, Bullocks?" asked the young jackeroo.

"Aw, a joke we played on a chap," "Wild Bullocks" explained. "Me an' Jack 'ere thought we was goin' ter have the trip on our own. It's a long ride, half a day an' all night, so I gets six o' rum an' a dozen o' beer. Jus' as we're leavin', a little ches'nut bloke with eyes like a poley steer with sandy blight hops aboard. He says he's a Guv'ment Inspector, goin' ter Lake Cudgellico, so we has ter take him. At the first gate we offers him a rum, it bein' the custom o' the back-blocks ter 'wet it' at every gate. Well he roars like hell. Reckons that it's poison, an' that I'm boozed, an' that Buckley ain't fit ter drive the coach. He keeps this up, too, the cow, an' we has ter pull up at all sorts o' places so as me an' Jack can get under the coach ter fix smashes in the springs that ain't there, an' have a drink. After dark we gets sick o' it, an' Buckley puts up a good 'un on him.

There's been a lot o' heavy rain about a day or two before, an' the plains is covered with about a foot o' water. Buck drives off the road inter the thickest patch o' scrub, slaps the brake on an' lashes up the horses. O' course they can't shift the coach an' they stops. Then we tells the inspector bloke as we're bogged, an' has ter get horses ter pull us out. We wants him ter get down an' look fer spare horses, but he roars a treat, an' says he sticks ter the coach. Then me an' Buckley climbs along the pole, undoes the horses an' rides away, leavin' him there. We lobs up at the Kiacatoo homestead in about quarter of an hour, it bein' just on the other side o' the scrub about a mile away. We camps there all night, leavin' the inspector bloke on the box seat watchin' the mails. It's a terrible cold night, an' he's nearly perished when we gets back ter him in the mornin'. He's fair blue with the cold, 'cause he only has a thin overcoat on, an' can't get down ter warm himself. When he sees us comin' up with the same two ol' horses he looks surprised, but it ain't nothin' ter how he looks when they pulls the coach onter the road as easy as winkin', an' he can spot the Kiacatoo roofs half a mile away."

"Did he say anything?" asked Jack, with amused curiosity.

"Not a blasted word till we pulls up at the next gate," said the old man, with a smile. Then when I'm pourin' out a pannikin o' rum fer Buckley, he says: My Gor, I sees it all. I'm dyin' o' the cold. Will yer give me a drop o' that rum, only a little. I'll take it as medicine.' We fills him up prop'ly an' he lands at Euabalong prop'ly shickered, an' singin' bloomin' hymns."

Buckley did not join in the laughter that followed. Instead he burst out into indignant wrath. "The cow!" he exclaimed. "He reported me over it, after all, an' I nearly done me contract. Blarst him!"

Jack Burnside laughed still more heartily.

"An' a nice sort o' inspector he was," continued the angry mail-man. "I found out after that he was an inspector o' flamin' cemeteries!"

As the coach swayed and rocked down the road, "Wild Bullocks" pointed after it.

"Ol' Buckley has been drivin' coaches," he said, "fer fifty years or more. He was one o' Cobb an' Co's old whips when they run all the coach lines in the country, an' then when the firm went out he took out contracts on his own. He don't talk much, but he's had some times, I tell yer. He was drivin' gold escorts when Ben Hall an' his gang was about Forbes – they shot Ben near there, an' his grave's in the town cemetery – an' he's been stuck up by the bushrangers a dozen times. Him an' Fagin – he's a wealthy squatter now – Bill Crooks, Dick Oldfield, Jimmy Welsh, Paddy Power, an' a few others opened up the mail routes through the back country, an' the bushrangers used ter give 'em a rough passage. Ol' Buckley's got a hat at home with a few bullet holes drilled through it as was done by Johnny Gilbert, him as they shot over at Binalong. But it's hard ter get him talkin'. I mind once he was drivin' over on the Bogan side, an' he has a commercial trav'ler on board who does his damnedest ter get the ol' bloke spruikin'. Getting' near Dandaloo they passes a cultiva-tion paddock with a crop showin' up ter the top rail o' the fence. The commercial says, 'That's a fine crop o' wheat, driver!' Ol' Buckley never answers him, jus' keeps drivin' along. About a month later the same commercial is drivin' with Buckley again, but this time he don't try ter get Jack ter talk. They'd come sixty miles without a blanky word betwixt 'em, but when they's passin' the same crop Buckley says ter the cove, 'That ain't wheat, blarst yer, it's oats!' That knocked the commercial bandy."

This anecdote so highly amused Jack that he insisted on "Wild Bullocks" entertaining him further with similar stories, and the pair yarned far into the night.

18

ON OUR SELECTION

Jack Burnside and his now inseparable friend, "Wild Bullocks", who could not be induced by any means to permit himself to be known by the name given him in baptism, spent nearly a month in Condobolin. The old man occupied his time in caring for the colt that Jack had purchased at Parkes, putting him through a thorough preparation – for he could handle a horse – in anticipation of a race meeting that was to be held at Bogan Gate in a few months' time. The thoroughbred, which had been named Bullangarra by Jack, although apparently little more than a two-year-old, had certainly been handled skilfully and carefully by his former owner, and took naturally to galloping. After a few weeks he showed such surprising form that both Jack and his mate were confident of winning some valuable races with him in the future.

Meanwhile Jack had been searching for land. He had sufficient capital to finance the purchase of a small holding on the river frontage, where he would be enabled to put into practice his very decided ideas concerning irrigation, but he soon discovered that for hundreds of miles along both sides of the sluggish Lachlan the country was either locked up in big sheep stations or occupied by selectors who declined to sell. Greatly disappointed at this condition of affairs and his inability to acquire a block by purchase, he determined to select an area under the Crown Lands Act. A wide tract of country that had all the characteristics of ideal wheat land, and that had originally been held under improvement lease by Burrawang Station, had just been thrown open for selection as homestead farms, a special form of perpetual leasehold tenure, carrying a peppercorn rental. Jack lodged an application. There were some fifteen blocks available, and on his application form he indicated his order of preference of the whole number, this being customary, as in the event of a ballot, an applicant who was unsuccessful in securing his initial choice when the first lots were drawn would have a chance of obtaining one of the other blocks if his number turned up before the total was exhausted.

The day of the ballot was an important one in Condobolin. All the applicants were present, as a matter of course. There were young men, like Jack Burnside, seeking homes on the soil; old men who had tired of some other district, and desired a change; others who had been following land ballots all over the State for years, only hoping to secure any sort of block anywhere. For the fifteen blocks, there were eight hundred applicants, and the ballot was conducted in the big, stone courthouse, under the direction of the local Land Board. These boards, which exist in different districts, consist of a Government official, long trained in the complicated land laws of the country, who acts as chairman, and two local appointees, selected for their practical knowledge of their particular district, who are known as "members". All matters appertaining to Crown lands, fencing disputes, modification of conditions of leases, appraisement of values – in fact, everything within the scope of land law jurisdiction – are adjudicated upon by them, the chairman determining any legal points involved, and the members usually deciding those questions in respect of which their experience of local conditions enables them to arrive at an equitable decision.

The ballot was governed purely by the law of chance, and each applicant entitled to participate in it had an opportunity of winning if his luck stood to him. The names of those qualified to take part –

several had been excluded, on account of their already holding lands – were set down in order, and numbered from one to eight hundred. The clerk of the board then called out each person's name and number, at the same time exhibiting a marble bearing the corresponding number, to a small committee appointed from among the applicants, to see that all was fair. The marble was then dropped into a large box hung on a swivel, and when the whole of the list had been so dealt with and all of the numbered spheres were put in, this box was set spinning for ten or fifteen minutes. When it was considered that the marbles had been sufficiently mixed, the box was stopped. Then, amid a tense silence, the clerk manipulated the patent slot at the bottom of the receptacle, and a single marble rolled out onto the table. It bore the number 322. Referring to the list, the clerk called out, "Number 322 – Henry Devine, Wyalong!"

Devine's application form had indicated Block 12 as his first choice, so this was allotted to him accordingly. Another marble was then let out, a Sydney youth being the lucky one on this occasion. His first preference had also been Block 12, but as this was not now available, his second choice, Block 16, was allocated to him.

For the third time was the marble dropped.

"Number 702 - Jane Carroll, Condobolin!" called the clerk.

There broke out a cheer that shook the crowded building as a grey-haired, frail little woman, with tears of joy streaming unashamedly from her tired, wistful eyes, pressed forward to sign the necessary documents. Her husband had been killed about six months before by a berserk stallion he had been handling, leaving her with a debt-ridden selection and five children, the eldest a boy of sixteen, who had since endeavoured to shoulder his father's responsibilities. The selection had been sold to satisfy the creditors, and this brave little mother was seeking another block on which to make one more effort to defeat drought and want.

The fourth number that fell was Number 698, and it stood in the name of John Burnside, Condobolin. Jack was allotted the block that represented his fourth preference.

The young man was extremely pleased at his good fortune.

Although he would have preferred to have secured one or other of his first three preferences, his fourth selection, which incidentally followed in the order hit upon by all the other applicants, was a valuable property. It comprised an area of 2560 acres, the usual four-mile block, and although carrying a fair extent of stunted pine scrub, offered no great difficulty in the way of clearing. About four hundred acres were open country, ready for the plough. He received the congratulations of his friends with a pleasure that was sincere, and a happy party drank to the success of his future as a wheat "cocky".

The block was confirmed to him by the Board – that is, officially allotted – within a few days. A week later he and "Wild Bullocks" were camped on the holding in two tents that were to be their homes for several months. The colt had been left in the hands of Nipper Tough, a capable trainer and jockey, to be wound up for the races, this leaving the time of the two mates free for their work on the farm. "Wild Bullocks" having flatly refused to part company with Jack, the young settler delightedly admitted him into a partnership arranged on a basis that was satisfactory to both.

The first work of importance engaged in was fencing. Fortunately, a netted barrier that had at one time been a portion of the original Burrawang boundary ran along two sides of the block, thus leaving only two lines of fencing to be erected. With the assistance of hired labour, consisting of Billy the Dodger and Old Bart, together with McLeod and his team, this was soon completed. Jack and "Wild Bullocks" chopped down the ironbark trees on a ridge

At the back of the block, sawed them into lengths, and then with wedge and maul split out the posts ready to be carted by McLeod on to the line. Dodger and Bart sunk the post holes with bar and shovel, rammed in the posts, and then bored them to receive the Number 8 fencing wire. The job did not take half so long as Jack had anticipated, and he was able to erect a rough bark hut before commencing the ploughing.

Breaking up the virgin land was the task that the young selector enjoyed above all others. He had purchased two teams of active draught horses and wide disc ploughs for the work, and, as he set his own team in motion towards the peeled sapling pointer in the far distance and turned the first furrow, his heart thrilled with pride. And, accompanying that thrill was a wistful longing that Molly had been present to cheer him on. But there was work before him, and he faced it resolutely.

Through a cloud of dust, the horses trudged unswervingly across the paddock towards the sighting-peg, and in their wake they left long, even scars in the red bosom of the soil. Jack delighted to see these straight, regular furrows in the rich red loam, and to glance across at his mate, who, amid a cloud of dust that was often faintly profane, drove another team. They ploughed from early dawn, week after week, until the scrub was a dim mass of eerie shadow in the waning sunset – and turned the last furrow on the day before the Bogan Gate races. As they fed and dried the horses that evening Jack said, happily, "We have finished a big job in good time, old mate; so it is a holiday for us tomorrow."

They saddled up next morning ere the fiery circle of the sun showed up over the rim of the plains, and were well forward on their fifteen-mile ride when its first strong beams flared in their faces. They reached the collection of unpainted pine buildings that comprised the town before many of its residents had stirred from their beds, and straightway sought out their trainer at the stables behind the hotel.

When they rode into the yard they found themselves in the midst of an excited group of people. Nipper Tough, their trainer, was tearfully bewailing an accursed fate that had caused him to sleep so soundly through the night. He had intended to watch the colt all the night, he loudly mourned, believing, from something that he heard, that an attempt would be made to tamper with him by some of the evilly-disposed members of the racing game then in town. He had armed himself, he said, to deal with the desperadoes, and he flourished an ancient, rusty revolver in proof. But he had slept, and while he slumbered some scoundrel had fed Bullangarra with a bundle of green lucerne. The colt was now blown up like a frog, and could never win two races that day. In fact, he had no chance of winning one event, let alone the double. The proof of the villainy of Nipper's enemies lay in the track of green lucerne from the gate to the horse's stall that could be plainly seen by everyone. Some of those who heard the story and saw the few stray stalks of lucerne were convinced, and they hurried away to spread the news.

Jack was greatly incensed at the occurrence, and expressed his opinion loudly and in forceful language. "Wild Bullocks" was picturesque in his profanity. Nipper, however, maintained a staid demeanour, and as the crowd departed winked solemnly at Jack and advised him not to worry.

"Back him for all you're bloomin' well worth, Mister Burnside," he said, cunningly. "I'll have him in trim to beat them all. I know how to get him right, so don't worry. I've only got fifteen quid in the wide world, but I've put the lot on him for the double at 20 to 1. He'll take it out, you'll see! I'm going to walk him about a bit, to get the green stuff out of him." With that, he saddled up the colt and rode him out across the paddocks.

After breakfast, as Jack was sitting on the edge of the hotel verandah, a battered, ramshackle buggy, drawn by a broken-winded, goose-rumped horse, emerged from a cloud of red dust, and came to a standstill in front of the building. Immediately there was a roar of welcome from the crowd, and the burnt-up little man on the seat waved an unkempt shovel hat in acknowledgement.

"Arrah, what does the crowd be after doing here today?" cried the driver of the vehicle.

"The races, Father O'Connell!" roared the bushmen, in response.

"Races is it? Sure then, they always do seem to be having races wherever I am to have a Mass on the Sunday. Can I never escape them?"

A gale of uproarious laughter greeted this statement, for every man of them knew that the genial, big-hearted old priest had not missed a single race meeting in the district, wherever it was held, during longer than most of them could remember.

Espying Jack Burnside, the venerable cleric hailed him with delight. "Arrah, Jack, my boy!" he exclaimed. "Tis to confess to you now that I will be after doing. That fifty pounds you sent me to buy a new buggy and horse for myself came in very useful, and I'm very thankful for it. But twas for the poor devil of a selector out beyond the Bogan. My old turn-out will be good enough for many a long day yet, and the money did someone a good turn that needed it more than I. And now, I hear that you have got the colt entered for the double today. Will he be after winning?"

"I'm afraid not," replied Jack, disappointedly. "Someone fed him with green lucerne last night, and that will about settle his chances."

"Oh, the villains!" exclaimed the priest. "And what was Nipper doing to allow that?"

"He was asleep, so he says," explained Jack, "but he does not appear to be very concerned about it."

"Come here, my boy," said Father O'Connell, and Jack walked to the buggy. Then, speaking in a low tone, the old cleric said, "So Nipper is not worrying? Did he be after telling you to back the colt?"

"Yes, he did. And he backed him himself. I do not intend to waste anything on him, though."

"Arrah, my boy!" said Father O'Connell, with a knowing smile. "You take Nipper's advice. I know him, and if he says he'll win the double he will. I know him better than you, and tis a clever lad he's after being."

Jack could extract nothing more definite than that from the priest, who shortly afterwards, with many knowing nods and portentous unclerical winks, drove into the yard. The young man was impressed, however, and set out to find the bookmakers who were betting on the double. The metallicians welcomed him effusively, and, having heard of the lucerne episode, and calculating that Bullangarra could not gallop after such a banquet of relaxing fodder, they offered attractive odds. It was not long before Jack had taken all the available double money at 25 to 1, investing a hundred pounds for the purpose. These liberal odds, for the fields were small, could not be obtained when "Wild Bullocks" tested the market, so the old man had to be grudgingly content with an average of 15 to 1 for forty pounds. Father O'Connell had also made a few modest investments on his own account, the odds involved and the amount outlaid being discreetly kept to himself.

All and sundry for miles around had assembled at the racecourse by midday. There was nothing pretentious about the Bogan Gate races. The track was marked out in a farmer's paddock, a harrow having been run over it a few days before the meeting, and a ploughed furrow opened to indicated its direction. There was no grandstand, the public watching the events from vantage points on buggies, motor cars or fallen trees. The judge's box was a flimsy structure of saplings with accommodation for one person only; the publican's booth was an affair of green bushes and sawn flooring boards. A big crowd came from the eastern neighbourhood by the Sydney train, and Jack noticed Williams, the man who had suspected him of sheep and horse stealing among the number. Most prominent of the local horse owners present was Thomas, the stud master from the Baroo side, who had several entries standing in his name.

Jack Burnside's colt, Bullangarra, had been entered for the first race, the Flying Handicap, and also for the "big money", as the principal race is always described in the bush. When the horses went to the post for the Flying, Bullangarra was second favourite at 6 to 4, a superb-looking mare belonging to Thomas being the most fancied at odds-on. After a great race, Jack's colt managed to win by a head, much to the disgust of the crowd who had solidly supported the favourite. Strangely enough, the colt showed no visible ill-effects of the lucerne. As Jack took the horse from Nipper when the lad went to the scales for 'weight', the little jockey said with a wink, "I'll win the handicap by a furlong."

He was as good as his word. In the big event eight horses sported silk, the punters backing Wamboyne and Birralee at two's and four's. Bullangarra was available in the market at sixes, at which price Jack invested fifty pounds for himself, fifty pounds for Nipper, and ten pounds for Father O'Connell. "Wild Bullocks", who was a cautious gambler, debated long before he mustered up sufficient courage to invest fifteen pounds.

In the race Nipper made no mistake. When the flag fell he

hopped Bullangarra to the front of the field, and remained there until the end. There was a howl of disappointed rage from the crowd as he rode back to 'weigh in', but the red flag was hoisted and the book-makers proceeded to pay. The heavy betting on the losers had recouped them to some extent for the substantial win of Jack and his party.

Watching Nipper working on the colt with a drying cloth, Jack asked the lad how the horse had come to make such a quick recovery from the effects of the lucerne.

"He never had no lucerne," said Nipper with a grin. "I told that tale for the benefit of the mob, so that we could get a decent price about him. It worked all right. I didn't let on to you, because I knew you wouldn't stand for it."

Thomas, who owned the favourite that had been beaten, then walked up.

"Where did you get that colt, Burnside?" he asked.

"Bought him in Parkes for eighty pounds, about five or six months ago," replied Jack. "He's a good sort of horse, isn't he?"

"He ought to be," said Thomas drily. "I sold him about eighteen months ago for twelve hundred guineas!"

"What?" exclaimed Jack. "You sold him?"

"Yes," answered Thomas quietly. "And you came and took him away from my place. He was stolen from you, I believe!"

Jack Burnside was absolutely staggered at this announcement. Not for an instant did he doubt that Thomas was right, for he knew that it would be impossible for the old horse-master to make a mistake regarding the identity of any animal that he had bred. He could think of nothing to say. At that moment also, he noticed the inspector gazing at him curiously from a position where he must have overheard the conversation. Before he could frame an answer, Williams took the stud-master by the arm and led him away. As they walked off Jack noted that they were engaged in deep and serious conversation.

That night, as he was about to ride out to his selection with "Wild Bullocks", he was arrested on a charge of horse-stealing. Somehow, he had expected it, and in anticipation, had entrusted his substantial winnings earlier in the evening for his old mate to bank for him. Turning to accompany the sergeant to the police station, he said to "Wild Bullocks", "Start the two teams in on Widow Carroll's block tomorrow, and you and Billy the dodger break up as much ground for her as you can. I will be back in a few days – out on bail."

19

FIELDS OF RIPENING GRAIN

Bogan Gate contained no angrier man than Father O'Connell when he learned the news of Jack's incarceration in the local lock-up. Hurrying to the police station, he indignantly demanded to know on whose information such infamous action had been taken. Sergeant Bool told him readily that Williams, the inspector for the Commonwealth Mortgage Company, which owned Bullangarra Station, had issued the warrant on the identification of the horse by Thomas, the stud-master.

"Arrah, then," exclaimed the old priest, at the conclusion of the sergeant's story. "And it's after convincing Mr. Williams he's made a mistake I'll be, this very minute. Come with me."

Father O'Connell and the sergeant were not long in finding Williams and the horse-master. The priest then explained to them all that he had been present on the occasion that Jack had purchased the colt in Parkes, and had, in fact, witnessed the receipt by appending his signature thereto. Further than that, the seller was a stranger to Burnside, and to him as well, although he had subsequently seen the vendor of the animal in the company of Brummy Collins. He would vouch for this, he said, pledging his priestly word, and if they refused to withdraw the warrant as he requested he would

there and then hurry to Parkes, and find sufficient additional confir-
matory evidence to establish Jack's bona fides as a genuine
purchaser.

It was then decided to interview Jack Burnside. He corroborated
entirely the statement of Father O'Connell. The sergeant pointed out
that in the face of this new, and apparently incontrovertible testimony, there would be no possibility of a committal for trial, and he,
accordingly, strongly advised withdrawal; at the same time, he
pointed out to Jack that he had in his hands a splendid chance for an
action for wrongful arrest. The upshot of it was that Jack was liber-
ated at once, a local justice of the peace providing the requisite
authority.

Williams was greatly perturbed over the whole matter. Jack had
resigned all claim on the horse to him, saying that although he had
been caused some anxiety by the arrest he was gratified to know that
it was through his unwitting instrumentality that the valuable colt
had been restored to his lawful owners. He also added briefly that he
would seriously consider what action he would take in the matter of
recovering damages as suggested by the sergeant.

The inspector, realising that he had acted impetuously, and
without making even the reasonable investigations that his innate
caution had at first prompted, threw himself on Jack's mercy, and
pleaded with him to let the matter drop. This request being seconded
by Father O'Connell, Jack consented to take no action, and made a
promise to this effect. He, however, regretted that promise a few days
later, when he read in the Sydney papers a telegram under the
heading of 'Country News', detailing his arrest, despatched undoubtedly by the busy local correspondent of the daily, who had scented a
'scoop' in the affair. And quite naturally he did not see any further
news about the matter in that paper, for none had been telegraphed
down by the correspondent.

And his regrets would have been deeper had he seen Molly
Forbes shrink into a huddled heap of despair as she read the self-
same paragraph. The terrible indictment had burned into her brain
like a brand, and her sobs of grief brought old Mr. Penderby hurrying

from his room to her side. She pointed to the item of news, and the old man read it slowly.

"So that is the trouble, my poor girl," he said, patting her arm tenderly. "Don't worry, it may all be a mistake. I will find out at the police headquarters whether it is true."

Old Mr. Penderby was as good as his word. Molly learned, a few days later, that Jack had been arrested, but had been immediately set at liberty, it being clear that a grievous error had been made. Unfortunately, the brief report from Sergeant Bool that the lawyer had seen did not contain very full particulars of the affair, so that the girl was not yet to learn the truth. However, greatly comforted at Mr. Penderby's news, she went about her work with a happier spirit than she had shown for many a weary month.

And on Yarran Plains, for so Jack had called his selection, from the trees of that name that flourished along the main road boundary, the days sped quickly. On Mrs. Carroll's farm, an area of four hundred and eighty acres had been ploughed and farrowed by the neighbours, and the whole sown with wheat. Those who helped in this work, and they would have been astounded had they been informed that their action was out of the ordinary, were, with the exception of Jack, struggling settlers blessed with scarcely any resources save their own indomitable courage, and that unquenchable spirit to succeed that characterises the Australian pioneer.

They had worked day and night on their own half-cleared blocks to get in the crop that would mean success or failure to them, yet they spared time and the sweat of their brow to help the brave little bushwoman and her silent, hard-working sixteen-year-old son, who could find no words to express the gratitude that his eloquent eyes so plainly showed.

This same lad, with a man's strength and a man's courage, displayed a warm but not openly-expressed admiration for Jack Burnside, and often at night would walk across from his mother's rough home and sit beside he camp fire with the young selector and the old shearer, smoking stolidly, but never speaking, until it was time for him to go home and turn in. The longest speech Jack ever knew him to make was on an occasion when he had given the boy a horse, saddle and bridle. The lad inspected the animal and the gear with a critical eye, measured off the stirrup-leathers by the length of his lean, brown arm, and gravely mounted.

"You're a bloody good man, Jack," was all he said as he rode off, but his steel-grey eyes were swimming in tears.

Jack had cultivated his land thoroughly. Six weeks after plough-ing, the paddock was broken down with heavy harrows. Then the sowing operations commenced. He selected, on the advice of his neighbours, two varieties of wheat: "Bobs" and "Federation", and the seed was planted with drills, forty-five pounds being sown to the acre at a depth of two inches. He had not thought of the Agricultural Department of the State Government as being likely to assist him until one of its experts chanced to call at his farm just after seeding had been finished. On learning of the varieties sown, he had told Jack that he could have made no better choice. The "Bobs" he described as a dual-purpose mid-season wheat, eminently suited for both grain and hay, and the "Federation" as another mid-season variety suitable for grain only.

From this officer Jack learned that the Department of Agriculture would supply free, to any farmer that cared to apply, books and pamphlets compiled and written by scientists and experts dealing with every phase of primary production; that experts would visit any district to have talks with farmers and advise them on crop and culti-vation matters, or investigate pests and diseases; that seeds and plants for experimental purposes connected with any branch of agricultural science, grain, fruit, vegetables, fibres etc., were also supplied free on application if supplies were available.

Jack also learned for the first time that the department conducted experimental farms in centres typical of certain districts, where everything in connection with profitable production of the particular locality was tried and proven; and he learned with interest of the old farmer-scientist, William Farrer, who on his little property at Cowra had devoted a lifetime to the breeding and inter-breeding of wheats until he produced varieties that were rust-proof and almost drought-proof, and which were now used almost exclusively throughout Australia. He became, after this, an enthusiastic correspondent of the Agricultural Department.

While the crop was growing, beneficial showers fell at the critical periods until prospects were of the brightest. Jack had purchased a thousand crossbred lambs early in the season, and having fattened these and sold them at a handsome profit, bought another lot of fifteen hundred. There was plenty of grass for them, so they topped off quickly, and he enjoyed greatly the happy task of riding around his little holding admiring the tiny flocks. He also spent a considerable sum on clearing. The mallee scrub was eradicated by being rolled down with a steam roller hired from the shire council, and left to dry and be burned off in the following autumn.

A section of old ring-barked country – that is, where a scarf had been cut round the base of the trees into the sap to kill them – he cleared by "yankee-grubbing". He let a contract for this work, about five hundred acres, to a gang of Chinamen, at eight shillings and sixpence per acre, and the Celestials, as they do on this work, toiled faithfully. 'Yankee-grubbing' consists of piling small wood and limbs against the ring-barked trees and then setting fire to the paddock. The trees are burned out two or three inches below the surface, stump-jump ploughs being used to break up the ground subsequently.

The days were busily occupied through the winter and the spring. The crop was a veritable picture, rolling and swelling like a glistening emerald lake as the breeze rippled its surface, and Jack never tired of gazing out over its wide expanse. A few days after the wheat was in flower, Jack and "Wild Bullocks" put in the reaper and binder to cut a portion for hay. With the help of the silent Carroll boy they cut a chain-wide swathe around the four sides of the crop, this serving to form a fire-break in the event of bushfires. The sheaves were placed in long open stooks for rapid curing, and the boy, in a fortnight's time, silently demonstrated to Jack that the hay was sufficiently dry for stacking by pulling out a few straws from the middle of a sheaf and showing him that it was brittle and dry at the knobs or joints. A few neighbours helped the partners to build and thatch the stacks, so that by the beginning of October, Yarran Plains presented the picture of a cosy, prosperous farm.

At the beginning of December, the crop was ripe. Then began days of bustle and toil. Jack had bought a combine harvester, one of those huge machines that were conceived by an Australian brain to revolutionise the wheat industry, and two neighbours, who had acquired similar ones from the makers on time payments, came to his assistance. In fact, throughout the year these neighbours helped each other with horses, machinery and labour. The three machines were started. As they advanced behind the horses Jack saw the golden heads of the wheat caught into the teeth of the nine-feet-wide comb and go whirling into the winnower in a cloud of dust. At the back of each harvester was the chaff carrier, a huge receptacle to hold the screenings and to prevent the 'dirtying' of the field; whilst on the platform were the grain bags, slowly filling. His heart filled with a wondrous satisfaction to see thus the tangible results of his first efforts on the land, and he then and there registered a vow that henceforth the cities and their ways would know him no more.

That was a great year for the wheat farmers in the Lachlan Valley. Every crop was a bumper one; every yield a record for that particular farm. Jack's went twenty-two bushels to the acre, and Mrs. Carroll took off an average of twenty-five bushels.

This was more than gratifying to the settlers in view of the fact that the yearly average for the State for the previous decade had been 10.48 bushels per acre, and as uncertain weather in other districts had reduced the whole yield tremendously that season, prices were high for the times, and the settlers sold to the Condobolin mill at three shillings and threepence per bushel. Jack's total return was over sixteen hundred pounds. Out of that he had spent four hundred and fifty pounds for plant and horses. He estimated that the cost of producing the crop had run into thirty shillings per acre, or six hundred pounds, so that he congratulated himself heartily on the result. The return was far greater than either he or "Wild Bullocks" had anticipated, and he had the plant to the good as well as over a hundred tons of hay. This hay he subsequently sold at four pounds per ton to a speculator who owned a portable chaff-cutting plant, and who, with an oil engine and a team of men, soon caused the stacks to disappear.

Jack and "Wild Bullocks" were in Condobolin shortly after the end of the harvest, preparing to take the oft-deferred trip to the Dungog district, on the coast. They were to leave, via Sydney, by the next morning's train. When Jack had phoned Callister at Bullangarra Station, informing him of his intended journey, the genial manager had expressed a desire to talk privately with him ere his departure. Jack, on this particular afternoon, was awaiting his arrival.

Callister's motor car drew up before the hotel at three o'clock, and over a friendly glass the manager heard the story of his young friend's experiences since they had last met. The arrest over the colt was discussed, but with laughter on both sides, Jack learning that Callister had sent it to Sydney to be trained still under the name it first raced under, that of Bullangarra. After an hour's interested chat, Callister said, "Now about the business I have in mind. You are going to Dungog for a holiday, and as you will have some spare time up there I want you to go across to Port Stephens to see a brother-in-law of mine, Alex Campbell, who is in the timber business. He has been trying to persuade me for months to go into some saw-milling venture he has in mind, but which he can't finance. What I want you to do is get the hang of it. See if there is the money in it that he promises, and if there is I will go into it. If you fancy it, you can stand in with me."

"But I know nothing about timber," protested Jack.

"You can inspect his books, make enquiries with your eyes and ears open, and then form an opinion," said Callister. "I trust your intelligence sufficiently to be sure that your opinion will be correct, whichever way it goes. Now, will you do that for me?"

"Certainly," responded Jack with warmth, "and I'll put some capital in if the prospects warrant it."

Callister and Jack were standing, later on, near the Post Office, when Williams, the inspector, drove along the street in a pole sulky.

"I can't make that chap out," said Callister, glancing at the passing inspector.

"What's up with him?" queried Jack.

"That affair of the Circle Y wethers and the theft of the colt seems to have got on his mind," answered the manager. "He's been running tracks since that time he nearly yarded you at Bogan Gate. But, still, I believe he has something up his sleeve. And, by the way, he is making all sorts of inquiries about Ray Penderby. What it is for, I can't make out."

"Where is Penderby?" asked Jack.

"Horse-dealing in the East with little Jimmy Elliott, I have heard. Queer thing for a medical student to take on in his fifth year."

"It is queer!" assented Jack.

Three days later, Jack and "Wild Bullocks" arrived at Dungog. It cost Jack a considerable effort to wait in Sydney several hours pending the departure of the north coast train, without making an effort to see Molly, but he convinced himself that she would not welcome his intrusion into her affairs, and so devoted his efforts to entertaining "Wild Bullocks". That old bushman, not having been in the city for nearly thirty years, was so terrified at the frenzied hurry of the congested traffic in the streets that he could not be persuaded to leave the comparative safety of the railway station.

"They're like a mob o' flamin' brumbies!" he said as he gazed, awe-struck, at the hustling crowds. "They'd trample a man ter death if he was mug enough ter get out among 'em. No! Let's stop here, where they're quiet as young scrubbers with their first calves."

20

WHEN WANDERERS RETURN

T he homing instinct is strong even in a bosom that harbours the most inexorable wanderlust. After two years crowded with hectic and varied experiences in the East and the tropics, Raymond Penderby returned to Sydney, partly on account of inclination, but chiefly owing to the importunate attentions of people he had victimised. During that space of time he had thrown himself wholeheartedly into life as he found it in the bizarre cities of the Orient, living hard, gambling hard, and drinking hard. His partnership with Jimmy Elliott had been a remarkably profitable one to both, for that shrewd horse buyer, opium smuggler, etc., had an amazing knack of skimming a handsome profit from every enterprise in which the firm engaged.

But, whereas Elliott seldom drank and never gambled, Raymond recklessly dissipated every penny that came his way. The astute Elliott had correctly gauged his partner's character early in their association, so there had been no shortages in the partnership funds for the simple reason that the young medical student was never permitted to handle them. Penderby's usefulness lay in his social qualities and the ease with which he gained access to the confidence of the notabilities for whom the firm executed commissions. He was able to conclude contracts that would never in any other circumstances have come Elliott's way, his gentlemanly demeanour and cultured conversation gaining him an entrée in circles where the rough, but more honest, horse dealer found scant toleration.

But Raymond's unscrupulousness and utter lack of principle rebounded on him in the long run, inasmuch as by the time he set sail from Singapore, amid the execrations of an unfriendly crowd on the wharf, there was not a port on the Eastern seas that he dared show his nose in again. Thus it was that he landed in the city of his birth after two years' absence, only richer by a hoard of experience of doubtful worth, and with not a friend to bid him welcome.

On the night of his arrival in Sydney, Raymond proceeded direct to his father's suburban home, not because of any sense of filial duty, but because he had long ago let out the flat he had formerly occupied. The old lawyer was overjoyed at his quite unexpected appearance.

"Two weary years," said his father, "since you left. It has seemed centuries to me. And your letters have been so brief and uninformative."

"But I'm back at last, dad!" exclaimed Raymond heartily.

"Yes," assented the old man, "but you do not look as though your health has benefited."

"I'm fit, father, fit as a racehorse," was the reply. "I look a bit off colour, true, but that is due to malaria. I had a recurrence of it during the last week. My heart is strong enough. A few weeks' rest will pull me together."

Raymond's glib explanation belied his looks; he appeared anything but healthy. Indeed, his whole being had undergone a very tangible alteration in those two years. The fresh healthy colour had departed from his face, the youthful eagerness from his eyes. Instead, his cheeks were sickly-hued, and his eyes hard with a cold, calculating glitter. There was a subtle suggestion of furtiveness in his appearance, that the old man, taught by a life-long business association with malefactors and offenders against the law, was greatly disturbed to note, and that caused him a vague uneasiness for many a day.

The young man probably sensed something of this in his father's manner, some fugitive, indefinable antipathy, as it were, that jarred, and so he set himself actively to dispel the feeling. Eloquently he told the old man of his experiences, stories of good fortune and of bad, of pleasant days, and nights of danger. He rivetted his father's interest speedily, and sustained until long past the midnight hour. At last he ended.

"So, you have been making money, and losing it," said his father. "I often wondered why you did not ask me for more than the thousand pounds I first gave you."

"I could not have done that, dad," answered Raymond, virtuously, "I determined to earn my own living at the same moment that I made up my mind to remain away until I was thoroughly recuperated. I would have starved rather than impose on your good nature again."

"There would have been no need for that," said the old man, with a gruff kindness, rising to retire for the night.

Next morning father and son repaired to the city together. At the office Raymond lingered to speak with Molly, who was still in her old place. Pressing her hand affectionately, he said in a tender voice," Molly, dearest! I would have been back ages ago if I could have hoped for one welcoming smile from you."

"I am pleased to see you again, Mister Raymond," the girl said simply, but avoiding his gaze.

"There is no welcome in your voice, Molly," he chided.

"I do welcome you most cordially," she said, and after a pause, added, "for your dear father's sake. He missed you terribly."

"But on your own account?" he persisted.

"Yes," she said doubtfully, "and for... my sake."

"I only want your welcome, darling," he said, his voice vibrant with passion, "and your love."

The girl drew her breath sharply; the colour left her cheeks and her lips quivered.

"You must never speak like this again," she commanded. "I forbid it!"

"Do you still love Jack Burnside, then?" Raymond asked, and there was an anxious look in his eyes. "I suppose you hear from him often?"

"Jack Burnside has forgotten me, if he lives. I never hear from him, nor do I know where he lives. I do not think that love will ever enter my heart again." And saying this, Molly turned such anguished, pleading eyes on the young man that, utter scoundrel as he was, he was impelled to walk away abashed.

When he entered his father's room he found the old lawyer gazing thoughtfully at a letter that he held in his hand. It had been in the pile of mail lying on his desk.

"This is strange," said his father, indicating the letter. "I have never bothered to tell you much of your family history, but this communication, coming as it does at this juncture, prompts me to say something to you concerning it. The letter is from your Uncle Tom, who lives at Dungog, and it is the first that he has written to me for over twenty years. We Penderbys have never been a very united family, I am sorry to say, and all of us have been to blame. Your uncle tells me that our older brother Raymond, who ran away from home as a lad and was never heard of afterwards, has returned to Dungog, apparently well-to-do, and is spending a holiday there. It appears that he has led a rough life in the west, for he is described as a rude, uncouth bushman, but, nevertheless, they have made him welcome, and propose that I should run up while he is there. And the strangest thing of all is that he is accompanied by a young man who is undoubtedly well-to-do. The young fellow is named Jack Burnside."

"Jack Burnside! Good God!" exclaimed Raymond, involuntarily.

"Yes; it is a remarkable coincidence," pursued the old lawyer, musingly. "It must be old Amos' son. But how can he have ever made money enough to be considered well-to-do? Maybe he turned out well, after all. I pray that he has."

"We can settle it easily, dad,' said Raymond, eagerly, "by running up at once. A few days will do you good, and I may make a month of it if they will have me. I can get properly right there."

"We will go tomorrow, then!" cried the old man, delighted that his son had so readily fallen in with the idea that had been forming in his own mind.

Thus it was that the Penderbys, the legal branch of the family, father and son, found themselves at the Dungog railway station next afternoon, making enquiries concerning the location of Mr. Thomas Penderby's property. They had not forewarned their relatives of the visit, intending to surprise them pleasantly, a circumstance that they regretted on learning that their destination was actually some seven miles out of town. Raymond had brought a good deal of luggage, in contemplation of an extended stay, for he had again resolved to make an attempt to gain Jack Burnside's money by hook or by crook, and the luggage was left at a hotel. A motor car, hired from a garage in town, whirled them rapidly over smooth sealed roads to 'Kirrawilla', Thomas Penderby's estate. Both father and son were astonished when the driver, saying nonchalantly, "Here y'are," swerved the car into a Norfolk pine-fringed carriageway, winding to a wide-veran-dahed bungalow set amid a bewildering beauty of garden beds. The appearance of solid and indisputable wealth about the place struck both simultaneously.

"Tom has been getting on," muttered the old lawyer, as he alighted.

"By Jove!" said Raymond.

The meeting of the brothers was not characterised by any great show of emotion. Thomas was a typical farmer: bluff, hearty and healthy. He was also a man of blunt speech, and incapable of being astonished at anything.

"So you're Jim, eh?" said the farmer, shaking hands with his brother. "You haven't shown your nose around here since the law gripped you, nigh on thirty years ago. Well, you're changed since we were lads."

"The years bring their changes, Tom," said the other, briefly, and then presented Raymond.

"So this is young Raymond, eh?" said Thomas, inspecting his nephew with a scrutiny that was disconcertingly direct. "Twenty-one years since I saw him in Sydney as a kid. You're not like your uncle Raymond, anyhow, nor like our father, whose name was Raymond also."

"Where is our brother Raymond?" interrupted the lawyer, with some impatience.

"Gone. Cleared out," said Thomas, waving his pipe argumentatively. "He's a queer bird altogether; as wild as hawk. He told me that for twenty years out in the back-country he never answered to any name other than "Wild Bullocks", and I'll bet they christened him that on account of his ways. He's gone over to Port Stephens with that mate of his, Jack Burnside, and won't be back for a week or longer. But come inside and see Nellie and the girls."

As they entered the house Raymond experienced a feeling of intense relief that both Jack and his mate were absent, and on that account unlikely to meet and talk with his father. He feared that the old man might discover the fact of his deliberate suppression of the knowledge of Burnside's whereabouts in the days when he was visiting Bullangarra, and awkward questions might follow.

Thomas Penderby's wife was a buxom, handsome dame of fifty, who greeted her relatives with restrained cordiality. But his two daughters gave the visitors a most agreeable surprise. The eldest, Doris, a tall, stately girl with serene brow, fine eyes, full red lips and perfect figure, was strikingly beautiful in a noble way, and presented a remarkable contrast to her sister Millie, though exquisitely moulded, and with charming, piquant features, resembled some radiant sprite of the woodlands. Both girls were unfeignedly delighted with Raymond, and in a very short while had lured him from the company of the older folk out into the garden.

Here they made him tell them of the city and city life, a topic of which they never wearied for, truth to relate, neither of them, though women in years, had ever been in Sydney. This remarkable admission from the girls caused Raymond much wonder, but they explained that it was quite a natural thing thereabouts, and quoted the instances of dozens of their girlfriends, whose parents were even wealthier than theirs, who had never seen the ocean. Indeed, the young man later discovered that in old-settled districts such as Dungog it was not an uncommon thing that men and women were born and lived and died there without having, during long and honoured lifetimes, ever ventured fifty miles afield from their homes. The young visitor found his two cousins bright, talkative, and very well informed on most subjects, despite their lack of travel. They made a merry party, these young folk, and as they returned to the house arm in arm, all three could not fail to note the extreme satisfaction with which their respective parents greeted their public display of cousinly affection.

That evening after dinner, while the girls and Raymond amused themselves in the spacious drawing-room with music and mirth, the two brothers sat and smoked on the verandah.

"Ray and Doris would make an ideal couple," said Thomas enthusiastically, after a long period of silence.

"Yes," said the old lawyer thoughtfully. "Yes, perhaps so."

"What's that?" asked his brother, enquiringly.

"I was thinking of Doris, Tom," James replied gently. "She is a beautiful girl, and a good girl, and may she have all the happiness that life can give her."

Thomas was plainly puzzled, but forbore to say anything.

"What about this young Burnside?" asked the lawyer, after another long silence. "Who is he, and what is he?"

"He appears to be a fine young gentleman," said the other warmly. "Old Ray swears by him, for they have been mates at mining, droving, shearing, farming – everything. He seems to have his head screwed on the right way, for he started with nothing a few years ago, and he has something like ten thousand pounds now, I believe, and a property out Condobolin way. He's got some sort of secret, so it seems, or at least, the girls say so, but neither he nor our brother has ever dropped a hint of it. The girls argue that it is a love affair, and that his heart is broken, but that is because he won't flirt with them. He was here for a week, and spent every evening yarning with Nellie and me. A broken-hearted man couldn't stand that, could he? He's a terror for asking questions about irrigation and farming, and I could never tell him enough. He seems to have read a lot about agriculture, for he showed me a few wrinkles and I'm no new-chum at the business."

The brothers talked long into the night, the lawyer continually returning to the subject of Jack Burnside. But the other could give him very little definite information, and confined himself to praising the young man, who had evidently made a very favourable impression on him, and commenting on the queerness of their brother, who, so he mentioned casually, was still called "Wild Bullocks" by his youthful mate.

The brothers, after a 'nightcap' of whiskey and soda, went to bed to dream of the happy days of a childhood spent in the pleasant, peaceful Williams Valley, and perchance to live again, in that mysterious realm of slumberous fancy, the half-forgotten incidents that their reminiscences had called from the misty past.

Raymond gallantly kissed his cousins an affectionate goodnight, causing thereby much blushing and a quite disproportionate amount of banter, half-joking and half in earnest, among them. This circumstance aroused a train of thought in his active brain as he sought his room. His country cousins were infinitely more attractive from a purely physical standpoint than he had ever conceived in those days from the past, when his father had suggested a probable matrimonial alliance between the families. Better still was the attraction of their financial position. By deft questioning he had learned from the girls that each already had ten thousand pounds in the bank in her own name – they explained that their father had invested this for them simply to escape taxation, for he was a cautious man – and that each would receive another ten thousand pounds on marriage. Either, he thought, would make an admirable wife for a young doctor, but unfortunately they had both given evidence of the possession of old-fashioned ideas regarding courtship, and had indicated to him, on being questioned, that they would as soon think of marrying before a year's engagement as they would of flying to Melbourne. And the firmness of character that both exhibited in their conduct and in their countenances convinced him that even his persuasive eloquence could not demolish these ridiculous notions.

Considering his whole position from every standpoint, he admitted to himself that he was in a serious predicament. The bookmakers, as soon as they knew that he had returned, would be on his track for the unpaid balance of those old gambling debts. Collins and his gang would seek his life. He would have to deal with Burnside, he decided, but how he could not determine. His father, he knew, was only moderately wealthy, being of a speculative bent, and also, for years having been liberally bled by his son. There must be a way out, he thought, and that he must shortly find.

The lawyer returned to Sydney after spending two days at Kirrawilla, pressing business demanding his presence in the city. He, however, extracted a promise from his brother that the wanderer, "Wild Bullocks", should be brought to Sydney, by force if necessary, as soon as convenient, together with Thomas' children, in order that the family reunion might take place after all.

Raymond remained behind, ostensibly for reasons of health, but actually to lay siege to the heart of one of his winsome cousins – which one, however, he had not decided.

21

IN THE TALL TIMBER

"So you are glad to be among the trees again," said Jack to "Wild Bullocks", as their saddle-horses plodded up a steep hill on the road between Sawyer's Point and Tea Gardens.

"My colonial oath!" exclaimed the old bushman. "It was very nice ter see Tom an' his missus an' the girls, but there's too much damn frill about 'em fer me. I was always uncomfortable at their place, an' the way they eyed me when I ate was a caution. It wasn't my fault if the blasted gravy wouldn't stop on the knife, and kept runnin' down me beard."

Jack smiled. "But you were glad to see the old place again, eh?" he asked.

"When I first spotted them ol' hills, Jack, all blue about the bottom where the valley spreads, an' with little handfuls o' clouds about the tops like new-clipped lambs' wool, a bloomin' lump kept chokin' in me throat. Yer mind when I walked down ter the river from the station? Well, damn me if I didn't howl like a kid when I seen the clear, clean water foamin' over the stones under the willer trees there by the ol' swimmin' hole where we played when we were youngsters. It was years since I seen a real clean river, but I got broke up alto-gether when I seen an ol' bloke fishin' jus' like ol' Jimmy Doolan used ter do, at that very same spot, forty years ago. But somehow when I got about the town things seemed different altogether. I couldn't find none o' the old places I used ter know, an' nobody remembered me. I might jus' as well been a wanderin', mateless swagman trampin' through, fer all anyone noticed. I felt like a stranger. An' then when we got up ter Tom's place, the valley an' the ranges got diff'rent. The blue o' 'em I first seen seemed ter disappear, an' instead there was yellow colourin's an' miles o' rung country like the ghosts o' the forest. An' little homesteads was hangin' on ter the sides o' the hills, where there was solid bush in my young days. I never seen the little valley clouds again, neither, fer there was always the wind blowin' or a thunderstorm smashin' through the ridges."

"You would find a change in forty years," said Jack gently.

"Yair, there was a change," the old man answered sadly, and his eyes took on a dreamy far-away look. "But I s'pose it was me as was changed; I been away too long. After a few days them hills seemed ter come creepin' an' sneakin' in on me as if they was tryin' ter crush me. The flats got so little that I come ter think they was ashamed o' bein' so small, an' was tryin' ter hide. Then, the day when that bush fire started up in Tom's back paddock, an' the smoke o' the grass an' the stinkin' smell o' the burnin' gum leaves got in me nose, I sees it all. The flamin' coast country was too small fer me. When I was beltin' that fire out it wasn't the smoke as made me eyes smart. I was wantin' ter be out on the big open plains where there ain't no blarsted hills, where the sky keeps blue fer months an' the sun leaps up sudden in the mornin', like a frightened kangaroo outer the scrub, an' drops down in the west at night glarin' at yer like a snake, without a blink. I've got the west in me bones, an' it's callin' me now jus' like yer hear the tinklin' o' the horse-bells through the mallee in the dusk, callin' yer on ter camp at some ol' bend on the Lachlan, where the teamsters is sittin' yarnin' round a yarran fire. This is a good enough country, with its dairy cows, an' its little patches o' corn an' lucerne no bigger'n a tarpaulin, an' its short green grass; but I want ter be where there's miles o' wavin' wheat; where the sheep is lost fer weeks in the barley-grass an' corkscrew when it's up ter their girths; where there's big wide billabongs sleepin' all day in the lazy sunshine, an' where the dirty, muddy ol' Lachlan creeps like a sad ol' sundowner out toward the sunset. I'm goin' back there, Jack, jus' so soon as you're ready."

"It will only be a few days, then," said Jack, deeply moved by this unsuspected evidence of feeling in his old friend, and stirred by the responsive echo in his own heart. "I believe the west has got a hold of me, also."

Just then they topped the rise, and both pulled up their horses as though at a given signal. The panorama spread out below them was sublime in its magnificence. They gazed over the expanse of a wondrous harbour, Port Stephens, whose shores on every side were deeply wooded and seemingly untrodden of man.

Far away to the west they saw the wide sweep of bay after bay, where the emerald shoulders of many hills thrust themselves into the water. To the south, on the opposite side, probably three miles across, a similar succession of inlets and sand-lipped coves indented mile after mile of the foreshores. In the middle were tiny islands, crested with cabbage palms, that seemed to have been flung there in sport in the far-off fabled days by a mischievous giant's hand. To the east they saw two noble headlands that guarded the narrow entrance to the hidden beauty of the harbour, and beyond that, the sea. The great, wide port below them could accommodate the navies of the world, yet they espied not a solitary sail on its bosom.

After the first wondering glance, the travellers began to discern more distinctly, amid the wild primitive beauty of the harbour, the presence of man. Nestling beneath the southern headland, far in the distance, was a tiny cluster of houses that betokened some little settlement, and a jetty sprawling out into the water. This, they learned later, was the township of Nelson's Bay. On the western shores they saw a few sparse clearings and two or three settlers' homes.

Below them, scarcely seen through the timber, was a quaint, old-fashioned church, a group of squat, stone outbuildings, and a rambling house. This, they also learned later, was Carrington, now a rich man's summer residence, but once the first settlement made by the Australian Agricultural Company, which had a grant of a million acres extending up to Gloucester, in the dawn of recorded Australian history, nearly a hundred years before.

"So that's Port Stephens!" said "Wild Bullocks" at last. "It's a bit bigger'n Lake Cudgellico, anyway."

Jack, who had heard of races being held in the bed of the lake referred to after the drought had dried it up, laughed heartily at the comparison. "It is a wonderful harbour," he said at length, "but it is hard to understand why they don't use it. Newcastle is only a dozen miles away, the biggest industrial centre in Australia, with no port to speak of, and it has this in its back yard. I'm afraid, 'Bullocks', our statesmen are a short-sighted lot."

An hour later they reached Tea Gardens, an unpretentious village built on the low banks of the Myall River, where it flows into the harbour. There was nothing to indicate the reason of its name. There were no gardens, and the popular liquid refreshment, so far as they could judge from the surroundings, was something more potent than tea. They found Alex Campbell's home, and sawmill, half a mile up the river, where, after they had attended to their horses, they were taken indoors by the old Scot. When he had enquired affectionately of Jack about his sister and brother-in-law, Campbell mentioned the subject of the young man's trip.

"Duncan wrote me of your visit," he said, "and I have prepared everything for you, so that you can size up the matter speedily. It will need three or four days to show you everything, but in the meanwhile I will give you an outline of my proposal."

"I will be pleased to hear what it is," said Jack.

"Well, as you have no doubt heard," proceeded Campbell, "this is one of the biggest and richest timber districts in the State. North of here lie the Myall Lakes, a chain of shallow sheets of water that are the most picturesque from a scenic point of view in the State. On the shore, however, grows the finest milling timber procurable, and the areas set apart by the Crown for forestry purposes extend for miles to the south, west and north, embracing hundreds of thousands of acres. It means that there is an unlimited supply of 'mill sticks', as they call the logs, waiting to be felled and hauled out.

"What I propose is to acquire from the Forestry Department a concession, or as they call it, an exclusive right, to cut over a certain area, hitherto untouched, shift my mill up there, set it going, get big contracts for sawn timber, poles, piles and girders, and then sell the whole thing out as a going concern. I have very little capital of my own, but my plant is worth two thousand pounds. I should have been a rich man, but I fought the timber 'ring', that is not supposed to exist, and have been crippled. So that is why I want Duncan to put up four thousand pounds in cash, and I will put up a thousand pounds, and the plant.

"The profits we will divide equally. When I get the concession and have ready money to pay the timber-cutters and haulers I can secure plenty of labour. The venture will then be on a sound basis, and there will be something tangible to sell. With the contracts I can sign up in Sydney for sawn timber, and in New Zealand and South Africa for telegraph poles, piles and girders, we can sell out for fifteen thousand pounds easily. If we work it ourselves for three months, we can net over three thousand pounds, so that the proposition cannot fail.

"I could have secured financial help in other directions before this, but as Duncan cannot be got at by the 'ring', I preferred to deal with him. Tomorrow we will inspect the forest that I propose to acquire, and as an evidence of my bona-fides I will have an officer of the Forestry Department, a forest guard, accompany us and give his expert opinion."

Jack was greatly interested in the old Scot's proposal, which they discussed exhaustively until tea-time, and after that long into the night. "Wild Bullocks" spent the night with a party of fishermen who were 'shooting' their nets on the sandbanks near the river entrance, and so enjoyed the experience that he lingered with the bare-footed fisher folk during the whole of his stay.

Accompanied by Jim Barker, the forest guard, Jack and Campbell set out next morning at daybreak to inspect the timber belt. At ten o'clock they reached the first lake, the Broadwater, and halted at a sawmill that stood at the mouth of Dirty Creek. The mill proved to be an affair of some importance. It greatly interested Jack to see the huge mahogany and messmate logs urged implacably towards the vertical "breaking down" saws that tore a passage through their hearts, amid a shower of red dust, and with protesting shrieks that deafened. The giant logs were handled with astonishing ease and rapidity. The hurrying, sawdust-spattered men wasted no single moment, and it seemed but a brief second that elapsed between the first attack of the upright saws and the assault of the whirring, biting 'circulars'.

But as they passed through the timber belt where the cutters were at work or this mill, Jack beheld something entirely new to him. The trees, giant hardwoods, reared their mighty crests far into the heavens, with clean, straight boles, without a limb for two hundred feet. Every variety of timber appeared to flourish in this forest – tallow wood, mahogany, messmate, blue gum, black butt, ironbark, yellow jacket, and a prodigious supply of soft woods. It was amid these surroundings that the hitherto silent forest guard waxed enthusiastic.

"Look at these beautiful sticks!" he exclaimed., pointing to the stately forest that stood around them. "This is what our department is looking after and caring for. It will be years before the big milling logs about here are cut out, but we are taking care to see that the supply will never become exhausted. Our licences will only permit of timber above a certain girth to be cut, the intention being to give the younger growth an opportunity to mature, and the cutters are bound by the regulations to stack the heads and limbs about the stump to keep the forest floor clear, and give the young saplings a chance to thrive. Where there is no young timber coming up we re-afforest by planting out seedlings."

"What advantage does the State gain by its supervision and work?" asked Jack.

"Well," said Barker, "we are ensuring a supply of timber for posterity. The forest of wealth of this country has been squandered recklessly in the past because few have realised the demands of the future. Countless millions of pounds worth of logs have been destroyed – burned up – by settlers clearing their farms, and it is still going on; but our educative efforts of forest protection are having results, slight it must be admitted, but nevertheless definite. We hope in time to bring the people to realise to the full, the wealth that lies in the timbered land."

"But does the State get any revenue from this?" was Jack's query.

"We charge licence fees to all cutters and sawmills. Royalty at varying rates, averaging about a shilling per hundred feet, is charged on all timber hewn or sawn, and we sell concessions, or exclusive rights, such as Mr. Campbell proposes to acquire, and grazing rights to reserves. The department is not conducted to make money, but to pay its way and exercise a strict supervision over the forests."

As the forester finished speaking they came upon a party of men engaged in felling trees. Two were at work at the base of one mighty woodland monarch with a cross-cut saw; farther on, two big-muscled axemen were perched precariously some thirty feet high on poles morticed into the trunk of a tree, cutting great chips with their keen-edged axes as they balanced on these frail supports. At regular intervals of about two hundred feet in a straight line, men were at work with axe or saw on the trees, and Jack expressed aloud his fear that some of the cutters might be injured when the giants fell.

"Just wait a while!" said Barker.

Some ten minutes later a loud "Coo-ee!" from the rear workers caused a cessation of the cutting. Presently the men, carrying bright-bladed axes or keen-teethed, springing saws, stamped through the undergrowth towards the spot where the horsemen had halted, at the first tree of the line, and disposed themselves in careless groups among the fern. The two men at the saw on the first tree continued to push-pull, push-pull, with rhythmic deliberateness, until an ominous creaking heralded its impending downfall. At first there was a gentle swaying of the giant bole, then a shuddering, as though it sensed approaching doom, and at last a rushing sound, like the whirring of the wings of the black swans on the lake, as the towering trunk hurtled downward. But before the tree reached the ground it struck into the spreading branches of a neighbour that had been nearly cut through by the axemen, and this, too, toppled and fell. It, in turn, brought down the next in line, and so each falling tree toppled over another, until a dozen were lying, end on end, in a long straight line. This, Jack was informed, was a "drive".

"You do it well!" said Jack to one of the axemen.

"Wot?" was the brief response.

"Why, making one tree knock down all the others that are in the line that are partly cut through," answered Jack.

"Aw, that's dead easy," said the uncommunicative bushman, shouldering his axe and starting off to work again.

Jack Burnside spent four days in the forest country with Campbell and Barker, returning to Tea Gardens firmly convinced that the old Scot's proposition was eminently sound. Having authority from Callister to give a decision, and, if favourable, to make the money available at once, he paid his own cheque over to the sawmiller, and signed, on Callister's behalf, the deed of partnership that Campbell had cautiously provided against such a contingency. Jack told his host nothing of the arrangement between himself and his friend at Bullangarra concerning the transaction, preferring to remain quite in the background.

When they were nearing Dungog a day or two later, Jack and "Wild Bullocks" were considerably surprised to overtake, lounging in the saddle behind a small mob of cattle, Brummy Collins and Joe Brady.

"Hallo!" said Jack. "What are you doing over this side?"

"Good-day," replied Collins. "I'm takin' these studs ter Hooke's from ol' George Lee's place at Merriwa, near Condobolin. They was bought there last year. An' what are youse doin' here?"

"Getting' a fill o' the coast, so's we'll appreciate the back country better," answered "Wild Bullocks" for his mate.

"By hell, you're right," said Collins nastily. "They're too damned inquisitive about here for me. I'm off back as soon as I deliver these bulls."

Jack was greeted by Raymond that night at Kirrawilla as though he were a beloved brother from whom he had been parted for many years.

22

"DAMNED WHEN THE DEVIL DRIVES!"

A carelessly-dropped remark by Jack Burnside at the dinner-table on the night of his return with "Wild Bullocks" from Port Stephens, that Brummy Collins of Condobolin was in the neighbourhood, had sent an icy blast of fear into Raymond Penderby's heart. That young man had been in the act of raising a cup to his lips when Jack spoke, and became so violently agitated at the news that his nerveless fingers refused their grip on the vessel, and it fell with a crash to the floor. All eyes were directed to him on the instant, but before any of the astonished diners could utter a word he staggered to his feet. Clutching the back of a chair to steady himself, he mumbled in a choked voice, "It is just a turn; the effects of malaria. If you will excuse me I will go to bed."

As he lurched towards the door the two girls hurried to his side, and with sympathetic ministrations and not a few tears they supported him to his room. Raymond was so overwhelmed in his panic that he had no word of thanks to offer the weeping maidens, and they promptly retired in extreme dejection, speculating mournfully as to their cousin's chance of seeing the night through. After the girls had passed out of earshot, Raymond locked the door, lighted the big kerosene lamp on his dressing-table, and threw himself onto the bed.

This unexpected appearance of Collins, he thought, could only portend one thing – murder, with himself the victim. Never before had death seemed so terrifying, for he had faced it with a laugh many a time during those reckless days in the East. Now that success seemed within his reach, when he was on the verge of evolving some scheme to grasp Burnside's inheritance, together with the portion of one of his cousins, he was to be murdered in cold blood by a gang of brutal bushmen for mere revenge. But was it revenge? This thought encouraged others more hopeful that flashed through his active mind, and within an hour he had succeeded not only in subduing his feeling of terror but in formulating a bold and simple plan that would be likely to ensure his safety, at least as far as Collins was concerned.

Raymond rose at dawn next day, and was urging his horse at top speed along the Dungog road before the folk at Kirrawilla had risen, and his absence disturbed the girls greatly. At seven o'clock he was riding across the camping reserve at the back of the town, where he guessed that Collins would be with the bulls. In the far corner he found the drovers, Brummy and Brady, preparing a meal at the camp fire. He rode up to them boldly.

"Good day, Brummy!" he called out.

Collins and Brady stared at him in stupefaction. For a full minute there was a tense silence, broken at last when the elder bushman burst into a torrent of blasphemous profanity. The fury of the explosion did not abate for five minutes, during which Raymond sat on his horse, the figure of stoic endurance. When at last Collins ceased for want of breath and further adjectives, the young medical student spoke.

"Now, if you have quite finished, Brummy, perhaps you will listen to me," he said, and then impatiently waved aside a further profane interruption from the infuriated drover. "You think that I have robbed you, and from your point of view you are perfectly justified. But you have never heard my side of the business. That night I had you arrested I was preparing to clear out of the country, because the detectives were after me. I never received a penny of that money on account of the sale of the sheep, because someone else collected it."

This colossal lie staggered the others completely.

"Who got it, then?" they both yelled, confounded by the announcement and the vehement sincerity with which it was uttered.

"I have never found out!" answered Raymond steadily. "When the last draft of sheep was being sold I was around the yards at Homebush, posing as Burnside. There were four or five Condobolin squatters there, who recognised the sheep as coming from Bullangarra. One of them spoke to me, calling me Burnside, and mentioned the fact that our sheep were selling well. I could not explain that I was not Burnside, nor that the sheep did not come from Bullangarra – those men could not be fooled – so I walked off.

"As I went I heard one of the auctioneers explain to the man that the sheep had been consigned by Collins, from Wyalong, and there followed the loud words of an ensuing argument over the matter, during which the squatter angrily declared that he knew the Bullangarra sheep, and that if anyone named Collins had consigned them they had been stolen.

"Later on, I saw this inquisitive Condobolin man with the auctioneer who sold the sheep, and a detective. Naturally I left hurriedly, but I mustered up sufficient courage to demand the cheque next day. The firm refused to pay me until further enquiries had been made. The detective interviewed me two or three times, but I succeeded in bluffing them for several weeks.

"Then, one day, when I went again to collect the cheque, I was told that it had been paid to me the day before. My indignant denial that I had received it made the agents more suspicious. The night that you came in on me I had just been warned that I was to be arrested on the following day.

"A friend of mine, a detective, who was under an obligation to me, had given me the hint and advised me to clear out. He had the case in hand, and promised to give me time to slip away. I left next day for Japan, not waiting to make inquiries or say good-bye to a soul, because I naturally believed that you all had been arrested, or that someone had 'put the pot on'.

"I had to give up everything, my career, my home, my prospects, and live like a dog among filthy savages in a climate hotter than hell. Do you think I would have done that if I had gotten the money? I was afraid to return, and I drifted around those God-forsaken wilds for two years, working at anything that offered, often starving, and always in terror of being recognised and arrested.

"It was only after a chance overhearing of a talk between two drunken grooms who had gone over to Samarang with horses, that I mustered up courage to return to Sydney. They spoke about the Circle Y ewes, and how no one had ever been traced in connection with the matter, and I, who was then working as a fireman on the steamer, felt easy for the first time in those awful years, when I over-heard their talk."

"Well, I'm damned!" said Collins, evidently impressed by the emotion that Raymond evinced in his recital, but still doubting. "Ain't yer got any idea who got the cash?"

"To tell you the truth," said Raymond with a great show of candour, "for a long time I believed that you had 'double-crossed' me and somehow got it yourself. Then I began to see that I must be wrong, and when I found that it was safe to return to New South Wales I registered a determination to ferret the matter out and deal with the man who swindled us. I only landed in Sydney three days ago, and from something I heard then I determined to come up here on the track of the man I suspect – Jack Burnside, that damned jackaroo."

"That bloke!" exclaimed Collins. "How the devil could he be in on it?"

"I have found out that he was in Sydney," explained Penderby, glibly, "about the time that the cheque was collected, so if I could impersonate him, what was there to prevent him doing likewise in regard to me and collecting the money? He has got plenty of cash. Where did it come from? You know he's no fool, and he might easily have got onto our game without our knowing it. If he did, and I can get even the slenderest evidence in proof, I will put him behind bars."

"He won't get there," said Collins, with a savage oath. "If it's him I'll fix him fer good an' all. You leave that part o' the business to us."

Raymond was surprised at the ease with which he had so completely hoodwinked these men. A great elation filled his heart, for he had already formulated another scheme that would assuredly crown his machinations with success. He was about to ride off, when Collins commenced to cross-examine him regarding Burnside's movements on Bullangarra after the theft of the sheep, and the open doubt evidenced by the other disconcerted him momentarily. Putting a bold face on it, however, he announced with a certainty that brooked no contradiction that he had ample proof that the jackeroo had been in Sydney as he had stated, no matter what Brummy might say or think to the contrary. Further than that, he agreed to prosecute his investigations and furnish conclusive evidence of Jack's guilt within three months, the same to be submitted to the assembled gang at the Wongonga pub. With that Collins appeared satisfied, and Raymond, with a curt "S'long," rode off towards the town.

At Kirrawilla, Jack, "Wild Bullocks" and Thomas Penderby spent a pleasant day inspecting the property for the twentieth time. The old farmer never tired of admiring and praising his farm, nor did Jack feel wearied at listening to his rhapsodies. "Wild Bullocks" was bored, and boasted of it, but he preferred to accompany them rather than to loiter about the house to be annoyed by "them flamin' women".

Thomas Penderby's property comprised a little over two thousand acres, with some three miles of double frontage to the winding Williams River. He fattened cattle, ran two dairies and cultivated about a hundred acres of maize and lucerne, the profits from which had made him a wealthy man. He told Jack how he had first purchased the property, as a young man, for two thousand pounds, and had struggled to make a precarious living as a maize-grower for the cornflour mills at Dungog. Then dairying had become an established industry, and, being one of the first to seriously engage in it, prosperity came to him quickly.

"Dairying is wonderful, Jack," he said, "and the farmers that are well-to-do men around here today were so nearly starving thirty years ago that they had to go out looking for road-work to keep themselves in food. I had to do it, and I'm not ashamed of it. But the milking cow made us rich. The cow and co-operation. If it were not for the co-operative factories the industry would not be nearly so profitable."

"How is that?" inquired Jack.

"The farmers are the co-operative owners of practically every butter, bacon and cheese factory along the coast," explained the old man. "That means that all the profits go back into their own pockets instead of into those of the middlemen, and as farmer directors elected by the shareholders manage the business affairs there is little chance of leakages. Then there are big co-operative distributing agencies in the cities that sell the output of the factories locally at a figure that represents London parity.

"In the flush seasons the exportable surplus goes to England in the refrigerating chambers of the ships, and realises big prices there. This profit gets back to the shareholders also. Then there is a co-operative box factory that makes the butter-boxes and saves the factories money. The cheese and bacon are handled co-operatively as well. All we want now is a co-operative buying house, from which we can purchase all our supplies, and there is a move to establish that now among all sections of the primary producers. Co-operation has made the dairy industry, right enough, and we are the only men on the land that have never had to go cap-in-hand to the government for concessions. We are so united that we can demand our rights."

"But dairying is tedious and tiresome, isn't it?" asked Jack.

"What work on the land isn't?" was the reply. "When I first started here with thirty cows, I had two boys from the State Reformatory and the missus to help me. We got up at daylight to finish the milking by seven o'clock. I did the separating, and then drove the cart in to the factory with the cream on board, while the missus and the boys cleaned up, fed the 'poddies' – the young calves – and got ready for the evening milking. The separating and washing-up was generally finished by half-past nine, and then we went to bed. It was seven days a week: milking, 'poddying', a bit of ploughing, messing round generally, but it paid. I soon had a hundred cows and plenty of hired labour – which is very unsatisfactory, I must say – but I kept getting richer."

"You don't dairy yourself, now?" said Jack.

"No," the old farmer replied. "I gave it up. The dairies I run are on the shares. I provide the land, cows, plant and residence while the farmer supplies the labour. I take two-thirds of the profits of the cream, half the pigs and half the poddies. It pays well, for last year from No. 1 dairy, the one that Kelly runs, I took sixteen thousand pounds as my share, and from the other, eleven thousand. They have less than two hundred acres between them, but it is good country. I was offered fifty pounds an acre for the lot lately, and I laughed at it."

The old farmer then pointed out the model dairy that Kelly managed. The yards, with cobbled floors, were spotlessly clean. The bails, ten in number, were under a high iron-roofed open structure, on a cemented floor, and the connections and tubes of the milking machines were neatly hung on the white-washed uprights. Labour-saving devices were prominent everywhere. The engine that provided power for the milking machines also drove the separator, and the milk was gravitated to the separator room through pipes that could be removed easily for cleaning. The skim-milk was carried off to the feeding troughs, where the young calves, taken from their mothers when two or three days old, were fed. A man and three boys did the whole work of the place, including sufficient farming to provide winter feed.

After old Thomas Penderby had explained the working of the plant, he showed Jack a set of charts that greatly interested him. These contained particulars of the daily testings of the cows. Each animal was numbered, and every day its milk was tested, whereby the dairyman was enabled to locate any cow whose milk was deficient in butter-fat, and which was consequently reducing the average value of the yield. There were no non-payers on the farm, the old man said.

When they were proved to be poor yielders, they were culled, fattened and sold.

But although Jack was impressed by what he had seen and heard, he told his host that dairying did not appeal to him. He had also seen a few farms in the vicinity where the milking was done by hand, and where little children, from the age of seven years onward, handled half a dozen cows before they trudged wearily to the school three or four miles away.

"To tell you the God's truth," said the old farmer, "I hate it myself. The kiddies are slaves on too many places, and it's no credit to the parents that they are rich at the expense of their children. My girls, thank Heaven, have never had to milk a cow in their lives, although their poor old mother spent many a morning in a wet, muddy yard, with me, 'teat-pulling' in the old days."

When they returned to the house late in the afternoon, they found Raymond Penderby on the verandah with the two girls, all in a state of supressed excitement.

"Oh father," exclaimed Doris as the old man came up, "Raymond has persuaded us to go to Sydney when he returns, and we are not going to wait for you, because he is leaving tomorrow."

"Well, bless my heart," said her father, "this is very sudden. What will your mother say?"

"Mum is busy packing," said Doris in tones that clinched the argument.

"Yes, and I'm going to make my will," laughed Millie. "Raymond says that a lion might eat me at the Zoo."

This matter of making a will, quite a common topic of conversation in the country, provoked an extremely good-natured discussion, the upshot of which was that, at the suggestion of Raymond, and dared thereto banteringly by the vivacious Millie, Jack and "Wild Bullocks" also agreed to make their wills on the spot. The old shearer made no secret of the disposition of his estate: he bequeathed it unconditionally to Jack Burnside. Jack, however, frowned long over the neatly written form that the skilful Raymond had prepared. At last he wrote a few brief sentences, and calling on his old mate and

Mr. Thomas Penderby to witness, he attached his signature along with theirs at the foot of the document. Raymond, straining eagerly to read its contents, saw at a glance that Jack Burnside had devised all his worldly possessions, after death, to Molly Forbes.

When Jack folded up the document, he handed it to "Wild Bullocks", saying, "There, old chap! If I'm 'knocked out' at any time, see that my wishes are carried out."

"My oath I will!" said "Wild Bullocks".

"And I'll help you, Uncle," supplemented Raymond.

"Yair, when yer flamin' well asked," snapped the bushman, angrily.

On the following afternoon, Thomas Penderby, Raymond, and Jack Burnside were sauntering by the river in search of wild ducks. Each had a gun, and each was keen on the chase. The old man was openly anxious concerning his nephew's careless handling of his weapon, and took occasion to reprimand him sharply several times as they walked quietly along the banks. Raymond, however, treated the warnings with scant heed and much levity, claiming that what he didn't know about guns could be told in two syllables.

They had entered a small patch of wattle fringing a wide pool, on which a small flock of ducks were swimming, when the old man whispered to his companions to steal silently to the water's edge, in order to get a clear shot as the birds rose. Jack led the way, Raymond following, with his uncle in the rear. As they reached the bank, the old man whistled, and the ducks rose in front of them, and flew downstream with a great whirring of wings. Raymond flung his gun up, and at the same instant Jack Burnside, half-turning towards him, fell in a flash to his knees, and with the explosion his hat was blown yards away, riddled with shot. Some subconscious instinct had warned him to fall; what it was he could never understand. Had he remained standing, or had he himself attempted to shoot, his head would have intercepted the charge from the other's weapon.

As Jack dropped, the old farmer cried out in horror. Raymond stood, rooted to the spot, gazing at Jack, his face livid with a terrible fear. Then the young man rose deliberately, and, looking Raymond coldly in the eyes, he said in even, steady tones, "If you ever set out to murder anyone again, I would advise you to be quicker on the rise."

And picking up his weapon, he walked away.

Next day, Jack and "Wild Bullocks" left Kirrawilla for Sydney. Raymond had postponed his departure for a further day.

23

"PRAY LESS - DAM MORE."

"I've got ter damn well stop in Sydney fer a fortnight," said "Wild Bullocks" to Jack Burnside, as they were seated in the smokeroom of the Australia on the night of their arrival from Dungog. "I'd go straight back ter the Lachlan, only I promised Jim I'd stop ter the flamin' shivoo he's givin' in me honour. Why won't yer stop with me? All Tom's family is comin' down."

"I want to see Callister," said Jack, wondering whether, if he decided to remain, he would have sufficient fortitude to refrain from seeking out Molly. "No," he continued, "I am afraid that I will have to deprive myself of your company for a few weeks, old mate."

"Burnside! By Jove, this is lucky!" This interjection, in a jovial voice, caused Jack to turn sharply. The speaker was Callister himself. As they shook hands warmly, Jack inquired the reason of the other's presence in Sydney.

"I am sacked from Bullangarra," said Callister, smilingly.

"Sacked. You?" exclaimed Jack incredulously.

"Snatched yer time," put in "Wild Bullocks".

"Well," explained Callister, "it is not so bad as you imagine. Bullangarra is on the market for forty-five thousand pounds, a low figure for such a good place, and when it is sold, as it is sure to be, my occupation there will have gone. The company has offered me another billet on a west Queensland property, but I am too old to face the far out-back again. I intended to go up to Port Stephens and catch you there if possible before you concluded any deal with my brother-in-law."

"I have settled everything, and committed you for two thousand pounds," said Jack.

"If you have done that it cannot be helped," Callister went on. "I have not much capital to command, and that two thousand just now would have enabled me to carry out a plan that I had formed; but I can wait for a year."

"If the deal with Campbell has embarrassed you," said Jack, "and you would rather not invest the money in that spec., I will relieve you. From what I saw, however, I am convinced that you could not get so good a return from the capital elsewhere."

"Tell me about the proposition," demanded Callister.

Jack thereupon detailed the arrangements entered into between him and Campbell, enthusiastically describing the great forests about the lakes, and assuring his listener that within six months they would more than double their money. Callister heard the particulars of the project with intent interest.

"It was my intention to buy an irrigation farm at Mildura," he said, after Jack's explanation had ended, "for I have promised myself for a long while that I would retire and settle on an irrigable area, where I could grow fruit and vines. I will put the money into Alex's scheme now, but when I withdraw my capital I'll buy a small farm on the Murray."

Callister and Jack discussed their business arrangements for some time, satisfactorily settling the financial part of it. Over a drink, later, the old manager announced his intention of paying a visit to the Mildura settlements, and asked Jack if he would accompany him.

"When do you start?" the young man inquired.

"If you will come, I am prepared to leave tomorrow night, by the

Melbourne express. We can spend a week or two looking around, then get back to Condobolin, around by Blayney way."

"I'll come," announced Jack.

"Lor' lumme!" said "Wild Bullocks", querulously, "Wot are yer goin' ter do about me?"

"Your brother will look after you," said Jack smilingly, "and perhaps your nephew will lend a hand."

"That blarsted swine! No fear!" said the old bushman decisively. "I'll roll me bluey first, an' waltz her home, before I knock around with Mister bloody Raymond Penderby!"

"What?" exclaimed Callister in surprise. "Are you an uncle of Ray Penderby?"

"Yairs, worse luck!" assented "Wild Bullocks" in great disgust.

Jack then explained several matters of the family history of the Penderbys, informing Callister that he had not mentioned it to him before in deference to the wishes of his mate.

"Do you know?" said Callister at last, "I'm hanged if I could stand that Raymond towards the end of his visit to Bullangarra. When I first met him in Sydney I saw a good deal of him, and was so charmed with his manner that I invited him up for a holiday. He certainly did not improve on acquaintance."

"He's a fair mongrel!" asserted the uncle.

Three days later, in the afternoon, Callister and Jack Burnside were nearing Mildura. For several hours their way lay across mallee-covered stretches that rivalled in monotony the dreary plains on the Lachlan when drought held sway. As the train rolled onward they eyed the landscape dubiously.

"We're only a few miles from Mildura," said Callister, "and if this is a fair sample of the country it is the poorest I have ever seen."

"I don't know how they can grow anything about here," added Jack.

The stunted mallee scrub, with the hungry red soil in between the trees made the landscape a dismal one, and the haze of a fierce heat hung over the land. Here and there willy-willies rose in red columns and remained poised in the air, trembling and swaying.

"The true signs of a drought-stricken land," said Callister, indicating the spirals of dust.

Just then the train, as though alive to the dramatic possibilities of
the moment, perceptibly increased its speed, and, bursting through
the last scrub belt, rushed without warning on the most picturesque
scene of rural beauty the two men had ever beheld. On every side,
and stretching away far into the distance, they saw a bewildering
array of orchards and vineyards, the rich, deep green of the trees, the
lighter shades of the vine leaves, and tints of the purple amber of
luscious grapes blending in a harmony of colour that was enthralling.
Around them lay a land of undreamed-of richness, a veritable garden
gleaming with a wealth of wondrous munificence.

"By Jove!" enthused Callister, at length. "It's a miracle, that's what
it is!"

Jack nodded agreement. He had no words to express his
emotions.

That evening, seated on the balcony of the hotel, they learned
something of the history of the Murray irrigation area, the "Sun-
raysed Settlements" as they are now known throughout the wide
world. They had met a newspaper man, a voluble individual who had
spent many years on the area, who knew every farm and every man
within a thirty-mile radius, and who was eager to enlighten strangers.

Mildura, they were told, had not always been so fruitful or so
prosperous. The very name was a local Aboriginal word, meaning "a
place where flies get in your eyes". Its history was one of struggle
against handicaps that had daunted all but the lion-hearted and the
optimistic.

In 1886 two Canadians, W. B. and George Chaffey, had entered
into a contract with the Victorian Government whereby they agreed,
in return for a grant of fifty thousand acres of the then scrub-covered
land on the banks of the Murray, and the right to subsequently
purchase a further two hundred thousand acres at twenty shillings
per acre, to spend over six hundred thousand pounds over twenty
years, to open up the area, to put in pumping plants, construct drains
and channels, erect canneries, etc., and generally transform a wilder-

ness into a garden. The deed of the land was executed to them on May 31, 1887, and the great work commenced.

The task before those far-seeing brothers, both of whom were equipped with a thorough knowledge of irrigation as it had been successfully applied in America, was a herculean one. To create a fruitful settlement on an area only 153 feet above sea level, and with an annual rainfall of but six inches, seemed impossible. Yet they persevered.

Settlers came, orchards were planted, and success hoped for and prayed for. But success was long in coming. Ill-luck dogged the settlement, and failure seemed inevitable. George Chaffey, disappointed and sick at heart, returned to America; his brother, with an abounding faith in the potentialities of the settlement, remained and set about finding some practical way of wresting success from obdurate Fate.

For years the grim and determined struggle went on, and at last W. B. Chaffey, who had become the dominating figure of the settlement – "The Boss", they called him – saw Fortune smile. Farms that a few years before could hardly be given away came to sell for over a hundred pounds per acre. Settlers who had lived for years on the very verge of bankruptcy had become wealthy and prosperous. New land was being cleared and planted everywhere; new settlements had sprung up across the Murray, in New South Wales, and across the border in South Australia, until there was, as the visitors could see, one wide, smiling garden, nearly fifty miles across.

The river, the wide, muddy Murray, provided a seemingly inexhaustible supply of water for the irrigated farms. The main pumping plant, a mass of never-idle machinery, was perched on the edge of the stream at the White Cliffs, and the life-blood that it poured over the red, loamy soil was spread through countless arteries in the form of channels, ditches and drains. The pumping, being costly, meant that the water rate was two pounds per acre, as against five shillings per acre at the Yanco irrigation area on the Murrumbidgee, in New South Wales, where the water was distributed by gravitation. Yet in the face of these high rates, settlers could make an income up to a hundred pounds per acre from their blocks.

In reply to Callister's query, the loquacious scribe stated that the principal products of the area were dried peaches, prunes, apricots, pears, sultanas, lexias and raisins, and wine and brandy. He described how, in the harvest season, fruit-pickers from all quarters denuded the trees of their luscious burdens. How the stone-fruits were seeded, dipped and dried in the sweat-boxes in the rays of the summer sun. How the grapes and berries were similarly treated. How the wine grapes were pressed and converted into table wines; how the residue was converted into brandy at the distilleries.

He told them of the other settlements – Curlwaa in New South Wales, where one man, Tolley, had brought prosperous order out of chaos; of Wentworth, of Renmark, of Merbein, all practically within sight of where they sat.

Jack and Callister were absorbed. The story, told as it was in simple but forceful language, illustrated with interesting reminiscences and adorned with tales of success or failure, thrilled them unspeakably. Both were impressed, and quite emotionally, with the possibilities of the wonderful, but undeveloped back country that they knew so well. At last, Jack broke a long silence.

"Tell me," he said, "how is the tremendous output of this area marketed?"

The old journalist rose to his feet. Leaning far out over the railing of the balcony, he extended his arms as though to embrace his beloved settlements, and gazed out into the night.

"We sell our products now," he said, "where best we can – mostly in Australia, competing against the foreign product that, I don't know why, Australians too often prefer to the better, cleaner local article. But," and his voice took on a prophetic tone, "I see great days ahead. Days when every article that we produce will be sold co-operatively. When some far-seeing, dominating man with the energy of a Hercules, the will of an Alexander, and the executive capacity of a Napoleon, will seize hold of things, and so direct them that the disunited settlements will combine to buy and sell as one man. I see the day when the products of our orchards, raised by the glorious rays of the sun, our sun-raysed fruits, will be known throughout the world, and will oust the foreign products from every market. Then will the settlement smile truly."

This enthusiasm was contagious. Jack, aroused by the note of prophecy, and greatly in earnest, asked if the days hoped for were far distant.

"No," replied the journalist. "The dawn is here. The settlers have awakened, and the man who will accomplish what for years has been my dream can be found. Within a very few years you will find that all that I have predicted, and more, will come to pass. I am an old man now, but I will live to see thirty thousand settlers making comfortable and easy livings here, where once was nought else but barren scrub and desolate plain."

The visitors spent the ensuing week driving around the settlements, the old pressman having appointed himself as their guide, and friend. He conducted them to homes innumerable, and from the contented settlers they verified all that he had told them. They found that the orchards ranged in area from ten to fifty acres, that the red soil, though far from rich, was wonderfully responsive to moisture; that no man who was industrious and enthusiastic need fail.

As they were returning to the hotel one evening, Callister gave expression to the thoughts that had been running through his mind.

"This place has made a marvellous impression on me," he said, "and I have made up my mind that I will buy a property and settle here. It is going to be a wrench for an old man like me to leave the Lachlan district, where my life has been spent, and where my people lived and died. It is going to hurt me more when I realise that the opportunities exist there for this same sort of thing; that half a million people could be settled on irrigation farms along its valley, where today only sheep-walks exist. The Lachlan land, or all that part of it along the river, with its many creeks and billabongs, is too valuable for sheep; it should be producing something of greater worth to the country. Sheep produce wealth, it is true, but not population, and we want our empty spaces peopled by a sturdy race of vigorous, prosperous pioneers."

"They will irrigate on the Lachlan someday," said Jack hopefully.

"Someday!" the old manager continued, bitterly. "Yes, some day, when you and I are dead and gone. Someday, after a foreign race has cast envious eyes on our unpeopled lands and seized them for their own! Someday, when the nations justly decide that this vast continent is no longer to be entrusted to the care of five million people, mostly crowded into cities on the sea-board, who do not realise the value of the gift they hold. Someday, when it is too late!"

"Amen!" responded the old journalist.

At the hotel Callister found a telegram, which resulted in his deciding to return to Bullangarra immediately. He and Jack left Mildura by train on the following morning, and arrived at Condobolin some three days later. They were greatly surprised to see "Wild Bullocks" at the Royal Hotel as the bus deposited them at the door of that establishment.

"Thought you were still in Sydney!" cried out Jack to his old mate.

"No flamin' fear," said "Wild Bullocks". "If youse ever catch me in that place again, yer can have me hide. When I sticks up a 'Travellin' T' again it's goin' ter be ter some place where they don't trample over yer in the streets, an' run yer down with cabs an' trams an' motors, an' where a bloke can eat his flamin' tucker how he likes without the whole damn mob starin' at yer as if yer were a double-headed yeller dingo."

"Was Sydney too crowded?" asked Callister, with a smile.

"Blimey!" exclaimed the old bushman in horror. "The people was as thick as galahs on a crop! I only went out once with ol' Jim, me brother, an' I got near killed so often that I wasn't game ter risk it again. I stuck ter the house fer three days, and then I hears me beautiful nephew talkin' over the phone ter Brummy Collins about comin' up here. From what I heard, I reckon Brum was leavin' that night, so I makes up me mind an' pulls out without nary a goodbye. Me an' Brum travelled up that night, an' I expect they're havin' me 'Welcome Home' down at Jim's without me."

"Hmm," said Callister, "Penderby and Collins were talking together! Did you hear much of the conversation?"

"Not much," said "Wild Bullocks", but they was goin' fer a long while. From the little I heard, though, I reckon Raymond, me beautiful relation, is comin' up here in a week or so."

"Rather strange," said Callister.

"Very strange," commented Jack, thoughtfully.

24

EUCHRE!

The Forbes mail coach deposited Raymond Penderby and his luggage at the Wongonga Hotel one afternoon in mid-February. Peg-leg Costigan limped out from the bar to give his guest a hearty welcome, for he had been apprised of his intended arrival days before.

"Have you got the 'strong' of the business?" Costigan asked, confidentially, as he showed his visitor into a shabbily furnished bedroom.

"I have!" exclaimed Raymond, emphatically. "It was that jackeroo – Burnside – right enough. I have sufficient written proof in my bag to convince Collins, although it might not satisfy a jury."

"If you can show us, plain enough," said Peg-leg grimly, "we'll settle him. Gun accidents happen out here, you know," he concluded with an evil leer.

"Er – yes!" said Raymond, confusedly, thinking of a former incident in this category.

"I never liked that bloke," added the publican. "I took a set on him the first time I spotted him and mistook him for you."

"Well, we will deal it out to him before long," commented Raymond, as he set about unpacking his bags. The publican retired to his bar to serve a clamorous customer.

Left alone, Raymond reflected with satisfaction on the manner in which his plans were making for success. He had successfully diverted the suspicions of the gang from himself onto his bitterest enemy, and he keenly appreciated the fact that their vengeance would take the form of such violence as would end Burnside's life. With Jack out of the way, the will held by his uncle, "Wild Bullocks", which bequeathed everything to Molly Forbes, could be sworn for probate and then he would put it to his father to hand over the amount that he held in trust for the deceased to his legatee.

He did not anticipate the slightest difficulty over this part of the affair, nor did he fear that the girl would reject his advances once the other was dead. He could fake a ceremony with a bogus clergyman, after which Molly would be as plastic as clay in his hands, and would permit him to handle her money. Once he had that in his grasp he would desert her, take a trip to America for six months, and on his return marry one of his cousins, Doris or Millie, he did not care which.

He had mapped out his course of action carefully, and with deliberate unscrupulousness. He could see no weak link in the chain of events that he was forging. There was no possible chance, he assured himself, of any of his plans miscarrying. With a feeling of warm elation, he met Collins in the bar-parlour an hour later, and proceeded to completely convince that worthy of Jack Burnside's guilt over the matter of the sale of the Circle Y wethers.

Believing that thoroughness was an excellent axiom, Raymond had made elaborate preparations to saddle Jack with his guilt. He showed for Brummy's inspection a statement purporting to have come from the auctioneers, declaring that they had paid the money to a man who, they admitted now, resembled Mr. Penderby but was not actually that gentleman. He showed letters, apparently having been written by Jack Burnside to Molly Forbes, intimating his intention of visiting Sydney on business for a few days about the time of the alleged wrongful collection of the cheque. He showed signed statements, seemingly from a dozen prominent Sydney men, setting out that they had seen Jack Burnside in the city on certain specified dates. As a trump card, he produced a receipt, on the form used by the selling firm, signed "T. Collins", in a handwriting that he declared to be that of the young jackeroo.

The documentary evidence clinched the matter. Collins was no scholar, and knew so little of the written language that he was easily convinced. As an afterthought, he suggested that Peg-leg might be permitted to scan the evidence, but to this Raymond entered an emphatic objection, for a number of various reasons.

"Well, that settles Mr. bloody Burnside!" said Collins, with deadly menace in his tones. "Me an' Bill M'Bean will fix the cow; but you've got ter help."

"Me?" queried Raymond, uneasily.

"Yes, you, yer blarsted swine. If it hadn't been fer your damned flashness, there'd have been none o' this. I'm sorry I ever let yer in on it."

"But I'm not going to assist in any violence," asserted Raymond, firmly.

"No," said Collins quietly. "I think yer too damn much of a cur fer that. But yer goin' ter go over ter his selection an' fix him, so as we can pot him from the scrub, an' so as yer can give evidence that he shot himself, or else met with an accident."

This proposal did not at all suit Raymond's plans, and he argued heatedly with his companion over it. Collins, however, proved inexorable, and finally secured a reluctant consent from the other after it was darkly hinted that it was not altogether a too difficult matter to remove from existence more than one troublesome person. It was decided, therefore, that Raymond should ride across the Burnside selection under the pretence of a friendly visit, and so arrange matters that on a fixed day, and a certain hour of the evening, he should contrive that Jack was to be at the road boundary gate of Yarran Plain. There, in a patch of scrub, Brummy and M'Bean would be waiting to do their part.

Greatly fearing for the success of his machinations with this errand of treachery and murder in front of him, Raymond rode to Yarran Plain next day. As he approached the hut that was the young selector's home, he came upon "Wild Bullocks" and the silent Carroll boy grubbing out a stump.

"Hullo, uncle!" he called out. "Where's Jack?"

The old man, who had recognised the horseman as he had ridden up, entirely disregarded the greeting, and went on calmly with his work.

"Not pleased to see your affectionate nephew, eh?" Raymond sneered.

"No! He's too much of a damned mongrel."

Young Carroll broke his usual silence with an outburst that bore a striking family resemblance to the cachinnation of a kookaburra. Raymond dug in the spurs and cantered off to where he saw Jack at one of the hay stacks.

As "Wild Bullocks" spat on his calloused hands and grasped the crowbar again he muttered, half-aloud, "I wonder what his game is. He ain't up ter no good wherever he is, but what he wants with Jack beats me."

Jack was more than astonished when he saw Penderby ride up, and, like his mate, he speculated as to the reason for the honour of this visit. However, he greeted the young man coolly, and enquired his business.

"I have just come up here for a few weeks on a health trip," lied Raymond, glibly. "I have been staying across at Jemalong, and I promised the dad that I would run over to see how you were getting on with your selection. As he is very interested in you, he asked me to find out how you were shaping. I'll stay for a few days, if you don't mind."

"I am sorry," replied Jack, "but our accommodation for visitors is so limited that I have nowhere to put you."

"Don't worry about that," laughed the other. "I am used to roughing it, I'll camp under the wire fence if needs be. I came here to stay, so you cannot get rid of me thus easily."

Realising that Penderby was determined to force his presence on him, Jack surrendered with a bad grace.

"All right," he said. "But don't find fault with us if we live roughly.

You can camp in the hut in my bunk, and I'll tackle the machinery shed."

After some spirited debate, during the course of which Raymond virtuously and absolutely refused to dispossess his host of his bunk, it was arranged that the visitor should be quartered in the aforementioned shed, and he was to assist in the cooking if he felt, at any time, inclined to work. On these terms, Raymond Penderby was admitted to the routine of life on the selection.

For several days, matters progressed uneventfully on Yarran Plain. "Wild Bullocks" maintained an attitude of vituperative hostility towards his nephew at all times, a course of conduct that, naturally enough, forced the young man to seek Jack's company. For his part, Jack had developed such an antipathy towards his unwelcome guest that he experienced the greatest difficulty in maintaining even a semblance of civility in his speech with him. The silent Carroll lad, evidently with deep suspicions in his mind, said nothing and remained neutral. Nevertheless, he watched Penderby closely but dispassionately day and night, as though he expected some sudden manifestation of violence from him towards Jack.

Thus it was on the sixth day, and on account of having received a letter by the mailman, who passed the selection each night just after dusk on his trip to Bogan Gate, Raymond rode towards the Yarrabandai siding, followed, unobserved, by the silent boy. At the railway shed the lad saw the man meet and speak with two horsemen who had ridden from the direction of the river at the back of Burrawang homestead. Creeping stealthily to the shelter of a row of empty trucks, he clambered into one and strained to overhear the conversation. Only a confused murmur of their speech came to him, and he was not able to distinguish anything until Raymond turned to leave his companions.

Then he heard Brummy Collins, who he had recognised, say, "You have him at the boundary gate tomorrow night when the mailman is due, and we'll fix him. Joe and Tommy will block the coach a couple o' miles down the road, so there won't be no witnesses." Raymond had expressed assent and ridden off.

Half an hour later, the silent bush lad crept from his hiding place and ran towards his horse, which was tethered in the scrub a half a mile away. In his mind, already filled with suspicions of Raymond, he had become certain that Jack's life was to be attempted by these men, for it seemed clear to him that their words could refer to nothing else but that, and he now knew – what had caused "Wild Bullocks" so much wonder – the reason of Raymond's presence at Yarran Plain. He would forestall the plotters and warn Jack.

Mounting his horse, he turned away across country in the direction of the selection at top speed, hoping that the short cut would enable him to reach the place before Penderby, who would keep to the road. Through the scrub and over open patches of plain, the lad urged his stock-horse at breakneck speed. It was dark as he neared the western boundary of Jack's little farm, and he was forced to dismount from his horse to untie the wires at a spot where he could enter.

Impatient at this very brief delay, he rushed the horse through, and, not waiting to re-tie the wires, mounted hastily and spurred across a tiny clearing. The horse was galloping hard, with its rider sitting loosely in the saddle, and lightly holding the rein, in order to let the animal have his own head in the dark. Suddenly the horse faltered. One of its forefeet struck a rabbit hole, and in an instant it was floundering in a network of burrows. Its two forelegs sank down deeply, and pitching forward with its head doubled underneath, it fell heavily. Nor, beyond a few convulsive struggles, did it move again. Its neck had been broken. The lad was thrown forward as though propelled from a catapult, and he landed with a heavy thud. Nor did he move for many hours.

When the boy regained consciousness, it was broad daylight. For a long while he lay motionless, wondering dully how he came to be in the scrub at sunset. Suddenly there flashed across his understanding the recollection of his errand to warn his one friend of the danger that threatened, and he attempted to rise. As he did, his frame was wracked with the fiercest pain, and he sank back, limp, helpless, the sweat of agony starting from his forehead. For a long while he remained inert, watching the sun sinking out of sight behind the horizon of scrub. Then again, through his brain came the insistent reminder that Jack must be saved, and collecting his thoughts he realised that this was the evening of the deed, and that he must have lain in the bush a whole night and most of the day.

With a supreme effort he raised himself to a sitting posture. His head swam dizzily, and then slowly cleared, but a sharp stabbing pain in his right leg told him that something was seriously amiss. He looked down, and saw that the limb was lying in a queer, twisted fashion on the ground. He knew then that it was badly broken. A raging thirst burned at his throat, and he was sick with agony.

But the boundary gate was less than half a mile away, and he would get there somehow, in time to warn his friend. This driving thought filled his mind to the exclusion of all else, and he commenced his journey of torture. Crawling along the ground, dragging the shattered limb over the rough surface as he moved, the bush lad crept forward. The intensity of his torture, the excruciating grate of the shattered bone, wrung no cry from him. Silently he endured the wracking torment, and won yard after yard. Twice Nature succumbed beneath the awful strain, and he lay fainting. But always did the subconscious urging of his mind arouse and spur him onward. It is not surprising that in an hour he had gained only fifty yards. It is to be wondered at that he was ever able to move from where he fell.

As the stars showed like glittering points of fire in the darkening sky, he made his last effort, and as he lapsed into unconsciousness again he cried aloud in his anguish, "Jack! For God's sake, Jack!"

Jack Burnside was riding from his hut towards the boundary gate, a mile distant, to meet the mailman and post some important letters for Mr. Raymond Penderby, who was indisposed. As his horse ambled along the thick carpet of grass, sad, sweet memories of Molly filled his mind. He was conjuring up visions of the future, those moving pictures that so often flashed across his brain, and in every one of them there was Molly – and happiness. Even as he determined to seek out this girl of his heart, he heard, distinctly, in the still night air, that agonised appeal: "Jack! For God's sake, Jack!"

Turning his horse in the direction of the sound, he spurred forward, calling out loudly. For a quarter of a mile he rode, but found nothing. He reined up and listened intently; nothing stirred in the sombre, forbidding bush, and he was preparing to turn away when there fell on his ears a low, drawn moan of agony. Again, his horse plunged forward, but within a few hundred yards it propped, and with a snort of terror wheeled aside.

Pulling up, Jack saw a huddled form, black against the grey of the long, dry barley-grass. He leaped from his horse and rushed to the prostrate body. Gently he raised the head, and then recognised the silent boy of Mrs. Carroll's.

The lad opened his eyes. "Don't... go... boundary... gate tonight, Jack. They're goin'... ter... fix... yer!" The lad forced out the warning with a last despairing effort, and then collapsed into insensibility.

At the same instant, the dead, still silence of the night was shattered by two gunshot explosions from the direction of the boundary gate, and later by the sound of galloping hoofs on the metalled road.

As soon as Jack Burnside had left the hut to ride to the mail-box, Raymond Penderby emerged from his quarters in the machinery shed, and. Springing on his own horse, which was already saddled for the purpose, he followed quietly. He was wretchedly nervous as to the outcome of the plot, and, although he knew in his heart that it was madness for him to be abroad that night, an irresistible impulse drove him towards the spot that would soon be the scene of his rival's murder. As he kept Jack well in view, it was with the profoundest astonishment that he saw the young selector suddenly turn his horse and gallop into the bush, for no apparent reason. This strange action greatly disconcerted him, and when Jack did not return, but, instead, appeared to be going further away, he became fearful that his plot had been discovered. What was he to do? He must warn Collins and M'Bean at all hazards before Jack, with probable help, approached them from the road. He spurred up his horse and galloped towards the boundary gate.

25

THE PRICE THAT WAS PAID

The sun had not been visible over the rim of plains for half an hour when Father O'Connell neared the boundary gate of Jack Burnside's selection. As he turned around the patch of scrub near the gateway, the broken-winded, goose-rumped pony stopped dead in his tracks. This unusual procedure startled the old man out of a deep reverie, and, looking up, he beheld the body of a man lying in a pool of blood just inside the gate.

"Arrah, tis some accident," he muttered as he hurriedly clambered to the ground.

As he viewed the body he saw the gunshot wounds in the breast and in the head.

"Foul play, there's after being," he said aloud.

Then, taking care not to make fresh tracks near the body, he walked rapidly to Jack's house. There was no one about when he arrived, so, philosophically lighting up the fire, he prepared to brew a billy of tea. As he was engaged in this occupation, turning over in his mind the matter of the tragedy that he had just encountered, Jack and "Wild Bullocks" came up from the direction of the Carrolls'.

"There is after being a dead man at your front gate, Jack Burnside," said the old priest, in grave tones. "Shot in the head and chest with a shot-gun."

"Good God!" exclaimed Jack. "Who is it?"

"Tis a stranger to me," said the priest, "but come down at once."

The three hurried to the scene. There, on his side, lay the dead man, the ants and flies already swarming over the body.

"It's Penderby," exclaimed Jack. "Who could have shot him?"

Disturbing thoughts raced through Jack's brain. He had heard two shots and then galloping hoofs just after the Carroll boy had warned him not to go near the boundary gate. Had someone intended really to shoot him? He had thought that the boy's words had been the disordered ravings of delirium, and the shots he had forgotten. And how had Penderby come to be abroad when he was supposed to be lying ill? There was something behind it all that he could not understand.

"Tis a matter for the police," said Father O'Connell. "Someone had better ride to Burrawang to ring them up."

"I'll go," said "Wild Bullocks".

At that moment there was a clatter of approaching hoofs on the road, and the three men waited to see who the early travellers might be. In a few minutes there came into sight Sergeant Cahalan, the black tracker Moolbong, and Williams, the tall sunburnt inspector of the Commonwealth Mortgage Company.

"Hallo!" cried the sergeant. "What's up?"

"Raymond Penderby has been murdered," said Jack, shortly.

The three horsemen were out of the saddle in an instant. The sergeant, after a cursory inspection of the body, spoke to the tracker, who immediately commenced scanning the ground round about for traces of the murderers. After ten or fifteen minutes the grinning blackfellow returned to report.

"By cripes, boss!" he chuckled, in the cheeky, good-humoured fashion of his kind. "Ol' feller Brummy Collins an' Bill M'Bean bin sit down alonga this place long time. Bimeby that feller bin ridin' up to the gate; they bin walkin' alonga scrub little bit, an' then bin shootem. Then they bin gallopin' like hell alonga road."

"How does he know the names of the men?" demanded Jack of the sergeant.

"Oh, that plurry easy," the blackfellow put in, with another chuckle. "We bin chase'm two, three, five days now. I been goin' to 'rest 'em soon for stealin' sheep along Circle Y."

"Yes," said Williams. "We have been on their tracks for some days now. We lost them at Yarrabandai two days ago, but picked them up last night. Moolbong was running them down when the trail brought us here."

"But," said Jack, greatly puzzled, "did they steal those sheep from Bullangarra? I thought that was forgotten long ago."

"By mostly everyone but me," said Williams, gravely. "I don't let a thing beat me once I start, and I have gathered enough evidence to convict two or three men."

"But why on earth should they shoot Penderby?" demanded Jack, still bewildered.

"Supposing he was one of the gang, and they mistook him for you?" said the inspector, cryptically. "I believe that mistakes have occurred before respecting your identity." With that he left Jack in a state of extreme stupefaction.

An hour later the last mortal remains of the young medical student were being conveyed in a bumpy spring-cart to the police morgue at Condobolin. Father O'Connell and the doctor had set the Carroll boy's leg, and that young lad maintained his usual silence through the torturing ordeal. To Jack and the inspector only did he tell the story of Raymond's meeting with the gang, and of his own subsequent attempt to warn his friend. The simple tale of heroism brought tears to the eyes of the young selector, and they brimmed over unashamed down his cheeks as he wrung the hand of the young bush boy.

"I will never be able to thank you sufficiently, nor do enough for you," said Jack in a hushed, broken voice, for he realised fully the agonies that the boy had endured for his sake.

"Garn," whispered the lad. "You'd o' done the same fer me, I know, because yer a bloody right bloke!"

Old Mr. James Penderby was present at the inquest on the body of his murdered son held at Condobolin two days later, but he was a broken, aged man, as he heard the verdict of wilful murder recorded against Collins and M'Bean, both of whom were present in custody. Collins had maintained a defiant and sullen attitude from the hour of his arrest, but M'Bean, who was at heart a craven, had confessed to the murder, besides telling also the story of the sheep-stealing and of the theft of the colt from Jack by the gang.

The same evening, Jack, Williams, Callister, and the old lawyer were seated in a quiet parlour at the hotel, discussing the story of the tragedy. Mr. Penderby scarcely spoke; but, though there was a far-away look in his eyes, he paid the closest attention to all that Williams was saying. The inspector was explaining his activities in the matter.

"I did not suspect Raymond Penderby definitely," he said, "until after Mr. Burnside's arrest at Bogan Gate, when Thomas told me much that set me thinking. I knew from the commencement that Collins and his gang were guilty, but every clue I followed brought me up against a dead end. I discovered that Raymond had lost heavily at the races just after the sheep had been sold, but I never dreamed for an instant that he would be likely to rob the robbers. Then his trip to the East seemed quite natural, in view of what you told me, Mr. Penderby." He turned to the old man.

"It was after Jack's arrest at Bogan Gate," continued Williams, "that I took up the chase again. I came here, and spent over a month making searching enquiries regarding the young man's movements while he was at Bullangarra, for by that time I firmly believed that he was the link needed to complete a chain of evidence that would lead to the capture of the whole gang. I learned sufficient to know that Raymond had impersonated Jack Burnside at many places, even with the stolen sheep when they were being travelled towards Wyalong.

"The only thing that remained was to clear up the matter of the collection of the cheque from the auctioneers. I experienced but little difficulty in this. I was able to identify the endorsements on the back of the cheque, as well as the signature to the receipt, as Penderby's handwriting, for both the firm and the banks assisted me greatly. I also discovered that the young man had a separate account in the name of Philpotts in another bank. This, together with the information I obtained from a few bookmakers, enabled me to complete my case.

"The only thing that remained after that was to get hold of my man. He was still in the East, as far as I could learn, and his father did not know when he might return. I decided, therefore, to wait, knowing that he was bound to come back sooner or later."

"Why did you not inform me of this?" asked the old lawyer.

"He was your son," replied the other, gently. "You would never have believed me."

"No," assented Mr. Penderby, brokenly, "no, I would not. But go on!"

"Well, I bided my time," continued Williams, "and a fortnight ago I learned that the young fellow had returned. He had arrived much earlier, I found out subsequently, but had gone to Dungog, where he spent some time, and afterwards while he was in Sydney he kept away from those places where he would be recognised. Only that he was in love with your head typiste, Mr. Penderby, a girl named Molly Forbes, I would not have heard of him when I did. He used to take her about a lot before he left for Japan, and I understood from him that they were to be married."

At this, Jack gave a great start. A horrible suspicion was forming itself in his mind, and the pictures that flashed vividly before him were very disturbing.

"Yes," went on Williams, gravely, "he used to haunt this young girl's home after his return from Dungog, and every night he visited her. I passed the two of them, one evening, and I could not help overhearing the girl tell him that she would marry no man until she was sure that someone, whom she spoke of as Jack, was dead."

"My God," groaned Jack, who now realised the treachery of his supposed friend and the loyal true-heartedness of the woman he loved.

The others were astonished at his ejaculations, but he controlled his feelings quickly, and bade Williams to proceed.

"The rest was easy," the inspector went on. "I called to see the girl next day, but she was not at work. The day afterwards, however, I found her, and learned that Raymond had left for Wongonga on the previous evening. I was then on his track, and coming to Condobolin I obtained warrants for his arrest, and that of the two Collins brothers, M'Bean, Brady and Gillett. I accompanied the sergeant to Wongonga to be present at the end, but there we were told that they had never been seen there. Old Peg-leg Costigan, the publican, swore to us that he did not know Penderby, but when Thomas came along he altered his tune, although he declared that the man we called Penderby was known to him as Burnside.

"We got no satisfaction from him, however, so we set out after Collins and M'Bean, who, we learned from Thomas, had just ridden to the river across his place. We followed their tracks for days, for they doubled about all over the place, a circumstance that encouraged the belief that they were aware we were after them. This was wrong, however, as their doubling had more to do with some of the Burrawang sheep than with us. Anyhow, we ran them down eventually to Burnside's gate – and you know the rest. The lot left alive are under lock and key, including that villainous old publican, and M'Bean's confession will make convictions easy."

"But why did they intend to kill me?" asked Jack, curiously. "I never did one of them a bad turn in my life, not even Ray."

"That baffles me completely," said the inspector. "There was no earthly reason for it."

"Perhaps I may enlighten you," said the old lawyer. "In looking through my poor boy's papers that were brought in from the Wongonga Hotel, I came across a number of very strange documents. I will not disclose their nature at this juncture, but I am convinced that he knew about a certain business matter in which I am interested, and which affects Burnside here, and wished to get Jack out of the way. This would have left him a clear field with the girl, for Jack is the one whom she loves."

"Did he love her so deeply, then," said Jack in an awed voice, "that he would encompass my death, in order to gain her?"

The old lawyer replied with another question. "Did you ever make a will, bequeathing everything you possessed to Miss Forbes? I have reason to believe that you handed it to my brother, whom you know as "Wild Bullocks". As a matter of fact, he lodged it with me for safe custody."

"I forgot that will," admitted Jack. "But still, I cannot see how my few thousands would have benefitted him."

"Perhaps not. Not just now," replied the lawyer, musingly. "You will know before many days; in fact, just as soon as you seek out the girl who has waited for you so loyally through all these weary years."

"I am leaving for Sydney tomorrow morning," announced Jack, decisively.

At this, Callister and Williams went to their rooms, leaving Jack and the old man alone.

For a long while there was silence. Jack smoked stolidly, and the old man polished and re-polished his glasses, until no speck of dust could possibly have dimmed their surface.

"This has been a terrible blow to me, Jack," the old man said at length, pausing in his polishing of the pince-nez, "and the more so because of its ghastly suddenness. When Raymond returned from Japan I feared there was something amiss with him, but never for a moment did I dream of a chapter of crime such as has been unfolded to me. It seems that he has led a double life, deceiving me for years and bleeding me for money that I too easily parted with.

"I blame myself greatly for my wilful blindness to his nature, and I ask your forgiveness on his account, and my own, for what you have suffered. Whilst I believed that you would prove a failure, my own son turned out... a criminal. You have a home, and, I believe, a substantial sum of money – he is dead. My heart is so numbed that I can feel no active sorrow, and I must forgive the unfortunate boy, for he has paid for his folly, his deceit, and his crimes, to the uttermost – with all that he had – his life."

Jack uttered a few sympathetic words.

"You cannot realise my feelings," continued the old man, "and the heart-emptiness that I feel. My poor son's nature was uncontrollable, and it was heredity that inclined him towards evil courses. There was one woman in my life that I truly loved – Jack, it was your mother – but when I realised that she was not for me I married, in a sort of blind rage, the woman who bore Raymond.

"Our married life was brief and unhappy. She was a bad woman in every sense, and when the lad was three years old she left me to live with another. After that she drifted from bad to worse. She became a criminal of the most dangerous type, and a few years ago she was sentenced to a long term of imprisonment on a charge of murder. She only died in gaol a year ago. Raymond never knew of her, for, perhaps the one good action to her credit was her renunciation of the child and my name. I hoped that he would never inherit her character, and I took every precaution to guard against it; but, it was not to be. I want you, Jack, to be a son to me as you would have been had your dear, saintly mother preferred me to Amos."

"I will, Mr. Penderby," said Jack, greatly moved. "I will try to do my best."

Raymond Penderby's body was conveyed to Sydney by train on the following day, Jack Burnside accompanying the broken-hearted father on the long and dreary journey. The interment was conducted very quietly, and it was not until mid-afternoon that Jack found his way to Mr. Penderby's chambers in Elizabeth Street. The old lawyer, overwhelmed by the events of the past few days, had driven directly to his suburban home after the funeral.

Jack Burnside halted nervously at the door of the office. His heart was beating at a furious rate, and his hands shook. Fear was upon him that Molly would spurn him after his inexcusable silence and his ungenerous doubts. He hesitated long before entering, appalled by the doubts that he felt; but at last made the plunge.

He walked quietly in, and found her bending over some papers on a table.

"Molly," he said softly, his voice tense with emotion.

Turning slowly, she saw him: a lithe, bronzed bushman, with the glamour of the wide spaces deepening the love-light in his eyes, his clean-shaven, clear cut face alight with a wondrous yearning for her. The same man that had left her years before – but not the same. This indeed was a man to love, and be loved by. The colour faded from her face; her lips quivered, and her body trembled violently. Then, with a burning blush that rose to stain her cheeks, and the light of a glorious exultation in her eyes, she rushed into his outstretched arms.

"Oh, Jack! My own man! Don't ever leave me again!" And she sobbed as she clung to him.

"Never again, little sweetheart," he said, and kissed the tears away.

26

"THE WEST WAYS CALL."

It was the day after his arrival in Sydney from Condobolin that Jack Burnside, tall, lean and sun-browned, a typical bushman, even to his 'shaped' trousers, broad-brimmed felt hat, and soft-collared shirt, sauntered happily along Pitt Street with Molly Forbes, both of them the picture of radiant happiness. The girl halted at the inviting doors of a big drapery emporium.

"You run away now for an hour, Jack dear," she said, blushing rosily. "I have to buy such a lot of pretty things for the wedding, and you have only given me two days. It's not fair, Jack, you know. I should have had six months at least."

"We have waited too long as it is, little sweetheart," said Jack, squeezing her arm lovingly. "But buy your pretty things and I will be back here within the hour. I must see poor old Mr. Penderby this morning about some important business that he claims to have with me, so I will put in the time with him."

"Cheer him up, Jack," the girl said, earnestly. "He was always so good to me, and I don't know whatever he will do now. Run away, darling, like a good boy, and let me do my shopping."

Jack took quite an affectionate farewell of her, and stood in the middle of the footpath, his eyes, tender with love, following her graceful form as she tripped into the shop. His detachment was so complete that it was not until a near-sighted old man collided with him violently that he aroused himself and hurried to the lawyer's chambers. He found Mr. Penderby seated at his table, wrapped in thought. In front of him was a black tin box bearing in white letters, the legend: "Estate of Amos Burnside, d'csd".

"Sit down, Jack," said the old man, his voice tragically vibrant. "I have just been going through some of your father's papers, and I have prepared a statement that you will be interested to hear. I thank God that you have proved to be the man your father hoped that you would one day become, and the man that I knew you were capable of being. What I am about to say to you concerning your father's affairs will no doubt astonish you. In the first place, your father was not a poor man when the end came."

"What?!" exclaimed Jack, involuntarily.

"No, he was not well-nigh bankrupt, as I led you to believe," said the lawyer. "True, he had lost very heavily on the Exchange, and with mining speculations in his later years, but before he died he entrusted me with the care of twenty thousand pounds on your behalf."

"Twenty thousand pounds," echoed Jack in a dazed voice.

"Yes," continued the lawyer. "The money was vested in me by a properly executed, duly attested and registered instrument, the sum being represented by shares in several reliable commercial concerns in the city. You will see from this document that I have power to hand this money to you at the end of six years if, in my opinion, you are a fit and proper person to be entrusted with it, or, on the other hand, to devote it to certain charitable objects. Although the six years have not expired, I am about to take it upon myself to come to a decision as to your fitness to have this money."

"Yes?" questioned Jack, breathlessly.

"From enquiries I made when in Condobolin from your friend, Callister, and from my own scapegrace brother, whom everyone knows, and strangely enough respects, as "Wild Bullocks", I am convinced that you now have sufficient judgement, steadiness of purpose, and firmness of character, to be entrusted with the handling of your own money. I have, therefore, prepared the documents necessary for the transfer of the shares and securities from me to you."

"But why did I not know of this before?" asked Jack, somewhat bitterly, as he recalled many unhappy memories of the past three years.

"It was for your own sake, my boy," said the old man, gently. "That day when you came here for a final settlement, and I drove you forth with hard words and bitter censure, you were really what I then described you. There was no ambition in your soul, no love in your heart, no determination in your will. Had you been given that money, then and there, it would have been recklessly squandered by today, and God alone knows what you might have become – perhaps something like my ill-starred son, who sought to obtain this money through Molly Forbes. I succeeded in galvanizing into activity the spirit to conquer that both your father and I knew lay dormant within you. I stung you into action, and you fared forth into that great university, the bush, and graduated – a man. Is not this true?"

"It was that – and other things," murmured Jack absently, thinking of the sweetheart who had remained true through the years of sorrow and loneliness, and of his dead, and dearly loved, father.

"Now," said Mr. Penderby, more briskly, "let us see how you stand. This statement shows in detail the accrued dividends and interest, and the total face value of the securities. The amount is £24,362, plus seventeen shillings and ten pence. Of this sum, the odd money above the original twenty thousand pounds is available for your immediate use. The shares and other securities, if realised, are worth considerably more than their face value, for some of the companies are now gilt-edged investments, and the shares are selling well above par on the Exchange. I should say that, roughly, you are worth over thirty-two thousand pounds from this source."

Jack was dumbfounded. For a time, his mind failed to grasp the situation. Then he stammered out incoherent thanks to the old lawyer who had proved such a friend to him.

"Tut tut," said Mr. Penderby, blowing his nose violently. "Any lawyer would do that as a matter of business. Think of your father and thank him. Now tell me, what are your plans?"

Jack told him that just at the moment he could not think of any.

"You will live in Sydney, of course," said the old man. "You will not want to bother with that little selection now."

Jack started at the words. He brushed his hand across his eyes, as if his doubts and fears had cleared away; he said in a decisive voice, "No more cities for me. The west is my home, henceforth and forever. They need men in the bush, and my sons, if I have any, will live their lives and die their deaths out on the wide open plains, where God's glorious sunlight glows in the timber and on the tall, lush grasses. There is big work to be done for Australia out in the back-blocks, and I will be one of the toilers."

"But," urged the lawyer, "there is no occasion for you to work."

"If I had a million pounds a year I would never live in a cramped, crowded, heartless, hungry city again. The bush is in my blood, and I must be in the open air. It is the Lachlan for me, the dear, dirty old river that only runs once in a while, and the great rolling spaces that stretch to the Never-Never."

Jack's face was transfigured with enthusiasm as he spoke. Just as he paused for breath, the post office clock rang out the hour.

"Great Scott!" he exclaimed suddenly, in great concern. "I've forgotten Molly! Goodbye!" And, grasping his hat, he rushed from the room before the astonished lawyer could demand an explanation of his outburst.

Jack need not have hurried in such violent fashion. Molly did not emerge from the shop for a further hour by the clock, and the conspicuous bushman spent the time gazing mournfully at a number of gaudy window displays until she appeared. When the happy girl did come forth it was to explain that she had not half completed her purchases, and that it would probably be another hour before she dare leave.

"What about lunch?" asked Jack.

"Lunch!" exclaimed the girl in mock horror. "If I wasted a second on lunch I would never finish today. You run away and have something, Jack, and come back here at three. No, say four o'clock; and then we will have afternoon tea together."

As Molly could not be persuaded on any account to leave the shop for such a minor circumstance as a meal, at such an important juncture, Jack wandered off disconsolately towards the Australia Hotel to lunch and spend a quiet hour in the lounge. He was meandering along when he heard a hearty greeting and received a resounding clap on the back.

"Here, you moon-struck old bush-whacker! Where are you going?"

Jack looked up and beheld Callister and Williams.

Over their drinks, Callister told him that he had come to Sydney to settle up with the company before leaving for Mildura. Bullangarra was not yet sold, he said, but there were inquiries about it from different people, and it would certainly go before the winter. The price asked – forty-five thousand pounds for the station, plant, and twenty-five thousand sheep - made it a gift.

"I am sorry to leave before the place is sold," said Callister, "but I could not stay there to see strangers come in and take charge of it. I will hang about here for a few weeks, and then, heigh-ho for the Murray!"

"I wish I had twenty-five thousand pounds," said Williams. "I'd buy the run myself."

"Would twenty-five thousand pounds enable a man to buy Bullangarra?" asked Jack, with curiosity in his voice.

"The company will take twenty-five thousand in cash and allow the balance to remain on mortgage," explained Williams. Those are the terms. If I could raise that amount I'd hurry down to the office now and put in a hundred pounds to bind the bargain."

Jack thought quickly. Then, grasping the two friends, each by an arm, he hurried them to the footpath.

"Take me to the company's office," he commanded.

They led him towards Circular Quay, and presently entered the busy offices of the Commonwealth Mortgage Company. During their brief walk his two companions had endeavoured to discover, without success, what whim had urged Jack to drag them thither. Locating the manager of the property department, Jack addressed that individual.

"Is Bullangarra Station, on the Lachlan, still for sale?" he asked.

"Yes, sir," was the brisk reply. "Forty-five thousand pounds for the station, together with twenty-five thousand of the sheep; the rest are to be removed before delivery is taken. Terms: twenty-five thousand pounds deposit on signing of the contract; balance, if desired, to remain on mortgage at the current rate of interest."

"How long would it take to prepare the contract?" asked Jack.

"Two or three weeks," said the salesman. "There are a lot of titles to be searched against, and applications for the consent to transfer to be prepared in connection with the leases. Say, a month at the outside."

"Right, I will buy the place!" said Jack. "I will pay one hundred pounds now to bind the bargain, and the balance within a month." And he drew out his chequebook to fill in the slip.

"Good Heavens!" exclaimed Callister, positively flabbergasted.

"I'm damned!" exploded Williams.

Jack paid over his cheque and pocketed his receipt.

"My solicitor, Mr. James Penderby, of Elizabeth Street, will arrange all subsequent details," he said to the salesman, as he turned to his astonished friends.

"Yes, Mr. Burnside," said the clerk, smiling cheerfully as he looked at the cheque.

Outside, Callister and Williams demanded explanations with much assumed fierceness of aspect, withal absolutely bewildered at the extraordinary action of the young man.

"How the devil can you find the money to pay for the place?" shouted Callister, excitedly.

"Did you go mad, suddenly, Burnside?" asked Williams, anxiously.

Then Jack told them the story of his good fortune.

"You deserve it all, Jack," said Callister, huskily. "I don't mind leaving the old place now, not a bit." But Jack saw that the tired grey eyes were misty with unshed tears.

"You will not be leaving, old friend," said the young man, in a husky voice. "I want someone to pull me through the droughts and rains for many a long year to come, and there's no one else I'll have there but you. Bullangarra will always be your home, and between us we will show them on the Lachlan what irrigation means. Will you stay?"

"Stay on the old place!" murmured Callister in faltering tones. "Of course I will stay, Jack! It would have broken my heart to leave it. The thought that I had to go has nearly killed me. This is the happiest day of my life!"

"Well, said Jack heartily, "you are still manager, on the same terms as before if you like, whatever they were; and if you don't like them we will see if we can improve them."

"I would stay on for nothing, Jack," said the old man simply.

"What will you do about the selection, Yarran Plain?" asked Williams.

"I can transfer that," answered Jack. "I am not eligible to hold it now, I suppose, and I certainly cannot put in my five years' residence on it. I will try to secure the consent of the Minister for Lands to transfer it to young Carroll as it stands. You understand this land business, Williams, so you might fix the matter up for me, if you will."

"I'll prepare the forms today," announced the inspector. "Your reasons for transferring are solid enough for the Lands Department."

"But Jack," said Callister, "what are you going to do about old Penderby – "Wild Bullocks" I mean?"

"I have an idea," said Jack, "that the manager of Bullangarra will find some sort of an easy job for him about the homestead. What do you think?"

"I have an idea you are right," said Callister happily.

"If you squatters want to buy a few big lines of sheep," put in Williams, "don't forget that I can do something in the way of suiting you."

"We will want a few good lines of two-tooth ewes," said Jack, "so you had better speak to my manager. He will attend to that part of the business. Meanwhile, I am going to look up some pumping machinery for an irrigation plant that is to be installed at Bullangarra."

Two days afterwards, Jack Burnside and Molly Forbes were quietly married in Sydney. There were less than a dozen guests, all close friends, at the church as the bride drove up with old Mr. Penderby, who insisted on giving her away; and the ceremony commenced at once.

The clergyman had just reached that solemn moment when he asked Jack if he would take "this woman" to be his wedded wife, when there was a shuffling of feet in the rear pews, and a hoarse whisper from the owner of them, "O' course he will, parson! Wot d'yer think he come here fer?"

All eyes were turned on the interrupter. It was "Wild Bullocks", his bearded face wreathed in smiles, his old eyes twinkling with merriment. He had overcome his horror of the city to be present at the wedding.

"I'm a bit late," he explained loudly, for the benefit of the wondering guests, "but don't stop fer me. Hitch 'em up, parson!"

And the clergyman did so.

There followed a quiet breakfast at the Australia, where the healths of the bride and bridegroom were toasted with great enthusiasm. Old Mr. Penderby, although still much affected by his bereavement and the unfortunate circumstances surrounding it, showed a brave spirit and a cheerful mien to the end. His brother, the rough bushman "Wild Bullocks", openly wept tears of joy, which he naively attributed to the bubbling champagne that he had tasted, and disliked, for the first time in his chequered existence. His speech, too, was a most satisfactory one.

"I want yer ter back inter this toast," he declaimed, "as if yer flamin' lives depended on it. Youse all know Jack as a bloke what's right ter the hoofs, an' his missus is as pretty as a spring mornin' when the sun is sparklin' on the little drops o' dew among the barley-grass beside a Lachlan billabong. I hope they'll be happy. I knows they will, because they can't help it. Jack's as straight as the railway line from Byrock to Bourke – fifty miles with never a curve in it, an whether he's holdin' it or not, he gives everybody a fair spin. He ain't got no relations o' his own that I knows o', so I'm puttin' me brand on him here an' now, an' adoptin' him an' his missus. When the kids come along," – at this Molly blushed and hid her face shyly in the shelter of Jack's sleeve – "I'm goin' ter take charge of 'em an' teach 'em the ways o' the bush. An' if they take after their bloomin' ol' father, an' their gran'father by adoption, they won't be too dusty. Now, lay up this here fizzy tack an' give a cheer fer Jack an' his missus, God bless 'em!"

The uproarious applause that greeted this speech, and the enthusiastic vociferousness of the toast delighted "Wild Bullocks" as much as it did the young couple, and he beamed and chuckled as though it were in his honour as well.

As the party was leaving the hotel, Callister, who was in the lead, was gripped by a brawny arm as he stepped on to the footpath.

"So, I've got you, eh!" roared a deep voice. "And Burnside too! Why, it looks like a wedding party!"

"It is, Alex," said Callister. "Jack has just been married. This is the new Mrs. Burnside – Alex Campbell, my brother-in-law."

Campbell, the sawmiller, offered his warmest congratulations.

"I have a wedding present for you, Mrs. Burnside," he said, cheerily. "Duncan Callister told me all about your husband's partnership with him in our timber deal, so I will pay you Jack's portion of the profits. I'm settling up today. I sold out the mill, the concession, and the contracts to the 'ring' for sixteen thousand pounds. Here is a cheque for four thousand, two hundred and sixty pounds – the dividend, less expenses that I will show your husband later. That represents the capital invested, and his profits. Take good care of it."

"Hooray!" shouted "Wild Bullocks", waving his hat, to the huge edification of a crowd of curious passers-by.

That evening at the railway station, Jack bought two tickets for Condobolin. He had not told his wife where their honeymoon was to be spent, and she, with an abounding trustfulness, had not inquired. Nor had he told her of his inheritance, nor of his purchase of Bullangarra. After the train moved out, which it did amid the cheering of his friends, and showers of confetti, he turned to her. With his arms about her, his cheek close to hers, he whispered, "Where would you like to spend your honeymoon, darling?"

"Anywhere, my lover, wherever you choose to take me."

"Aren't you a little bit curious as to where we are going, sweetheart?" he asked.

"I don't care where we go. I am too happy to want to know anything but that I am with my own dear husband for ever and ever," she answered softly.

"Well, Molly," said Jack, after the fitting interval that he employed in kissing her rosy lips, "I have some wonderful news to tell you."

And then he told her of the manner in which his inheritance had come to him at last, and of how he had come to purchase the great fertile station on the Lachlan, that was to be their future home.

"Oh, Jack darling," exclaimed the girl rapturously. "Then it all means that you are terribly rich, and that we won't have to live in a bark hut after all. I could weep with joy!" And she proceeded to do so, very prettily.

"Yes," said Jack earnestly, and with a great decision in his voice. "I am the richest man in all the world, darling, for I have you."

And in that instant, even as he clasped his dear one in his arms, there flashed before his mind a vivid, momentary picture of the silent, sombre bush about the station homestead, where the white roofs gleamed in the quivering light of the blazing stars; where the long, dry, grass glistened with the sheen of molten silver, where the river brooded and murmured amid the eerie shadows of the gaunt, grey gum trees. And then the weird, alluring mystery of the west, that wondrous land of toil and travail, of joy and peace, sent forth to him its irresistible call – and he answered.

To his wife he said, "And now, darling, together we go forth, out to the wide, open plains of the western bushland, along the track that will lead us to Bullangarra – and to happiness supreme."

THE END

27

GLOSSARY

Bails – small enclosures in which cows are held while being milked

Billabong – waterhole or small branch of a river, often isolated from its source except in times of flood

Bluey – swag, bedroll and belongings tied up and carried (usually on the back) while wandering the bush

Boniface – the proprietor of a hotel or restaurant

Busted – penniless, broke

CHAIN – a measurement of 66 feet (22 yards), equivalent to 20.1168 metres. The name comes from an old surveyors' measuring tool.

CHINESE GARDENS – small vegetable patches established across parts of inland Australia by Chinese immigrants who'd arrived as part of various gold rushes across the country. Selling provisions to miners was often more lucrative than the fossicking itself.

COCKY - -A FARMER with only a small holding, often on the edge of a waterhole, like the supposed habitat of a cockatoo

DEAD RING, **dead ringer** – look-alike

EXHIBITION – Brisbane's annual agricultural show, run by the Royal National Association

FAIR DINKUM – true

FRACTEUR – gelignite

GUINEA – an amount equal to 21 shillings (a pound equalling 20 shillings), originally a gold coin of one quarter ounce of gold.

JACKAROO – a young man, often English and of independent means, working on a large sheep or cattle station, learning the practical skills and experience required to own, or at least manage, such a station.

Usually a privileged position, who ate with the owner, not the other workers.

JACK-SHAY - A BUSHMAN'S quart pot used especially for boiling water

KNOCKABOUT MAN – odd-jobs man, general hand

LEXIA – a soft, light-coloured raisin, originating in Spain

METALLICIANS – money-men, usually bookmakers

MOKE – horse

NEW-CHUM – rookie, new and unpractised arrival to work on a station

OULD ERIN - IRELAND

PITCH-AND-TOSS - a gambling game in which the player who manages to throw a coin closest to a mark gets to toss all the coins, winning those that land with the head up.

ROOT OR PIG-ROOT – the bucking of a horse, referring to the animal's tendency to duck its head down towards the ground as it jumps and kicks.

ROUSEABOUT – unskilled labourer in a shearing shed, often the 'odd-jobs' man

SELECTOR – owner/operator of a small farm. Under Land Acts in Australia's colonies, from 1860 people were able under certain conditions to select and buy land even if it was part of a big grazing property owned by a wealthy squatter. They were not allowed to rent out their selection.

SENT DOWN – expelled from University, usually for disciplinary reasons

SETTLING DAY – normally a day or two after a major race meeting, when bookmakers settle their accounts – paying out winnings and collecting bets made 'on account', or agreeing other arrangements when necessary.

SHICK – shickered, drunk

SHIRTY - angry

SQUATTER - SOMEONE who occupied a large tract of land theoretically owned by the government, and who then used it to graze livestock. Initially often having no legal rights to the land, they gained its usage by being the first (and often the only) settlers in the area. By the 1830s the term was used for large land-holders who had obtained a lease or licence to occupy Crown land.

STONE MORAL – a sure thing, a certain winner

STOUSH – to beat up someone, a fight

TATTERSALL'S CLUB – a social club, originally mostly comprising bookmakers, founded in 1858. The name is derived from Richard Tattersall, an English horse dealer who is credited with establishing the modern concept of horseracing with fair betting rules.

TWO-TOOTH – a sheep of approximately one year old. They start growing their adult teeth at about that age, first a pair of incisors, then a pair every year until they have four pairs. So a two-year-old sheep is a four-tooth, and a three-year-old is called a six-tooth.

TUCKER – food

WALER – ORIGINALLY 'NEW SOUTH WALER', a hardy type of stock horse from Australia, thought to be originally a mix of thoroughbred, Arab, Cape horse (South African), Timor Pony and perhaps Clydesdale. Noted for their endurance and hardiness.

WETHER – a male sheep, castrated when young, making him less aggressive and able to be penned with females. Used for wool production.

WHALER – swagman, wandering bushman

WILLY-WILLY – small spiralling wind-storm, usually carrying dust, like a very miniature tornado

YAKKA – hard work

YARRAN – a hardy small acacia shrub

ORIGINAL INTRODUCTION - 1922

This introduction is a composition of three such articles that appeared in Australian newspapers to promote the book's impending serialization: Sydney's 'Daily Telegraph' on Monday, 13 November, 1922; 'The Express' in Adelaide on Tuesday 21 November; and Brisbane's 'Daily Mail' of Friday, 1 December of the same year.

A NEW AUSTRALIAN NOVELIST. MR. GORDON BENNETT

We have purchased the serial rights of a story by a new Australian novelist, who gives promise of making a name for himself. It is entitled *The Boomerang of Destiny*, and the author is Gordon Bennett.

It is a story that will be talked about. It is one of the best that has yet been written with an Australian setting. The stones are laid in Sydney and the western and northern parts of New South Wales.

The author of *The Boomerang of Destiny* is a New Zealander by birth, and arrived in New South Wales as a child. He is a son of Mr. Walter Bennett M.L.A. for Maitland, and was reared in the valley of the Hunter, where he gained an extensive practical knowledge of farming and forestry.

Before he was 20 he went to the western districts, and subsequently purchased a newspaper at Condobolin, on the Lachlan, which he conducted for a number of years. He also edited other country journals. In the west he became interested in pastoral and mining affairs, thus coming into close contact with the conditions that obtain in the back country. At present he is engaged on the staff of the *Farmer and Settler* newspaper, Sydney, as writer on land and agricultural affairs.

His experience in the bush has been gained far from the roads travelled by the tourist and pleasure-seeker. It has come from the stock routes, the "Guv'ment" tanks, the dusty western towns, the drowsing grey rivers, the shearing sheds, the saltbush plains, the spinifex deserts, and lonely camp fires. His outback wanderings led him over the back tracks of four States on the far-flung fringe of the Never-Never, where he lived and worked with the people of the bush, and learnt their ways, and their hearts. He has been in turns compositor, journalist, drover, prospector, jockey, mail driver, land agent, valuator, railway construction tally clerk, and stock dealer.

As a writer Mr. Bennett has produced many short stories that have been published in Australian, American, and English magazines, besides much bush verse that has appeared in the *Bulletin* and elsewhere. He has also written a history of the aborigines of the Dungog-Port Stephens district, and his articles, printed under the title of *The Story of the Murray Lands*, have been reprinted in booklet form by the New South Wales Government for distribution among intending immigrants.

The Boomerang of Destiny is a graphic narrative of the experiences of a young, city-bred dilettante who, disappointed in his expectations of an Inheritance, is compelled to turn to work. This young man chooses to go on the land, and secures a position as jackaroo on a station down the Lachlan. *The Boomerang of Destiny* is a story that grips from the beginning. It is crowded with incident and vivid impressions of life in the back-blocks and on the coast. The author depicts the western country as it is, and he describes the types of people who toil and strive and live their lives far remote from the cities and the glamour of the crowded ways. Humour and pathos are skilfully blended in the telling of the tale, and from it, readers may learn something of the hidden and more intimate phases of life in the outer spaces, something of the heroic endeavour, the high intent, and the tireless labours of those who struggle to win a fortune from the land.

The types of bushmen that fill the pages are so strongly drawn that one may see into the hearts of the wandering swagman, the squatter, the cocky, the shearer, the boundary rider, the jockey, and the outback clergyman. The plot is exciting throughout, and the race-course incidents supply many interesting aspects of the tale. The love interest is a strong one, and the fortune of the young jackeroo and his faithful sweetheart will be followed with the keenest interest. The characters are very true to life, and two or three of them, including the heroine, a Sydney girl, are of a most lovable type.

www.ingramcontent.com/pod-product-compliance
Lightning Source LLC
Chambersburg PA
CBHW020404120726
47904CB00002B/704